MPLETE.

PRICE 1s.

THE

PEARL FISHER

OF

ST. DOMINGO.

A TALE OF THE BUCCANIERS

BY E. GONZALES.

LONDON:
GEORGE PEIRCE, 310, STRAND.

THE PEARL FISHER
OF
ST. DOMINGO

A TALE OF THE BUCCANIERS.

LONDON:
GEO. PEIRCE, 310, STRAND;

THE PEARL FISHER.

CHAPTER I.

JOAQUIN REQUIEM.

URING the period when the incidents of this drama occurred, the maritime world presented a spectacle almost unique in its annals. The celebrated besom of Holland had not then swept every rival from the ocean. The British navy was only springing from the stocks. The French noblesse sent out to the colonies their choicest dependants, whose boasting surpassed that of the best cadet from Gascogne. The Spaniards could then ballast their ships with gold and silver ingots. They had exterminated or subjugated the Indians, or driven the bravest into the depths of the forest, lighting their path with the blaze of their burning lodges. The most docile and timid were employed in the mines and pearl fisheries of the Spanish conquerors. The Spanish Inquisition dominated over a hundred cities in the richest districts of South America and the Antilles. Each port at that time also contained fleets of merchantmen, richly laden, and bound for the Peninsula. However, during several months, the shipping remained at anchor without daring to put out to sea. Extraordinary event. The powerful and proud Spaniard was afraid of a few hundred buccaniers ranging the Caribean sea, who had chosen as their watch-tower a rocky island, about sixteen leagues in circumference, called the Turtle Island. The fabulous exploits and miraculous heroism of this handful of adventurers can alone enable one to comprehend the extraordinary contest which ensued between them and the Spaniards, whom they thus menaced in the very centre of their possessions. The most astonishing characters were developed by the manners, customs, and roving life of these semi-savages. We, instead of being accused of invention, cannot be charged with equalling historical facts of a romantic character, scarcely credible in themselves, unless supported by undoubted proofs of their authenticity. The Pearl Fishery, where our first scenes are laid, was called Rancheria, and was situated on the eastern side of St. Domingo. The prolific soil of the Antilles was there displayed in all the luxury of vegetation. The hatto, or pleasure-house of the Governor, Don Ramon Carral, rose gracefully above the splendid landscape with its pointed gables and its Moorish balconies. It was flanked with miniature towers or pavilions, painted in various colours, and over which wandered the tendrils of plants and flowers up to the very roof, festooning every window with their green and flowery drapery. Behind the hatto extended a thicket of orange and banana trees, spreading over a gentle hill their thick coaty fruit and flowers, and affording a back ground of purple and of gold to the governor's residence. The sweet perfume floating on the breeze, the profound azure of the sky, fringed with ruddy lines towards the horizon, the poetry of the whole rendered life enchanting—a sort of fairy dream upon earth. Nevertheless, a vague feeling of melancholy saddened the brow of a young girl, who, at the opening of a lovely May morning, sauntered negligently on the balcony of the hatto, attended by a negress. This young girl, whose movements possessed all the undulating grace peculiar to the creoles, was the Queen of Rancheria, Donna Carmen de Larates. In a few minutes she seemed fatigued, and leaned her arms on the balcony, awaiting the departure of the pearl fishers, who commenced their labours every morning at six o'clock.

Before we proceed with the plot of our drama we shall make a slight digression to describe our principal heroine. Donna Carmen was seventeen years of age. Her beautiful countenance expressed a calm mind, but a true and resolute spirit. She had been reared by her father (whose death had taken place only a few months back), in pride, pomp, and rigid devotion, which, however, had not altered the natural beauty of her mind. She was not a coquette, although she liked to be admired. Lively, impetuous by turns, but ever kindly, she always, by a smile and a word, healed those wounds which an imperious command or ill-timed reproach had created. Her beauty was placed in strong contrast with the dark and tattoed countenances which generally surrounded her. Donna Carmen inherited from her mother one of those melancholic countenances so pale when undisturbed, but so fiery when the spirit becomes excited. The resplendent freshness and bloom of health rendered all decorations of the toilet useless, and, with a simple flower at her breast, she seemed more lovely than when decorated with diamonds. On the morning of which we speak, the unpowdered curls of her long chesnut-coloured hair fell in profusion over her shoulders. Her large black eyes were fixed upon the sea, their brilliancy bearing testimony to an energetic soul within, whilst their smiling expression enlivened her exquisite beauty. She was a being worthy of the scene which surrounded her. As the day broke, the flowers opened their petals, and the forests and hills exhibited fresh beauties, widening and enriching the magnificent landscape.

Donna Carmen seemed absorbed in the contemplation of the sublime horizon, when she suddenly heard a sharp and well-known voice behind her—

"So early on foot, senorita?"

She turned quickly round and perceived the hard cast and ironical countenance of Don Ramon Carral. He was a little, thin nervous man. His puckered lips, his sharp little eyes and red eyelids, his hooked nose, all indicated an implacable and avaricious spirit. The cousin and partner of Donna Carmen's father, he expected to marry the young heiress of Rancheria, and thus become sole master of that princely fishery. Always accustomed to command, and looking upon Donna Carmen as still a child, he was in the habit of treating her rather imperiously. Donna Carmen had hitherto supported that tyranny out of respect to her father's memory; but annoyed at that rude tone of voice in which she was now addressed, she felt her heart revolt at the indignity.

"I intend to watch the fishery to-day," said she, coldly, "since it is the only pleasure one can have in this dismal solitude. You will permit me to enjoy it. You have already interdicted my rambles in the woods under pretext of a hundred concealed dangers from imaginary serpents up to the blood-thirsty ladrones. I am a prisoner in my own house: surely that ought to satisfy you."

Don Ramon concealed his impatience, and, in a dry manner, remarked—

"What motive could I have, Carmen, in depriving you of a pleasure? But you know that your presence encourages the fishermen to demand a recompense, and the slaves to neglect their duty. They all trust to your indulgence."

"I am merciful, sir, and I detest unnecessary cruelty—that is all. These poor creatures were made by the same hand, and belong to the same family that we do."

"Romantic nonsense; believe me, Carmen. Time will cure you of such dreams, and, in the meantime, I shall be always ready to second the least of your desires."

He blew a shrill call upon a silver whistle, which was suspended on his breast by a chain. A crowd of slaves, of Indians and of fishermen, hurried out of the huts which lined the shore. The beach, previously deserted, was now animated with the bustling throng, dancing, singing, and shouting. As they passed under the balcony they respectfully inclined towards Donna Carmen, who replied by a smile to their affectionate regards, although she seemed sad and pensive. The fishermen then launched their six-oared boats and clustered around the great receiving bank. A single boat alone remained on the beach. The crew stood motionless and ready. Don Ramon made a signal for them to push off. Then a loud cry was heard at the utmost pitch of the voice—

"Joaquin, Joaquin."

No reply was made. The commander stamped his foot with rage, and blew his whistle a second time. This time a fine young man, about twenty-two years of age, appeared on the door step of the farthest hut. He wore strong calico drawers, his arms and chest being bare ; his hair cut close under his broad-brimmed straw hat. His figure was slender, although well built, and combining strength and agility. His soft blue eyes were surmounted by an ample forehead, which ill contrasted with his servitude.

"Oh !" said the commander, contracting his bushy eyebrows, " 'tis that sluggard, Joaquin. Always behind." But this reproach did not reach Donna Carmen, whose eyes brightened at the sight of the young fisherman.

Joaquin, whose countenance was pale and gloomy, advanced slowly. He bowed low under the balcony, and stopped as Don Ramon called out—

"Stay ; I wish to speak to you."
And the worthy commander added, between his teeth—

" This disobedience merits a most exemplary punishment."
But Carmen instantly interrupted him, saying, quickly—

" Pardon him, cousin ; hear me. I have a long time thought of asking such a favour. This pursuit of Joaquin is a terrible one. Is it not ?"

" Well," said Don Ramon. " Well, attach him to the household. He will make an excellent domestic."

The commander shrugged his shoulders.

" Indeed, I had quite forgot that Joaquin was your *protégé*. His position as a slave dishonours him. Ah ! what a dull head I have got. Some duty, more noble, and more gallant, must be found ; for instance, page, or master of the horse, to Donna Carmen de Larates ; " and he burst into a loud and ironical laugh.

" What is the meaning of that pleasantry, sir ? " demanded the young girl, haughtily.

" Oh ! " said Don Ramon, whose tanned countenance assumed its habitual calmness, " it signifies that you are very imprudent to ask such a favour. I would advise you to forget this fopling, who seems to occupy your thoughts rather too often. It is thus that the insolence of his breed augments."

" Cousin, you have deeply offended me," said Carmen, surprised, to the last degree, to have deserved such a reproach. " Was it not you yourself who vaunted the docility and devotion of Joaquin ? "

"I did wrong," replied the commander. "Although formerly he was one of our best fishers, he has changed for the worse for some time. His audacity alone has improved. You know that as well as I do."

"I know it as well as you!" mechanically answered Carmen.

"Yes," said Don Ramon, firmly. "The other evening, when we were conversing in the grove, who picked up your fan, just as I bent down to present it to you?"

"It was him," interrupted Carmen. "I paid no attention to it; but, thanks to you, I owe him a favour for it."

"Very good," continued the commander, whose voice trembled; "but, the day before yesterday, when you wished to have a sail by starlight, how did it happen that Joaquin was there, although the boat was not his, and the coxswain, too, got drunk, and could not attend?"

"What!" exclaimed Carmen. "Was that silent and mournful steersman Joaquin? I did not recognise him; otherwise I should have spoken to him."

Don Ramon impatiently bit his lips, for he could not mistake the sincerity of the young girl, who regarded a lie as the most degrading wickedness. Nevertheless, he made another attempt, and said—

"At least, you might inform me who the gallant is, who every morning attaches bouquets of flowers to the rails of the balcony?"

"Can it be poor Joaquin who is guilty of this great crime?" asked Carmen, laughingly, "whilst I dreamed of some unknown admirer, who had mysteriously visited Rancheria for that very purpose. You must grant, cousin, that you possess a singular degree of modesty, thus to reveal to me the existence of a rival."

Don Ramon understood, from her jeering tone, that he had rendered no good service to himself, by raising thoughts in Donna Carmen's mind which found no place there before.

"Seriously, cousin, are you jealous of this poor fisherman?"

"No," quickly answered the commander, "but do you not observe that it is your affability which encourages such forwardness? Can you deny that the look of this poor fisherman, as you call him, is ever upon you, and brightens on your approach?"

He made a sign to Joaquin to follow his companions.

Donna Carmen remained a moment silent and thoughtful, but the pride of her character soon resumed its sway, and she, with much dignity, addressed her cousin—

"We have had enough of this, Don Ramon. I consider your extraordinary jealousy as a pleasantry, not as an offence; besides, compose yourself, Joaquin loves me like a brother. We have, when children, played together; he obeyed my will, submitting to my caprice, was sad when I wept, gay when I laughed, and angry with himself when I was petted. This servitude attached him to me, and he, at least," added she, with a sigh, "if he does think of me, it is not to reproach me; my wildest desire is a law to him."

Don Ramon remained silent, fearful to exhibit his violent temper, and alienate still more the heart of his betrothed.

Carmen involuntarily looked at Joaquin, standing up in the boat, his arms crossed, and listening abstractedly to the measured song of his companions.

"Your father confided to me your happiness, and, like him, I counsel you, because I love you. Yes, if you knew it, Carmen, I love you with sincerity and devotion."

A smile of incredulity disturbed the lips and eyebrows of the young girl. "Do not profane that word, Don Ramon. Love, I think, ought to make a man just, good, and charitable, instead of ferocious and jealous. Besides, love is blind, even to faults."

"Have I not already forgiven Joaquin, to please you? You have only to order what you desire, and it shall be done."

As he spoke a long plaintive cry arose in the air, with a prolonged melancholy sound, which caused Donna Carmen to tremble, and lean for support on Don Ramon's arm.

"Again the same ominous cry, which has suddenly awoke me these two nights past!" murmured she.

"It is childish, senorita, to allow yourself to be so agitated by the whining of a crocodile."

"I have indeed reasoned with myself, but I cannot overcome the impression which that terrible sound produces within me. It is a weakness I cannot conquer."

"Our fishermen assure me that one of these monsters, of a most extraordinary size, has chosen for his retreat the Bay de la Hache, close by, behind the wood De Mangles."

"Would to God some bold hunter could deliver us of the monster."

"I take our lady of Pilar to witness, that your wish shall be executed, senorita," said the commander. "But you are too much moved to remain long on this balcony. Lean on my arm, and let us enter the room."

Donna Carmen made a gesture of surprise at the sight of a

monk, whose sallow countenance appeared at the same moment at the door of the saloon. It was Friar Eusebio Carral, brother of the commander, a rigid Dominican, and a fanatic, though sincere in his devotion. The strong affection he bore for Don Ramon, which he concealed under a rude and severe exterior, formed his greatest prominent virtue.

"What! you are returned from the Gulf of Honduras. Has your mission been successful?"

"Yes, the Indians are now subdued. We have visited all the scattered tribes of the Grandes Oreilles. They have paid tribute in corn and cochineal, and received the sacrament."

"And have you encountered any resistance?"

"No. Oby, a kind of soothsayer, who has vast influence over these poor idolators, tried to create a revolt; but we executed several of the most prominent, and the rest returned to their duty. As for Oby, he escaped, and lay concealed in some lair, where our blood-hounds could not even track him. We put to the flames their idolatrous temples, and succeeded in capturing Oby's daughter."

"And what have you done with her?" inquired Donna Carmen.

"As she obstinately refused to reveal to us her father's hiding place, or become a convert, we sold her as a slave."

"Is it possible!" cried the young girl. "That was a most horrible cruelty."

"Has the mistress of Rancheria," said the priest, with severity in his reproof, "learned during our absence to blaspheme God and pity the idolators?"

Donna Carmen made no reply. She even believed she had committed sacrilege, and smothered in her breast those sentiments which compassion had excited.

"But, would you believe it, brother," continued the monk, "we narrowly escaped being taken by the buccaniers, at Granada, which their Captain, Jean David, completely pillaged, with only four-and-twenty men."

"At Granada!" repeated Don Ramon, in an altered voice. "Granada, that is 40 leagues from the sea, and defended by 800 armed Spaniards. It is impossible."

"Nothing seems impossible to these men. Demons must protect them. Our countrymen are paralysed. These pirates march, without being betrayed, through an incredible extent of country, and suddenly appear where they are least expected. Grape shot seems powerless amongst them. They move amidst a shower of balls as unconcerned as if it rained down roses. After having surprised and killed the sentinels, in the middle of the night, Jean David and his followers awoke, one after the other, the richest citizens and the priests, from whom they took the keys of the churches. The pillage continued three hours amidst perfect silence, when the alarm was given ; but the adventurers had time to escape, with gold and precious stones to the value of 40,000 crowns. Their ships were attacked, but without success."

" What marvellous courage ! " exclaimed Donna Carmen.

" Courage ! " repeated Don Ramon, with contempt. " Say rather, that they had only cowards to deal with. Let them come to Rancheria."

" No idle boasting, brother," said the priest, with a severe look ; " and may heaven avert the consequences of your wish. Dreadful accounts are given of the cruelty of those reprobates. Roe-Bresilian, one of their heroes, whose countenance is always spotted with blood, has such an invincible hatred to our nation that he throws his prisoners on a red-hot gridiron, to compel them to produce their treasures, and finally destroys them by the sword."

" How can heaven tolerate such monsters?" said Donna, Carmen, shocked at the recital. " Are all the pirates equally ferocious ?"

" The buccaniers are not so cruel," replied Friar Eusebio, " but the bravest of their leaders has declared war to the death against every Spaniard. It is the famous Leopard, who is, they say, cruising about the Port de la Paix."

" So near us !" cried the young girl.

" Do not alarm our cousin with your gloomy tales," said the commander, moving from the saloon. " The fishery ought to be over. I will order preparations to be made for hunting the crocodile, a spectacle I promised you, Donna Carmen. Will you accompany us, brother ?"

The slaves and fishermen landed on the beach, bearing on their shoulders sacks of the pearl oyster ; and in spite of their fatigue, still joyous in appearance. But when the commander informed them of his intention to have a crocodile hunt in the Bay de la Hache, a dead silence reigned over the throng.

Such an occupation was extremely dangerous, and the crocodiles were formidable objects of terror to the slaves. Donna Carmen only noticed Joaquin's surprise, and the ironical smile which lifted the corners of his mouth.

The cavalcade was soon ready. Don Ramon and the friar mounted two magnificently harnessed horses. Two slaves bore a palanquin for Donna Carmen, but she preferred to proceed on foot, according to the custom of the Castilian creoles of that period. Four fiddlers marched at the head of the troop, creating a discordant noise, which, however, was speedily left behind. Before the bay could be reached, it was necessary to pass through a forest which stretched along the shores.

" Must we then force our way," said Donna Carmen. " through that intricate foliage? It is impossible to penetrate such a jungle."

" We have no other choice," said the commander ; "because, if my brother's information be correct, we should run too great a risk by proceeding by water ; and as for compassing the forest, who knows where we might wander to. These cursed branches are so interlaced with these wandering tendrils that we might, like the Indians, walk from branch to branch for many a league without putting foot to the ground."

" Senora," said Joaquin, who respectfully advanced when he observed the young girl hesitate before she would pass through the wood, " in a quarter of an hour we shall reach the place, and I can lead you there by a path I have hewn for myself. But it is absolutely necessary to walk."

" Let it be so," said the commander, " and let us lose no time."

Donna Carmen thanked the young man with a sweet smile, and Joaquin led the way, breaking and cutting the branches which stretched across the path. More than once she was obliged to lean on the fisherman's shoulder or cling to his arm. Only once he lifted her from the ground, over a dark and hollow tree, beneath which he imagined he saw the scaly sides and glittering eyes of a serpent.

Two prolonged and singularly plaintive cries attracted the attention of Don Ramon and the hunters ; but they could not discover from whence proceeded these mournful sounds. Was it from the sea, from the top of the trees, or from amongst the slaves that they originated. No one could divine. Finally, they all safely reached the bay, where Donna Carmen re-mounted her horse.

This little bay was surrounded with immense granite rocks, which lifted their calcined heads towards the sky, in points sharp and straight as needles. The sandy beach was spotted here and there with lakes of greenish water, left by the sea, and piled with fish. At the extremity of the bay a small brook discharged itself into the sea.

" This is the Bay de la Hache, is it not ?" asked the governor.

" Yes, master," replied Gongora, the boatman.

" The crocodile has not been a bad judge in fixing in this retreat," said Don Ramon, looking round with satisfaction ; " but the sluggard is asleep, no doubt. We must arouse him, and prepare some trap for him. I see no other way. Yes," continued he, " the animal is alarmed at our presence ; but we must drag him from his slumbers. Let two negroes wade into the sea, and throw stones to arouse him."

No one answered ; but the blacks mechanically recoiled with marked repugnance.

" Well," cried Don Ramon, " must I repeat my order ?"

" Master," said Gongora, the orator of the troop, advancing bonnet in hand, " if he hides himself, it is useless seeking him."

" What's to be done, then ?"

" If we had found the monster asleep on the sand," continued Gongora, " we might have transfixed him at once, and with the barbed lance succeeded."

" Very meritorious," interrupted the friar ; " but, fool, we have not found any thing asleep."

" Yes ; now that he has been advised concerning our visit, we can try the floating bait, to which we can attach a calf's lights. It is a favourite morsel for a crocodile. The moment the glutton perceives it in the water, he will soon commence to swallow it, when we can fire upon him from the shore, and finish him at once."

" Well said," remarked Don Ramon. " Let it be got ready at once."

" But, above all things," said the boatman, " let silence be preserved. The least noise will alarm him. Ask Joaquin Requiem. He knows them well."

" True ; Joaquin is with us. I had forgotten him," cried Ramon. " Why don't you speak ?"

" You have asked me no questions, master," said Joaquin, shortly.

" A zealous servant anticipates his master's wishes," observed the friar, Eusebio.

" Do you approve of Gongora's idea ? I charge you with the execution of it."

" Bah! I approve more of the harpoon; for the crocodile will not lift his head above the water for your amusement."

" Very good. Since there is no harpoon, you approve of the bait ?"

" Still less, master."

" Why so ?"

" Because of its extreme danger," said the fisherman quietly. " This crocodile measures at least sixteen feet, and is of such a strength, that he would drag the men into the sea."

" You are afraid, then, Joaquin?" said Don Ramon, with an accent of marked contempt.

" Fear !" repeated Joaquin, in a startled tone, as if doubting whether such a term could be applied to him. " Fear !" And his countenance became dreadfully pale, and his hands were convulsively contracted. But he made a violent effort; looked at his companions; and perceiving no sign of surprise or emotion on their countenances, so much does slavery familiarise the soul to every indignity, " Fear !" muttered he, between his teeth. " But I am a fool: a master cannot insult a servant—insult is his privilege." And he answered as if he had not felt the insult. " Why tempt fate in vain, Don Ramon ? If the crocodile had assailed you, it would be well; but since he is concealed as if dead, why seek him and irritate him in his concealment ?"

The commander heard him with an air of stupefaction.

" I permitted you to speak, did I not ?" said he, struggling to suppress his rage. " Now I do not want your counsel. I command you to obey, if you are not a poltroon. Refuse, and every one here will bear witness to the cowardice of Joaquin Requiem."

A singular agitation shook the limbs of Joaquin. Donna Carmen regarded him with surprise, as well as Gongora and the remainder of the troop. A violent struggle seemed to rend his soul—still he spoke not.

" I have promised my cousin," said Don Ramon, " to free her from the doleful whinings of this animal; and I am resolved to keep my word."

" It is then the senora who wishes it? I shall obey at once; but I doubt much our success."

Without knowing why Donna Carmen felt touched by the simplicity of Joaquin's remark, Gongora gave the bait to Joaquin, who slowly waded into the sea. The hook trailed on the surface, but no crocodile dashed at it from the deep. If there was one there, it never stirred.

" Well," said the fisher.

" Well," said Gongora, " how could you attract him with the hook bobbing about like a rope's end in a breeze ?"

" Will you try it ?" said Joaquin, ironically.

" Willingly."

The moment Gongora took in his hand the dangerous instrument, another strange doleful cry seemed to issue from the water, and froze the hearts of the negroes with terror.

Gongora was not more fortunate than Joaquin, and retired in spite, after half an hour's trial.

" It is just as I predicted," said the pearl fisher, with an air of triumph.

" All this does not seem natural," observed Don Ramon, to his brother and Donna Carmen. " Have you ever seen an expert hunter rejoice at the absence of game ?"

" A word, brother," replied the monk, whispering in Don Ramon's ear. " Did you hear that mysterious cry which terrified those slaves ?"

" Yes, Eusebio."

" I kept my eyes steadily fixed on Joaquin's countenance, and although his lips never moved, 1 could swear on the holy cross that that sound proceeded from his accursed throat."

" But for what purpose, Eusebio ?"

" A little lower, brother—a little lower. The fisherman, whom his companions surname Requiem, like his father Melchior, understands the habits of these animals. Do you believe he does not know how to kill them ?"

" What do you mean ?"

" Are you not aware, brother, that there are crocodiles who come at a given signal to receive any food that may be presented to them, without injuring the hand of the donor ? The Egyptian priests have also sacred crocodiles."

" I begin to comprehend you."

" Very well ; this cry of Joaquin's was unquestionably a signal. The fisherman wishes to save the monster you are pursuing."

" You are an astonishing man, Eusebio. But how can we force the wretch to confess it, or alter his resolution? A suspicion cannot bear the force of a proof."

" You want the means, governor, murmured the monk, casting a glance towards Joaquin. " Since this insolent fisherman resists your authority, it is necessary to make his pride kneel down before you."

He then conversed in a low tone with Don Ramon, whose countenance brightened up with a savage joy. He motioned to Gongora to approach.

"You believe, then, that we must abandon the hunt?"

"Yes, master; success is impossible; otherwise Joaquin would have rooted him out. Do you know what I saw him do, one day?"

"Tell it aloud to my brother and cousin, so that all may hear."

"One beautiful morning, during the bull-fights, Joaquin was washing his tent. He felt a crocodile gently dragging it through his hands. You, or any of us, would most likely have run away. He, however, perceiving the water clear, and the depth insignificant, put his knife between his teeth, and allowed himself to be pulled away with his tent cover. Once at the bottom, he tried to drown the animal; but finding it impossible, he dived under it, and ripped open its belly, retiring with his property."

"What courage!" cried Donna Carmen, with admiration.

"And yet, my brave hunter," said Don Ramon, "you refuse to rouse us the crocodile which infests this bay?"

"I do refuse it."

"You hear that!" said the commander, in a voice of thunder. "Very well, I have sworn to accomplish it, and once more I promise you shall witness the death of this frightful monster."

There was a dead silence, every one looking at Don Ramon.

"I have discovered the means of putting new life into you, young man. In a short time, you will pray me on bended knees to allow you to seek out the crocodile. Oh! I can excuse you; the young horses must be broken in by spur and bridle, before they will work submissively."

These words, the mysterious meaning of which no one understood, caused, nevertheless, a general alarm, Joaquin alone held down his head, and remarked—"It is folly to take an oath which cannot be kept."

The slaves expected to see the commander's whip descend on Joaquin's shoulders.

"Bring a solid log of wood," cried Don Ramon.

Gongora obeyed, and dragged before the governor a square log of mahogany.

"Jesu Maria!" cried Donna Carmen, "what are you going to do?"

"Silence," said Don Ramon, severely. "Silence, senorita, and do not betray before those slaves the secret of your unworthy weakness."

"Do not suppose, sir, that I am to be deprived of my liberty by violence. If you intend to torture this young man into obedience, I shall not suffer it. I am not your slave, sir."

"Patience, cousin; I shall not touch a hair of this fopling's head; I swear it. Will that satisfy you?"

"You swear it," said she, in a suffocated voice.

"And you, on the other hand, must promise not to throw any obstacle in the way of that which may occur, because I will not permit it; besides, no one will obey you. I am the commander."

"I give you my promise," stammered the poor girl, who, at the same time, accused herself of cowardice.

"Here is the log, senor."

"Drive it into the sea, so that one half of it may only appear above the surface."

The order was executed amidst general astonishment. Joaquin saw only a menace directed against himself.

"Are all the hunters here?" demanded Ramon.

"Only one is absent."

"Name him."

"Melchior Requiem."

"Melchior, Joaquin's father, the best of our marksmen, why is he absent at this important moment?"

"He has been sick these three days," Joaquin hastened to reply.

"What right have any to reply who are not spoken to?" said the commander, drily.

"The son has spoken the truth," hazarded Gongora.

"Pitch the tents under the shade of the trees," cried Ramon, amidst the general alarm. "And let a party of you bring Melchior here. We will wait for him."

"But," cried Joaquin, advancing, "you have misunderstood me. My father is in the very height of fever; to bring him here is to sentence him to death."

Don Ramon was deaf. He waved his hand to Gongora to set off, and turned his horse's head towards the wood.

"Stop," said Joaquin, seizing the boatman by the arm, "you are deceived. You see well enough that Don Ramon does not understand. Is it not so?" continued he, in a most moving accent. "Is it not a mistake? You cannot order such a thing. A moment, Gongora—tell him, master, to stop —do tell him."

Don Ramon was already at some distance, and Gongora endeavoured to disengage his arm for the purpose of proceeding on his mission.

" I must obey, Joaquin."

" Obey," said he, with a bitter smile. " Do you not see that such an order is impossible. You, Friar Eusebio, you, a man of God, I see are only waiting to countermand the order. One minute—one second, so that I may speak to Don Ramon. He cannot be serious. He merely puts me to the test. Is it not so ? My God, this man will not understand me, and the order is obeyed—a terrible evil, you will see, must be the result. The monk shrugged his shoulders. " It is true, then, that all abandon me. Ah ! their hearts are hard. No— no pity in them. My God—my God !" Then suddenly his eye brightened. " I am saved ! Donna Carmen is here."

" Donna Carmen," reprovingly observed the priest, " has already asked for mercy. Do you believe, then, that my brother, without her supplication, would not have punished you for your disobedience ?"

Joaquin was crushed with this reply, and fell upon the sand in the most frightful agony. He remained a long time insensible to the incomprehensible scene. Donna Carmen was seated in her tent, and the governor and the monk conversed in a low voice. Finally, Gongora appeared, followed by two of his companions, who bore the old Melchior. His bald front—his saddened countenance, bearing a noble expression, though rutted with the lines of old age ; his eyes almost robbed of their vitality, all contributed to arouse a feeling of veneration. He looked at the commander with surprise.

" What do you require from the old Melchior ? I suffer greatly, and I have been deprived of my son's attentions. My lips are parched ; but my arm is too feeble to reach the jar of water to assuage my thirst. Why, then, am I brought hither ? What has happened ? You are silent—some misfortune hath befallen Joaquin. Is it so ?" added he, clasping his hands with despair.

" I am here, father," said Joaquin.

" Thanks be to God ! Then, why am I here ?"

" You will soon know, Melchior," said the commandant.

" Your son does not know how to attract the crocodile to the beach. His attempts have all failed."

" That is impossible," said Melchior; "I have myself taught him.   He is an able hunter."

Don Ramon smiled.

" Be silent; for pity's sake, father, be silent," said Joaquin, in a low voice.

" Silence, fisherman!" thundered Ramon. " We will not

subject your son to so severe a trial in causing him to attach you to this log.   If the crocodile attacks you, your son knows how to defend you or to revenge you."

" Horror! horror!" cried Donna Carmen.   " Don Ramon, can you be guilty of such horrible cruelty?"

A general cry of horror burst from all the hunters and fishermen.   Joaquin was roused from his stupor; and marching

2   c

rapidly towards Don Ramon, he stood before him face to face, looking into his eyes.

" You dare not do that. It is an infernal idea to spring from the mind of any who bear the image of God, or who has been suckled by a Christian mother. It is an atrocious piece of raillery. That is all."

" Bind the old man to the stake," shouted Ramon.

" I will go to it myself," said the old fisherman, although the rigour of the fever trembled through every joint.

" Do not go, father; do not go. You see the governor only tests us. He makes sport of us as no executioner ever did of a criminal."

" Go," cried Ramon.

" It is an accursed work, senor," said the old man, " and God will remember it." Then he squeezed Joaquin's hands in his. " You tremble, my child," said he, in a soft tone. " Be calm; let us sustain our reputation, and dishonour not the surname of your father."

He advanced calmly to the stake, whilst his son shook his arms on high with grief and rage.

" Give him a musket," said the governor. " Well, young man, do you now refuse to fight the crocodile ?"

" Do you not see my hand is unsteady ? "

" It will be steady enough when the enemy comes."

" Do, for mercy's sake," begged Joaquin, " attach me to the stake, and let my father take the musket ; his aim is surer."

" His strength would fail him. We are too merciful for that. Bind the old man fast, Gongora."

" Do not approach me," said Melchior. " Do you not know me ? I have no fear." And he leaned against the post, crossing his arms on his chest; his countenance calm, without any defiance. Suddenly he shivered.

" You tremble already," said Ramon.

" It is the fever, commander. Have you forgotten that ?"

A profound silence reigned over all. Suddenly the water was violently agitated, and foamed and tossed ; the water dashing against the stake.

" Be calm, my son ; be worthy of my lessons."

They soon saw glancing on the water the shining carcase of the crocodile. Joaquin did not fire; he was adjusting his piece, but a shower of balls rattled on the mailed back of the monster. The crocodile plunged down, leaving a red spot on the waves, but little injured by the discharge from the hunters.

" Commander," cried Joaquin, desperate, " was that what we agreed upon ? I undertook to kill him alone. A hundred balls would not penetrate his coat."

" Let no one fire. I will have it so," said Ramon.

Joaquin then took a long breath, and whistled in a soft, melancholy manner. The frightful head of the monster surged up his mouth half open. Joaquin fired. He hit the animal right in the eye; and shortly the huge body rolled dead towards the beach.

Joaquin rushed towards the stake, and was about to lift his father in his arms. Melchior uttered a loud cry. Horror !— the perspiration stood on Joaquin's brow, when his father pointed to his leg, where the crocodile had succeeded in inflicting a frightful wound. Anxious to encourage his son, the brave old man had not uttered a groan, but spoke in a mild and tender tone. All the hunters looked on mute with admiration and horror. The friar proceeded to Donna Carmen's tent, to invite her to remount her horse. As for Joaquin, the blood rushed to his head, and he fell down.

" It must be a dream," muttered he. " Oh! my God ; when will these horrible visions depart ? When shall I awake ?"

He slowly arose and followed the slaves, who bore away Melchior, saying, in a convulsive voice,

" My poor father, you were silent and suffering—losing life slowly—whilst I calmly awaited the opportunity to fire. But how to be revenged ; and upon whom—upon whom !" cried he, pressing his brow with his burning hands. Then suddenly uttering a cry of joy, he snatched a musket from one of the hunters, and levelled it at Don Ramon. The commander had, however, been observing his movements; and on a sign given, Gongora and two slaves threw Joaquin on the ground, and bound him fast. Don Ramon leaned towards Donna Carmen as she approached, and, pointing to the crocodile, observed, coldly—" Senora, you are obeyed."

Firmly seated in the saddle, whilst the horse impatiently reared on the sand, Donna Carmen looked with a mournful eye on the dismal scene, and finally remarked to Ramon—

" I, nevertheless, senor, demanded forgiveness for Joaquin."

" You are too capricious, my beautiful cousin. You love courageous men ; and I have afforded Joaquin an opportunity in which his has shone to some advantage."

She regarded him with such a profound look of contempt, that he turned away to order the tents to be struck. At the same moment, Gongora, the experienced boatman, approached the commander, and said anxiously—

" Master, have you observed the sky ?"

" Well, it is most beautiful, and the wind low," remarked the friar.

" I do not like the appearance of that dark gray cloud, like a man's hand, on the horizon. We must pass the jungle, and should the tempest overtake us, we shall be fixed in the marsh ; besides, you know, that in similar cases the maroons or run-away slaves, as well as some other characters whom you know, take advantage of the difficulty, from their refuge in the thicket."

Don Ramon partook of Gongora's uneasiness ; and hastily glancing at the number of his hunters, he became re-assured, but ordered the boatmen to proceed in advance, and carefully examine every sign in the leaves, stones, or broken branches, as well as the humid soil.

The party pursued this time a much more circuitous route, and further from the sea than the first. The path they took was along the edge of a brook, which tossed and boiled beneath. Gongora acquitted himself with much zeal, but very little success. He suddenly stopped, and said in a low voice—

" Master, I cannot discover the smallest sign, yet I have a strange presentiment of danger, which I cannot account for. Ah ! if Joaquin would only assist us. The most wary Caribean Indian could not cover his track from his eye."

After reflecting a moment, Don Ramon turned towards the young pearl fisher, whom two robust negroes were carrying on a litter, to which he was tied.

" Hear me, Joaquin : if you will guide us to the hatto, I promise to forgive you, and will wave the punishment your offence deserves." Joaquin never turned his head, nor did he appear to listen. He seemed absorbed in contemplating his aged father, whose nervous shiverings, from time to time, alone announced the presence of life. " Will you, senorita, speak to this stubborn fellow ? Do speak to him, I conjure you." Donna Carmen shrugged her shoulders with disdain. The commander then feigned to disregard the pearl fisher, and, in a loud voice, said to Gongora, " I recommend you to use the utmost caution ; remember the safety of Donna Carmen is at stake." Joaquin heard him then, and with a look directed Ramon to his manacles. " Will you swear not to escape," said the commander. Joaquin inclined his head in the affirmative. The slave then cut the cords. "I confide myself to you," said the commander. "Your head will likewise answer for her safety."

After a few minutes' march Joaquin stopped; and, without lifting his eyes, which were fixed upon the ravine, he said softly—

"Buffalo hunters have passed here within an hour."

"Come," said Ramon, "you are either a fool, or you wish to deceive us. There is not a root bruised, a branch broken, or a single footmark before us."

"True."

"The Frenchmen," said the friar, sneeringly, "must then hunt the buffalo in the air."

"No," said Joaquin, without noticing the satirical monk; "but they make use of stratagems, learned amongst Caribeans, to deceive the Spanish lancers."

"Well, what signs have they left?"

"The signs are in the water," said the pearl fisher, with profound conviction. "We have not had a drop of rain these two months, and the muddy colour of the water could only be produced by numerous feet moving in the bed of the stream. Here comes the storm. To make up for lost time, all we can do, is to reach a clearance where we can pitch the tents."

In truth no time was to be lost. The sky became rapidly dark and gloomy, and a stifling heat indicated the necessity of profiting by the pearl fisher's advice. In the Antilles the tempests are sudden and tremendous, and the very instant the troop had reached a clearance, large hot drops of rain pattered around them, whilst the sudden claps of thunder burst close overhead. As they filed on to the clearance, they soon perceived sufficient indications to convince all of the infallibility of Joaquin's penetration.

"A drying shed!" cried all the hunters at once, in the utmost consternation. This hut, erected for smoking meat, was covered over with the stems and leaves of the palm-tree. Joists were stretched across, on which were hung the quarters of wild boar's flesh, the bones and skins of which fried beneath produced a thick searching smoke preferable to that of wood. In fact, the volatile gases, disengaged from the skin and bones, attaches itself to the flesh, whilst the smoke from wood alone escapes through the sides of the hut. The buccaniers prefer this cured flesh to any other, and consider it delicious, having acquired the custom from the Indians. The Caribeans roast their prisoners of war in the same manner, and call the place and manner of sacrifice Barbacoa and Borican.

Don Ramon, when he perceived the smoking shed, cried furiously to Joaquin—

"Wretch, you have betrayed us! You have led us into a snare. Confess. You have held correspondence with our enemies."

"But the shed is deserted—abandoned," said Gongora. "The heretics have not even left, according to their custom, a sick companion or a slave prisoner to cook their food."

"In that case," said the commander, "the pirates were afraid, and have fled at our approach."

"Say, rather," remarked Joaquin, "that they have watched us, and are now surrounding us. The French buccaniers and the British hunters are not men who run away and leave Spaniards to eat their dinner, if we were twice as numerous as they; but I do not fear their approach. They cannot behave with more refined barbarity than Don Ramon Carral," added he, as he heard old Melchior groan in agony, whilst Donna Carmen had been removed into the shed.

"Scoundrel!" roared Don Ramon, "on your knees," and he rushed towards him with his cane uplifted. The butt end of a gun stopped the blow.

"Cowardly rabble," thundered, in a hoarse voice, a man who suddenly appeared from a dense clump of bushes, and approached the commander.

"Who gave you authority to invade the shelter of honest buccaniers?"

A thunderbolt seemed to have fallen amidst the troop, who remained stupified before the unknown. He was between forty and fifty years of age. Tufts of gray hair were scattered over his head. His nostrils were dilated with passion; his eyes, keen and piercing, were injected with blood. His countenance might have appeared repulsive; but for the valiant and hardy expression of manners which removed all trace of savage or vindictive cruelty. He was little, and, to all appearance, possessed no remarkable degree of strength, so that his muscles and sinews must have been of steel to account for his harassing and dangerous occupation. It was astonishing to observe the degree of terror which this buffalo hunter produced. Instead of surrounding and seizing him, Don Ramon's hunters dare scarcely look at him. Joaquin alone looked upon him with an aspect of resistance.

"Not a man of you stir or touch his arms," continued the buccanier, "or else it will be an affair between them and me."

Donna Carmen remained an immoveable spectator at the entrance of the hut, the vapour and intolerable smell having prevented her from penetrating farther. She was surprised at the effect produced by the hoarse voice and savage look of one man over the ferocious Don Ramon and his troop. She watched with interest the movements of the first buccanier she had ever beheld. The dress of this personage, who is to play an important part in this narrative, was as singular as his habitation. He wore a strong canvass jacket, two shirts, and a pair of drawers, reaching half way down his thigh. His feet were defended from the thorny paths of the forest by untanned buffalo skin. His shoulders were marked with the blood of the animals he had slain, and which many of these active hunters could overtake by swiftness of foot, hamstringing them as they ran. At his waist hung a sheath made of crocodile skin, in which were ranged a bayonet and four long sharp knives ; whilst his waistband was composed of fine sheeting, which he could spread out in the woods as a covering. The beard of this odd being seemed, from its bushy appearance and length, to have grown at will for many years. His head was protected by a low-crowned hat, with a peak only in front over the eyes. He leaned negligently on his long-barrelled musket, and, after a short pause, which seemed sufficiently long to the Spaniards, he said, sharply—

" I wait your answer."

Seeing that Don Ramon was too much alarmed to speak, Joaquin replied, firmly—

" The shed seemed abandoned. We were surprised by the tempest, and could not allow this young lady to be exposed to its violence."

He pointed to Donna Carmen, whilst Don Ramon remounted his horse.

The buccanier regarded with melancholy interest the countenance of the young pearl fisher, and, in a softer tone, remarked—

" That is another affair, my young sir. In that case I offer you all hospitality, although I have an act of justice to perform. However, let the anger of heaven be first dissipated. On your behalf, and also that of the young lady, I suspend the execution of my vow."

" Bah !" arrogantly interrupted Don Ramon.   " If you had not offered hospitality we should have taken it without much ceremony.   Are you left alone here ?"

" No," replied the buccanier, with a meaning smile.   " I am protected by two faithful companions."

" Where are they ?" quickly asked the commander.

" My musket is one.   It is an old servant fabricated expressly for me.   Barrel four feet and a half, carries sixteen to the pound.   Here I have twenty pounds of good powder," said he, pointing to a calibash, stuffed with powder, and carried like a knapsack, surrounded with strong sheeting.

" And your other companion ?"

" My other one ?" said the buccanier, with immeasurable disdain.   " It is that fear which the name of a buccanier inspires in every Spaniard.   If you killed me I know how my companions would avenge me."

Donna Carmen and Joaquin could not help admiring a man who, surrounded by enemies, believed himself capable of repelling them solely by the force of his own courage and the terrible renown of his race.

" Ah !" cried Don Ramon, pale with rage, now that the band of buccaniers had vanished, and the prospect of taking a prisoner appeared in their place, " you wish to brave it out do you ?   Advance, there, and seize him."

Gongora and another fisherman approached, but with such reluctance and hesitation, that the buccanier smiled.

"You see, commander, where your power is.   Come on, my brave fishermen.   What are you afraid of ?   I lower my arms.   You may take me like a lamb from the fold."

This very seeming compliance, far from encouraging the two men, only led them to anticipate a snare, and they stopped short before him.

" Are you wearied, my brave hunters ?   Must I come to you ?"   Their feet seemed nailed to the ground.

" Obey !" shouted Ramon, " are you fools ?"

" Noble senor," interrupted the buccanier, " I have only to inform you that the moment your slaves touch me, you will drop down dead where you are now lording it with such authority."

" What do you say ?" murmured Ramon.   The buccanier uttered a shrill cry.   The rain was then pouring down, and the lightning zigzaging through the trees.   Another cry replied to the buccanier, apparently issuing from the heavens, and ringing in the ears of the commander and his troops.

" Here—here!" cried the buccanier. " Vent-en-Panne, take good aim at the Spaniard. Just break his arm. Tayan —Tayan, Curaçoa! As for you, Gerondif, you can seize him, and bind him to the tail of his horse."

Confusion and terror spread like a panic amongst the hun-ters. Many fled. Joaquin threw himself before Donna Car-

men, prepared to defend her at the risk of life. Don Ramon followed the direction of the buccanier's eye, and beheld, amidst the green leaves of the tree beneath which he was, the shining barrel of a gun, and holding it cross-legged on a bench, was a figure, having more the appearance of a large monkey, than anything else. It was Vent-en-Panne. Don Ramon trembled, and struck his spurs into his horse's sides, with the intention of flying. His horse would not move, for on each side of it growled two formidable dogs, such as are employed in hunting the wild boar. The commander was stupified, confounded, and alarmed, as if a tableau of alarming spectres had been suddenly unfolded. The buccanier advanced towards the two fishermen who were charged to arrest him. With his own hand he seized them, and bent them both to the ground.

"Mercy!" cried both at once.

"You are only slaves," said the stranger. "Begone! fortunately you did not touch me, otherwise—" They arose with hands folded in token of gratitude. "Now, go straight to your master. Go—seize him." They dared not disobey the fiery look of command which the buccanier gave them. "Now, an act of justice will be accomplished," said he, in a loud and haughty voice, to Don Ramon. "I have offered you shelter and hospitality; you have insolently repelled them—you are both cowardly and cruel. You must be humiliated, and punished."

"Holy mother of God!" cried Don Ramon, who began to recover himself, "are ye all mad that you permit a heretic to heap such abuse on your master?" Then he added with a ferocious look, "I shall never forget one of those who now abandon me."

Several of the fishermen and slaves began to take courage. The buccanier replied, calmly—

"Señor commander, I command you to observe a respectful silence in my presence."

"Fool! respect a pirate?"

"And to listen to your judge in a more humble attitude."

"You, my judge?" sneeringly said Don Ramon.

"Vent-en-Panne," said the laconic buccanier, "make ready!"

This peremptory order at once succeeded. The commander lifted his eyes towards the branch, where the marksman was sitting, and, fascinated by his look, as if by a serpent, he remained silent.

"All right, Leopard," replied the watchman.

When this terrible and well-known name was uttered, a movement of curiosity and terror agitated all. Don Ramon conceived his fate sealed, and repeated, with affright—

"The Leopard!"

The Spaniards pressed forward to look at this celebrated

adventurer, chief of the band of buccaniers, of the port De la Paix, who was renowned for his audacity and stratagems, and upon whose head a price was laid of 100,000 piastres. Joaquin and Donna Carmen then fully understood the assurance of this extraordinary man of whom so many fabulous things were related ; such as having, single-handed, and armed with two pistols, kept at bay 100 lancers.

"Yes," said the Leopard, coldly. "You, who have so long been judge and master, are about to find both in your host of the forest. You have abused the power you exercised over God's creatures, born of the same flesh and blood. There must now be some requital. But first dismount, unless you want these two valets at your side to assist you."

Don Ramon dismounted, foaming with rage.

"Now proceed to Joaquin Requiem, and remove those bands, which I see still on his arms."

"Never, never ! I would die first," said the commander, who observed the look of contempt which Donna Carmen threw upon him.

"Get the sulphur matches ready," ordered the Leopard.

These words soon restored agility to Don Ramon's limbs. These matches are lighted and placed between the fingers of each hand, where they are left to burn to the bone. Such is the punishment which the Spaniards experienced when the pirates put them to the torture, to compel a revelation of their treasures.

"Is that all ?" demanded Don Ramon.

"Certainly not," said the Leopard. "Joaquin Requiem, the poor pearl-fisher, who possesses a brave and generous heart, —you, whom this man has trampled under foot—you, whose spirit he sought to break, and whom he has played with without mercy—revenge yourself. Your father, whom he has crushed, is in that palanquin. Revenge him."

Joaquin stepped before Ramon, and measured him with his eye.

"Oh !" cried the latter, plucking out his sword. "Beware! take care, slave!"

"Not another movement," cried Joaquin, who had thrown himself instantly on the commander and wrested from him his sword, which he broke across his knee and threw at the feet of his trembling master. "A man of honour ought only to wear a sword ; there is yours converted into poniards ; these are the most fitting weapons for Don Ramon Carral." Then seizing the commander's arm, he continued in a stern voice, "Now we stand face to face—unarmed man to man. Your servants are no longer ready to chastise me at a sign of your hand, nor am I any longer bound. Well, master, strike me now." Don Ramon felt his hair rise with astonishment. He looked around him. Old Melchior attempted to rise from the litter, but he fell back with a groan. Powerfully moved, and excited by the cry of agony, Joaquin raised his hand to strike the commander.

"Oh! have mercy on him—no violence," cried Donna Carmen, stretching her arms in a supplicating manner towards the pearl-fisher. The sweet voice subdued Joaquin's anger, and he remained motionless.

"Be quick," said the Leopard, sharply, "I have other matters to attend to. Pronounce judgment on your master; it shall be executed forthwith, on my faith. I say, Don Ramon, do you hear? Down on your knees before Joaquin."

Again the commander would have resisted.

"The pontlet will bring him to his senses," cried Vent-en-Panne.

Under the Leopard's orders a cord was put round the commander's brow, and turned tighter and tighter, with two sticks. At the second turn Ramon fell on his knees.

"Pronounce judgment, Joaquin."

"But," replied he, "am I not amply revenged, by seeing him kneeling before me, and trembling like a coward in his humiliation?"

"Good, very good, my son," murmured Melchior.

"It is nobly done," observed Donna Carmen, with gratitude.

"You are wrong, my lad," said the Leopard, "you should never half crush a serpent. Take care—he will have his revenge when he leaves this place; but," continued he, with a sigh of regret; "you will have it so. Be it as you wish. Rise, Don Ramon Carral." The commander stood up. "Take particular notice of what I say, and remember my words. This lad is a fool, and I can read in your eyes how you will reward his forbearance. But, if any mischief befals him in consequence of this rencounter, you will settle it with me, Don Ramon, if I follow you over the last ember of Rancheria; ay, we shall know where to find you, if you dive into the bowels of the earth. Swear, then, by the sacred name of Our Lady, that you pardon Joaquin Requiem, and will make no attempt on his life."

"I swear," said Ramon, hastily, with a sardonic smile.

"I absolve you from the oath," exclaimed the monk, aroused from his long constraint.

"But, I will not," said the Leopard, irritated at this fanatical fervour. "Now you may go—the tempest has passed."

Whilst the commander, Donna Carmen, and the monk, re-mounted, the buccanier took Joaquin aside, and observed—"My brave marksman, if you have ever any reason to regret your generosity, depend always on the Leopard. He will not fail you in the hour of need."

They shook hands in friendship, and the pearl-fisher has-tened to overtake the troop, which departed in solemn silence. No sooner had the party disappeared in the depths of the wood, than the Leopard burst into a hearty laugh, which was echoed from the tree by Vent-en-Panne.

"Fools and cowards," said he, when his loud laughter had subsided. "We have had a narrow escape. We have im-posed upon them most excellently. I shall enjoy it a long time. It is decidedly the best hit I ever made amongst the Spaniards."

"Your summons to me," said Vent-en-Panne, "had a most admirable effect."

"Ay, they saw a buccanier hid under every leaf; but I shall never forget the frightful grimace Don Ramon made when he discovered you."

"It does not signify," observed Vent-en-Panne, sliding down the tree. "It is not so good as that back and back affair with the hundred lancers."

"Audacity, my lad, is the mother of safety. Surrounded, as we were by those lancers, no one was willing to become a sacrifice for the others. Without that we should not have been here. But it is time we were on board, and running round by Rancheria. I cannot trust that governor, and his hypocritical brother. I think of making a tour round to-night, and should anything happen to Joaquin, I should be unhappy. He is a brave young fellow. If he is in any danger, I must get him out of it, and enrol him amongst our fellows. He will make a first-rate recruit."

The two adventurers then loaded themselves with the smoked meat, and reached the Bay de la Hache, conversing about their exploits amongst the Spaniards.

CHAPTER II.

THE HATTO AND THE HUT.

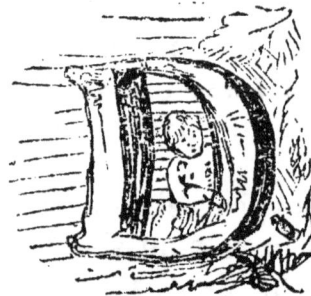 URING the progress of the troop, the commander did not address a single word to any one, not even to his brother ; but, when the hunters arrived in front of the hatto, he gave the signal to disband, saying to the pearl-fisher—

" Do you think I will keep faith with that brigand ? "

" I should have believed so."

" And do you think I shall forget that you threatened my life with a musket ? "

" People never forget that which they have feared, Don Ramon."

" And, after all, you expect that I shall not have my revenge ! "

" I await it, master, and so does the Leopard."

" Fool ! poor fool, to suppose that the heart can bleed from no other cause than the stroke of a poniard."

" Have you anything else to say to me, senor ? Old Melchior awaits me."

" Yes, your father is dying. Is it not so ? To calm his fever, and heal his wounds, to restore him to health, the services of a doctor are required. You would pay for them in your blood."

" The skill of Friar Eusebio will surely not be wanting when a fellow Christian suffers."

" Without doubt, my brother could carry life with him into the hut. There is still time ; but he sails this evening for the port De la Paix, to negotiate an exchange of prisoners."

" Serpent accursed ! " murmured Joaquin.

" So old Melchior will have his son for a kind physician, and you will reap the whole credit of the cure for yourself."

He turned slowly and deliberately away, entering the hatto. Joaquin spoke not. He saw that cruelty was premeditated and inexorable, therefore he would not implore Ramon's pity, but swore to be revenged this time, without scruple.

With the assistance of Gongora, Melchior was transported to his hut, and waited upon by his son, until the evening. About eleven o'clock, when Joaquin saw his father asleep, or rather prostrated by suffering ; he rose, and slipped into his belt a hunting knife, then, with a cautious step, prepared to leave the hut. The slight movement aroused the sinking invalid, and he murmured, " Drink, Joaquin."

The pearl-fisher returned towards the couch, and poured some drops of water on his father's lips, which were pale and parched. Melchior made another effort to raise himself, but his head was heavy, and he said in a disturbed tone—" Do not leave me, my son."

" I am beside you, father." But as soon as the forced respiration of the old man announced that he had fallen into a kind of half slumber, the young man threw a tender look upon him, and leaving the hut, proceeded towards the commander's mansion. The gates were closed, and a profound silence reigned around the hatto. Joaquin went twice round it, then stood before the Moorish balcony, half inclined to scale it, and see if any window was open through which he might penetrate to Don Ramon's chamber, He was at length about to put this resolution into effect, when he heard a sudden groan, like the agonised voice of death, proceed from Donna Carmen's apartment, where a feeble light still glimmered. Surprised and alarmed, he listened attentively ; but no other sound broke the silence.

We shall now describe what occurred at the hatto, during the evening. Donna Carmen, on her return, announced that she would see no one that evening, and retired to her apartment. This chamber was furnished in regal splendour, which, in the Indies, as well as in Spain, contrasted strangely with the miserable huts of their slaves and peasants. A velvet tapestry figured with gold, carpets of a most splendid pattern, and a silver lamp fed with perfumed oil, adorned the apartment. Mirrors were fixed in the wall, with burnished silver frames, sculptured in a masterly manner, as well as the oak plinths, and mouldings of the room. A velvet covered door at the bottom of the room, concealed in a partition of scented wood, the entrance to an alcove, which enclosed a private chapel, a bed of white damask, bordered with Spanish silver lace, and two small mahogany tables, covered with coral, gold filagree, precious stones, and various other curiosities in vogue at that period.

When Donna Carmen had confined herself to this chamber, where she had lived and dreamed since infancy, she endeavoured to gather together the confused recollections of the day, and judge between master and servant. The result of her reflections was anything but favourable to Ramon, and she determined anew never to give her hand to a man for whom she entertained such hatred and contempt. The evening passed away.   All the sounds around the hatto died away by degrees, although the young girl remarked it not. The silver lamp suspended from the roof, only threw a mournful shade around. All at once, the chamber door burst open, and the commander stood before her.   Donna Carmen, absorbed in her sad reflections, did not at first observe him, except with vague surprise. Don Ramon bowed, smiling, and shut the door behind him. The young girl then threw aside her torpidity, and, assuming all her natural dignity, arose, and said, very dryly—

"You here, sir, at this hour, and after I had declared that I would receive no one?"

Don Ramon appeared to expect this reception.

"Between relatives there is little need of ceremony. Besides, an important matter must be considered, which cannot be adjourned until to-morrow."

"Explain yourself clearly, commander."

"I wish to speak of our marriage, senora."

"You have admirably chosen your time and place to propose such a subject to an orphan still in mourning for her father."

"This marriage was his last desire, Carmen, and circumstances now render it imperative that you make known your determination ; and I tell you that I will have it."

"How bold you are, senor, when you have females to deal with. You know *then* how to terrify."

"I await your answer, my beautiful cousin," said Ramon, coolly seating himself.

"You ought to guess it," cried Donna Carmen, standing before him with a look of disdain.

"I have, then, a favoured rival?"

"A rival ! You know well that I live here secluded, between slaves and a tyrant."

"A thousand thanks, senorita, but why then refuse my demand with such haughtiness. I am not an old, gray-headed, wrinkle-faced man ; and I can neither bring to you misery nor dishonour. Besides, I love you to that degree to be jealous of you. What more do you require?"

Donna Carmen hesitated a moment, and then replied, "That which I expect, Don Ramon—ah! you may say I am ill to please, and foolishly romantic; but I desire a husband who will make me respect him."

The commander shook with impatience.

"Who then dare in this place show a want of courtesy to the wife of Don Ramon Carral?"

"I know you are a violent and remorseless master, but I repeat that I shall never choose for a husband either a coward or a hypocrite. Do you understand me?"

With an irritable gesture she pointed to the door, retaining a dignified and imposing attitude.

Don Ramon did not stir. "My dear Cousin, since we are

now in progress of explanation on both sides, and since you have rejected my proposition concerning this delicate affair, I shall put the question more simply. You have only to choose between the husband of your father's choice, or a cloister, where penance and want will occupy the place of riches and luxury."

" Do you speak thus and seriously to the daughter of your cousin, Don Juan de Larates ? "

" Most seriously."

" And you supposed I would for a moment hesitate between you and the service of God?"

" You, then, hate me ?" said Ramon, his lips pale and trembling with emotion. " But," suppressing his rage, " you cannot struggle against me; I must be absolute master of Rancheria, and the obstinate resistance of a young girl shall neither bend my will nor mar my projects."

" Such, then, is your pretended love. I knew well the mask would hurt your face in time. So this marriage is a sort of bargain or sale, where the heart counts nothing. You love me because 200 slaves are marked as my lot ; but we shall see what power can control me thus in my own house."

She stretched out her hand towards the bell-pull.

" It is useless, senorita ; no one will answer it."

The cord was cut. Donna Carmen uttered a cry of alarm.

" What infamous snare have you dared to prepare for me ? "

" What I have resolved to do must be done at any price, and therefore I have adopted my measures."

" I dream," said Donna Carmen; " such deliberate villany is impossible. But beware, sir ; my voice may reach my servants. Retire whilst there is time. If not, I shall cause you to be driven forth with ignominy."

" Let them come ; they will be good witnesses to the marriage," said Ramon, endeavouring to seize her hand.

" Wretch !" cried the young girl, retreating to the door of the little chapel, " do not approach me."

" As you will, senora, but let us converse rationally. Your choice is reduced now to marriage or dishonour; for I am resolved not to leave this chamber, except in presence of witnesses."

" My God ! my God !" murmured the young girl, bursting into tears.

" You may affirm what you please about violence and surprise, but men will not believe you. They will rather consider you fortunate in finding one who would cover such a stain with his honourable name."

"Just heaven! is there not enough of this? So you anticipated finding me alone and unprotected, and that I should implore for safety like a suppliant; but you are deceived," said the courageous girl, calling to her aid her whole strength of mind. "Listen to me, noble commander, I will not hesitate between the choice of yourself or ignominy ; I should prefer even dishonour to the still greater stigma of bearing your infamous name."

This time Ramon started up with fury in his countenance, and rushed towards her.

"Abuse not my patience, senorita. I must have your consent. Sign, sign!"

"In the name of God, do not approach me!" The commander was not more than two steps from the partition. "In the name of my father, who was your friend," cried she, trembling, and in a wild accent.

"Why implore in his name? It is him you oppose. Sign, sign, I tell you."

Pale as death, and nearly dead with fright, Donna Carmen pressed against the partition, to seek refuge in her sacred oratory, but at the same moment Ramon's hand touched her arm. He was about to seize her. She suddenly bowed down, slipped behind him with great agility, and, on turning, he saw her before him, holding a small dagger in her hand, her cheeks suffused, and her nostril wide. The commander hesitated a moment. The creoles generally carry a poisoned dagger, of the most venomous character. Ramon blushed at the idea of being intimidated by a girl, but sought first to snatch from her the weapon. "Children should not play with such toys," said he, attempting to wrest the weapon from her. But the poniard seemed glued to Donna Carmen's hand, she grasped it so convulsively. Indignant and horrified at a brutal gesture of the commander, Donna Carmen threw her hand forward to repel him. At that moment an agonised cry struck her ear (it was the same Joaquin had heard), and Don Ramon Carral fell dead at her feet.

The young girl remained motionless, without life or sensation, before the corpse. She then gazed around her with horrified consciousness. The dark and gloomy chamber seemed like a tomb, and that strange suffocating feeling known to prisoners pressed on her breast. As her reason returned, she experienced a strange fascination, an irresistible desire to look upon the body extended on the carpet. To escape from the dreadful scene, she pushed against the partition, pulled the velvet curtain aside, and staggered on to the balcony without daring to look behind her, and in her convulsive efforts imagining the hand of Don Ramon was planted on her shoulder, to drag her back.

Once on the balcony, she breathed freer. The night was beautiful, the stars alone watching over the calm and silent scene. Perfumes hung upon the air, and the softened influence of all around made her think the whole a dream.

She trembled as she observed a dark immoveable figure, like a shade, under the balcony. Hope, which her troubled spirit had first seized upon, instantly vanished. This terrible witness had, without doubt, heard the death-cry, and would accuse her of the murder. She was lost. Her fear was not of long duration, as Donna Carmen was endowed with a resolute spirit. Instead of allowing this incident to depress her, she determined to profit by it.

Deeply affected and troubled, Joaquin remained motionless as a statue when he recognised Donna Carmen appear on the balcony; but, what was his surprise, when the young girl leaned over the balustrade, and by a commanding gesture silently motioned him to ascend.

" Has she recognised me ?" thought he ; " but I am a fool; it is impossible. Does she guess my design, and seek to discourage me ?" He climbed up by aid of the trellis work, and when on a level with the balcony, Donna Carmen assisted him with her fair and cold hand.

" Whoever you are, before you go further, swear by the Holy Lady of Pilar that you will never reveal what you may see or hear. I will not put a price on your discretion."

" Have I ever required such an inducement, senorita, to serve you ?" said he, in a low voice.

" What, it is you, Joaquin ?" replied she, with surprise. " God has then pitied his humble servant. You have courage, Joaquin, and that alone can now save me. You would, surely, never seek my destruction ?"

" Why should you sport with me, senorita ?—a poor servant of your own. What can I do to injure any one ? And what has the mistress of Rancheria to dread from any one ? She is beloved by all."

" You do not know what this hand has done ; but come, we have no time to lose. You are about to know a terrible secret, Joaquin, which will place my life at your disposal." She advanced at the same moment into the chamber, followed by the pearl-fisher, whose heart felt painfully oppressed.

" Pull aside that curtain," said she, in a feeble voice.

Joaquin obeyed, and suppressed with difficulty an exclamation on perceiving the inanimate and bleeding body of the commander.

" This man has committed an outrage upon you, Donna Carmen ?" said he, after a moment's silence.

" Oh! I did not wish to kill him. I only defended myself. Don Ramon was pitiless. He derided my tears and supplications. Well, he dared to raise his hand against me. Fear gave me courage, and despair drove me to commit a crime to save myself from him."

" Good senorita, to defend one's honour is never a crime," said the young man, exultingly; " but should this corpse be found in your apartment——"

" I am lost, Joaquin ; nor could my honour outlive the exposure. They would ask why I did not raise an alarm. They would smile with incredulity at my statement. Who knows but they might say I was surprised by the commander in some intrigue, and that I had slain such an important witness ? My life, then, rests in your hands, Joaquin. You alone will have pity upon me."

" Such a prayer is unnecessary, senorita. Don Ramon was already condemned. If he had escaped your hand, mine would not have spared him."

" Indeed he has been cruel and unjust towards you."

" I have other motives than personal ones to hate him mortally."

" And these are—"

" Because I have often heard him address you in an imperious voice, whilst yours was submissive and soft. He has commanded, and you have turned pale and obeyed. I said, there is an executioner and a victim."

" And by what right did you make such remarks ?"

" What right ? Pardon me. I was no doubt foolish ; but the humble pearl-fisher was jealous of Don Ramon Carral."

" And do you consider it the price of your devotion now that I should listen to such language ?"

" Pardon me, senorita, I forgot. You have recalled me to my senses. Fear nothing, Donna Carmen de Larates, my folly will not have a lengthened existence. I shall know in future how to suppress my feelings."

" Time flies," murmured the young girl.

" We must speak of more serious affairs," said Joaquin, coldly. " I must remove the corpse. Is it not so? And remove all suspicion of the cause of death?"

" And if you are surprised? If you are stopped and questioned, what will you say?" asked she, anxiously.

" That I killed this terrible commander. Do not be alarmed—not because he loved you, but because he had no pity for my old father. Vengeance alone caused me to use the knife. That is all. Masters believe, senorita, in the hatred of slaves, if they do not in anything else."

" Silence! silence! Joaquin; but do you know what fate awaits you if you are known as the murderer of the commander?"

" A fate less cruel than the one to which I have been hitherto subjected. I will submit to the fatal sentence with joy when I can say, thanks to my death, Donna Carmen is free. God has ordained my fate because Donna Carmen had trusted her honour in my keeping."

The generous heart of the young girl was strongly moved by these simple words.

" But can I accept such a sacrifice? No, it would be an eternal source of remorse. Joaquin, do not touch the body; I forbid you."

" Well, and in a few hours your attendants will find it here. You will be accused, your honour calumniated, and your father's name disgraced."

" Say no more, Joaquin; I am but a woman, and that thought alarms me."

" Well, detain me no longer." He raised the body and enveloped it in one of the bags used by the pearl fishers. " Now I can escape the notice of all."

Donna Carmen still hesitated; whilst the young man had disappeared, and was sliding down the balcony with his strange burden. He proceeded towards the thicket, when he distinguished a slight sound, which would have been imperceptible to European ears. He stopped; but he was too late. Two men cautiously came out of the wood, and, in a low voice, asked him in Spanish—

" Where are you going, comrade?"

Joaquin replied not, but endeavoured to disengage himself from the vigorous hands which held him. He thought he had to do with the night rangers whom the commander charged to keep watch during periods of alarm. When he found his efforts vain he stood motionless and speechless.

" Here is a dumb customer," said one of the new comers. " Let us relieve him of his burden."

Joaquin trembled in every limb. They took the sack, and were surprised at its weight.

" What have we got here?—stolen piastres or pearls, no doubt."

" In that case," said the second, " we have met one of the slaves about to become a maroon."

Joaquin was still mute. The two men untied and quickly opened the sack. They with difficulty repressed an exclamation of horror when their hands touched the cold and inanimate face of a corpse.

" ' A corpse! Ah, comrade, what trade, then, do you pursue ?'

" That body is Ramon Carral's, formerly commander of Rancheria. Now do with me as you list."

" The commander ?" said one of the unknown. " The rogue could come to no other end."

It was Joaquin's turn to be surprised at this strange funeral oration.

" What do they call you, friend. Your voice is not unknown to me."

" Nor yours either," said the pearl-fisher.

" Why, it is Joaquin Requiem."

" And you are the Leopard."

" I did not expect," said the buccanier, " such a speedy meeting : but after such a masterly stroke, you cannot remain any longer here. You are a good pilot and a good marksman. Come with us."

" I was just about asking you. But my father, old Melchior, is dying, and I must take a last farewell."

" We will accompany you."

" Be quick, then," said Joaquin.

" We will do better than that," said the Leopard. " Let us proceed to the hut, where Vent-en-Panne will join us, after he has delivered us of this prey for the crocodiles."

Vent-en-Panne disappeared in the wood, whilst the two proceeded onwards. The hut was feebly lighted by a pine torch. The Leopard stood motionless at the door, so that Melchior could not see him. Joaquin approached, and bending on his knees, looked at his father. He was struggling against the death agony, and a deadly perspiration covered his brow. His hands were grasping the air.   When Joaquin pressed them he became more calm, and smiled.

"I shall soon die, my son; but I am tranquil. I have taught you obedience towards those whom destiny has placed over us.   Why did you tarry so long?"

"It was a necessary duty," muttered Joaquin.   "But I am beside you now."

"Your voice, my son, is bitter and sad.   Beware of hatred and vengeance."

"But when one is outraged, father?"

"Pardon then, my son.   Oh! that I, who am about to appear before my Creator, had done so—had been less cruel and unpitiable; but pride surrounds the heart with brass, and honour permits no stain on the escutcheon of a gentleman."

Seeing Joaquin's look of surprise, he said, with an effort—

"My head wanders.   We who are poor must not contend against the caprices of the rich."

"In future we shall have no caprice," said the fisherman sadly.

"What do you say, Joaquin?"   Then seeing the bloody stains on the young man's hands—"What have you done, unfortunate boy?   Answer me.   What have you done?"

"My father—yes, I ought to avow it.   This blood is that of the commander.   The executioner has gone before his victim."

"So, then," said the old man, lifting his feeble hands to heaven, "this is the end of my efforts to make your lot humble, and keep you far removed from the reach of vanity and ambition.   You have wished, then, oh God! that our race should not be extinguished in obscurity and forgetfulness."

"What do you say, father?"

"What I say, Joaquin, is, that you are by birth and blood a gentleman.   You are the heir of the Marquis de Cossé."

The Leopard made a movement of surprise.

"I a nobleman?" said the astonished pearl-fisher. "You surely cannot deceive me, father?"

"May God preserve my strength a little longer, and you shall know all."

The impassable buccanier made two steps towards the humble bed.   Joaquin saw him wipe the tears from his eyes.   Joaquin thought no more of him.   He listened to his father.

"Let the least details of this unfortunate history be engraven on your memory. My father was one of those old feudal barons who would have laid down his life for his king. He was proud and violent; nor did I ever see him smile, except twice, during my youth. His life was full of trouble. His wife, whom he ardently loved, died in giving birth to my brother, Petris; nor could my father ever see that child without evincing

uncontrollable hatred. Whilst he used to caress me, he drove my brother from his presence. Singular enough, my brother was not jealous of this preference; and in spite of all my caprice as a spoiled child, he loved me still: nor did he remark the difference in our dress, which the old attendant at the chateau always rendered sufficiently distinct from the vagabond's, as she termed Petris. He was more robust than me, and on one occasion testified his affection in a most striking manner. Our father permitted us to attend one of the village *fêtes*, and on our return, about eleven o'clock, the night being very dark, we saw two shining lights before us in the shade, like coals of fire. There was a good deal of talk at that time of a famished wolf, and I was greatly alarmed when it came suddenly to my recollection. We held each other by the hand, and trembled as the flaming eyes approached us. Petris let loose my hand, and cried—" Save yourself, my little brother," and advanced with his staff in his hand. I could not move a step. Petris struck the beast on the head, and knocked it down. It sprung up, howling tremendously and bounding irregularly. Petris then pushed his stick between its teeth, and held it down until it was suffocated. Petris then withdrew the staff, but his arm was dreadfully torn. He then came to me, and we ran breathless to the chateau, without speaking a word. When we arrived he said—'Don't tell my father, or he will never allow you to go out with me again.'

" 'You must be suffering much,' said I.

" 'A little,' replied Petris, smiling.

"I kept my promise, but could not help wondering how much he was afraid of my father's anger, and yet did not fear the wolf. So our youth passed amidst solitude, sorrow and happiness. When I reached my twenty-fifth year, my father called me into his chamber.

" 'Bernard,' said he, ' have you ever directed your mind to the future. Does your life here meet with your full desire?'

" 'Yes, father.'

" 'And you have never dreamed of what passes beyond this small corner of the earth, nor longed for a career more useful to your country?'

" I became thoughtful, and tumultuous ideas crowded my head.

" 'I often dream, sir, of more stirring events and more glorious deeds.'

" 'Bernard,' said my father, ' I shall ere long be in the tomb of my fathers; but you have a debt to repay your king and country. We must separate. His Majesty's son, Monsieur, will condescend to accept our hospitality the day after to-morrow. I will present you to him; and, if agreeable to you, he will enrol you amongst his gentlemen attendants.'

" I was struck with astonishment, and was unable to repress my feelings.

" ' It must be so,' said he, with severity. ' You are now a man, and must act as such.'

" I awaited the day of arrival with anxiety. I could not sleep ; and had resolved to act a part before the prince to cause him to refuse me. But already vanity and ambition had been gnawing at my heart. When the trumpets announced his highness's arrival, I felt my strength fail me ; how different it was when I beheld from a window the splendid cortége. My only fear then was that I might displease him. The circumstance of the absolute Marquis de Cossé holding his stirrup gave me a vast idea of the prince's power. The marquis presented me. Every curious eye was upon me. I reddened like fire. The gentlemen smiled. In a moment I discovered that they made sport of me on account of my ancient costume, which contrasted strongly with my youth. The prince himself regarded me with surprise. My vanity revolted, and I said—

" ' Monsieur, my coat is not cut in court fashion, like those of your gentlemen of honour; but it will stand fire as well as those in your highness's service.'

" My reply pleased him. Then turning to the most prominent of the quizzers—

" ' Well, Frontrailles, and you, Montresor, what do you think of the rejoinder ? Suppose we put him to the proof? Young man, you will come with us.' And without waiting my reply, he said to my father, ' Marquis, I do not see your other son.'

" My father was confused. He had entirely forgotten Petris until the last moment. They had sought him everywhere, but he could not be found. Humiliated, for the first time, at his humble apparel, he had concealed himself. A cloud rested on my father's brow, and he replied laconically—

" ' Monsieur, he is ill.'

" I must confess that I had not thought of my brother, so much was I occupied with the conversation of the gentlemen attendants. They spoke of balls, duels, sports, tricks played upon husbands, and women who were like angels, that I opened my eyes with astonishment. Next morning before my departure I asked for Petris.

" ' Mention his name no more, Bernard. That vagabond no longer belongs to the family. He has fled, no doubt, into some disreputable society. I renounce him for ever.'

" I besought mercy for him, but the prince made a sign to set out, and I had only time to embrace my father, to mount my horse, and to depart. At a turn of the road where we lost

sight of the castle turrets, the prince's servants were engaged
with a young peasant seated under a tree, holding a gun in his
hand, who refused to give up two hares which he had killed.
When we approached, I recognised Petris, and grew pale.   As
soon as he saw me, he ceased to resist; and seeming to leave
the decision to me, no longer regarded me.   I ought to have
embraced him, and acknowledged him as my brother, but a
false pride restrained me.

" ' You are wrong,' said I, rudely.

" He retired without saying a word, but with a look of
reproach so tender and so resigned that it might have melted
the hardest heart.   I contented myself with saying,

" ' Let him go; do him no harm.'

" Tears rolled down his cheeks when he saw us depart.
These, my son, are faults which God never forgives, and I have
expiated since then that excess of false vanity.   The next
time I saw Petris was under far more terrible circumstances.
I will pass rapidly over the life of folly and intrigue which I
led at the court.   I was there about three years, when one
evening the prince, who had been during several days taciturn
and disturbed, detained me after the gentlemen attendants had
retired, under pretence of reading to him.   When we were
alone he took my hand.

" ' You are attached to me, Bernard.   You are not one of
those spies whom the cardinal has placed around me, to report
all my movements, and mark every beating of my heart.   You
know that the old tiger-cat has banished my faithful servant,
the Count de Rochefort.   I understand he has written to him
to-day, for the purpose of securing him to his party, by
demanding the hand of his daughter for one of his followers,
Schomberg, Duke d'Hallain.   Now, the beauty of the count's
daughter is reported to be marvellous.   Well, I have found a
rival for Schomberg.'

" ' And this rival, monsieur?'

" ' Is myself,' said he, with a triumphant air.

" I could not believe this strange statement, and would have
opposed it.

" ' I will not hear a word, Bernard, the thing is decided.   I
will be married, without my brother's permission, and the
affair will enrage them all.'

" ' But the marriage will be dissolved.'

" ' We shall see that; but, before anything is done, I must
be assured of the lady's beauty: and for that purpose I shall
send you to Brussels to ascertain the truth.'

" An involuntary presentiment agitated me at these words, and I tried in vain to resist the proposition. Four days afterwards I was at the count's chateau, who received me in the most open manner, perfectly unconscious of my mission. But, when I saw his lovely daughter, having, until that time, my heart free, I felt confused, and remained speech-bound. I had always ridiculed those powerful passions which seize the heart at first sight. I then, however, understood them. I could not endure the thought of putting such loveliness in the possession of another, and I felt the extent of my passion by the jealousy I experienced. That same evening I wrote to the prince, that they had deceived him; and giving a most indifferent picture of the lady's charms, adding several political reasons against the match, which Montresor gave weight to, by proposing an alliance with the daughter of the Duke de Lorraine. These things combined induced Monsieur to forego the match. But this was not all. It was necessary to circumvent the prince in the most masterly manner, so as to make it appear that he had ordered me to espouse the beautiful Adelaide, so as to bind the count to his party by a closer link of union. I, consequently, pretended to assent to the union from pure obedience to the prince, and as if I made a great sacrifice. I was not displeasing to the young girl. The count bestowed her hand on the favourite of the Prince Gaston D'Orleans; and I passed, at Brussels, three months of the happiest period of my life. But soon after a letter from Monsieur, who pitied my *ennui*, recalled me. I then saw the full extent of my fault. I must tear myself away from happiness itself. When I announced my determination to Adelaide she grew pale and burst into tears, accusing me of want of affection in leaving her. I endeavoured to reassure her and reasoned on the necessity of watching over the prince's interests; and, if necessary, sacrificing life itself in his cause. She accused me of ambition and forgetfulness, and finally proposed, either that I should remain or she accompany me.

" Imagine the embarrassment into which I was plunged. I had then no other alternative save to confess all to her. She listened to me with an altered countenance, and became deeply thoughtful—

" ' Return to the court, Bernard,' said she, coldly; ' I will detain you no longer; I will remain in this tower, which, after your departure, will be to me only a prison.'

" I endeavoured to console her, but she remarked, with a strange look—

" ' So, then, but for you, I might have been the Duchess of Orleans ? Certainly I should never have dared to hope for, or dream of, such a splendid fate.'

" And, do you now regret it, Marquise de Cossé ?"

" ' No, indeed, Bernard.' But, a few minutes afterwards I surprised her brooding, and murmuring to herself, ' Duchess of Orleans !'

" She questioned me on the beauties of Paris, the splendours of the court, and the favourites of the prince. I took little notice of those trifling circumstances, at that time, which might have been to me ominous events.

" A year rolled by since my marriage, and my father-in-law informed me of your birth, Joaquin. Then broke out the grand rebellion of Monsieur and the unfortunate Duke de Montmorency. This time I took my part in the movement; but the irresolution of the prince lost us. When Castlenandry was subdued, the head was cut off, and Gaston D'Orleans espoused the daughter of the Duke de Lorraine.

" Whilst we were in exile, an Italian painter, named Gingoire, passed through Nancy, and paid court to Monsieur. The prince desired, for the sake of pastime, to see a gallery of pictures, which the artist brought from France to his master the Duke de Modena. We all criticised the various specimens of court beauties, upon whom we poured a shower of epigrams. But how was I struck, when I saw Monsieur all at once arrested by a likeness I knew too well."

" ' Is it possible,' said he, ' that such a likeness could be drawn from nature ?'

" ' Yes, monseigneur,' said I, anticipating the painter, ' for it is the portrait of my wife; but if the other ladies cannot be recognised, I can assure your highness, that no one could know the original from this copy.' The painter was surprised, but supposing I had some motive in view, he remained silent. I watched Monsieur attentively, my heart beating violently. He said nothing, but remained absorbed in the contemplation of the picture, changing colour frequently. Finally, he said sharply—

" ' Tell me candidly, Bernard, has your wife such blue and languishing eyes ?'

" ' Yes, monseigneur.'

" ' And this charming turned countenance—and this mouth, so rosy and small, and that beautiful black hair ?'

" ' True.' My brow was bathed with a cold perspiration.

' But she wants that charm which enlightens beautiful features.'

" He was silent a moment—then exclaimed, ' I must see this prodigy—If Madame de Cossé can be ugly with such a countenance, I know not a greater rarity. Bernard, we shall set out for Brussels in a few days.' Had a dagger been driven to my heart I could not have suffered half so much. I wrote to Adelaide, to inform her of our new misfortune, and to recommend certain precautions in dress and manner. She profited by my instructions so far as to appear in the most splendid and attractive manner she could.

" He had hardly conversed with her many minutes before he looked at me in a manner I shall never forget.

" ' This is the woman, then, in whom you found neither mind nor beauty, Bernard? Well, I pity you.'

" He said no more, but mutely pardoned me. Adelaide returned with us to the exiled court at Lorraine. Every day I advanced in the prince's favour. I lodged at the ducal palace. I dispensed all the favours. Beloved by my wife and the prince, I believed myself the most happy of mortals. I remarked a singular change in my wife's behaviour. Sometimes she sought me as if to confide some secret to me. Again, she avoided me as if with abhorrence. I watched her movements; and my jealousy was aroused. One night I awoke and I saw her as white as marble, her hair in disorder, and kneeling before her oratory. The following days she pursued every court pleasure in splendid robes and with an unnatural gaiety. Then she shut herself up for some time, and would see no one. I could not comprehend her malady. One day, when my mind was disturbed by these events, I heard an officer in the court speak very lightly of Gaston d'Orleans. I took up the quarrel, glad of an opportunity of showing my devotion to the prince. The rendezvous was at nine o'clock. I concealed the meeting from Adelaide, but that evening she informed me she would not join the fluchess's circle. She tried to detain me.

" ' Sit down, Bernard, I am very much indisposed,' and she took my hand and placed it on her burning temples, where the arteries beat violently. ' Remain with me.'

" I arose, took my mantle, and was about to depart.

" ' Where are you going, Bernard?'

" ' To Monsieur.'

" ' You deceive me. I know all.'

" I looked at her and said severely—

" ' I must listen to the call of honour. I must avenge an injury done to my benefactor, Gaston d'Orleans.'

" ' Your benefactor !—that feeble and capricious prince ?'

" ' Not another word, Adelaide.' She would have cried, but her eyes were dry.

" I buckled on my belt, pulled my hat over my eyes. She threw herself at my feet, and, in a piercing voice, exclaimed—

" ' You risk yourself for him—for him?' said she, in a strange accent.

" ' Nothing can prevent me. It is my duty.'

" ' Nothing ! Will nothing do it? You do not then know.'

" ' What would you say ?'

" She was silent. I moved towards to the door.

" ' If you die what is to become of me ?' The clock struck seven. I trembled. ' Every knell strikes me to the heart,' said she.

" ' Pray for me, madam,' said I, in a ferocious manner ; but she bounded like a panther, threw herself into my arms, and cried—

" ' You shall not go—no, you cannot go. My God, only give me strength.'

" I repelled her rudely. She remained on her knees. I said then, with emotion—

" ' Is it the woman who bears my name who would wish to see it dishonoured ?'

" I know not what sense she applied to it, but she fainted. I called her attendants. I found my adversary at the place appointed. We fought: I wounded him in the right arm. Monsieur himself spoke to me of the duel that night, but in a voice much constrained.

* * * * * *

" Cardinal Richelieu, finding himself indisposed, and desiring to have new concessions granted by the King, resolved to surprise him by a reconciliation with his brother ; for which purpose he sent to Nancy his secretary, M. de Chavigny. We gave a grand reception to the cardinalists at the hotel of the Trois Mores. I was charged to negotiate confidentially with the Bas Rouges the terms of the amnesty, all of us being tired of our banishment. We drank, talked politics, and conversed about the news. I laughed at the confusion of subjects, and was in high spirits at the prospect of Monsieur's return to the court. Chavigny, a profound politician, sought to environ the affair with difficulties.

"' Mort Dieu! my dear Cossé, the court will mend by the settlement of this affair. There is an eclipse of the stars at present. A most marvellous report is spread of the beauty of the marquise.'

"' She is Venus personified,' cried de Suze.

"' You can only know her from hearsay, M. de Chavigny,' said Villemore.

"' But, fortunately, the marquis is not as jealous as a tiger,' remarked one of the Bas Rouges, with a loud laugh.

"There was a moment's silence. My friends seemed embarrassed, and I knew not why. I answered Chavigny, smiling,

"' If you will sup with me to-morrow night along with your

friends, the Marquise de Cossé will receive you with every attention.'

" ' Such a woman is a perfect treasure for a man,' said Lanbardemont, with a sinister smile.

" ' Beautiful and devoted, M. de Cossé is sure to live happy in this world, as well as certain of heaven in the next.'

" I did not comprehend the meaning of all these pleasantries. I felt a sudden tumultuous motion at the heart, but I laughed with the cardinalists. My friends were, however, by degrees, more and more silent, and I saw them regard the other party with looks of anger and impatience.

" ' We have had enough of this,' said Frontrailles. ' Let us talk on more important subjects.'

" ' Come, come,' said I. ' You are pale as a corpse. Drink on with us, as we do.'

" He shrugged his shoulders, and made no reply ; but Chavigny leaned towards me, and said in my ears—

" ' I find you, marquis, in the humour I expected. His eminence has charged me to make you the most brilliant offers if you will influence Monsieur to accept our propositions. You understand me ?—If the conditions are honourable.'

" ' You deceive yourself, M. de Chavigny. I have no such influence as you suppose.'

" ' Come, come, you must not play with us in that manner,' and he accompanied his words with a smile of intelligence which I could not comprehend.

" ' What is the use ?' said Lanbardemont, who sat on my left. ' All can be arranged if you only speak to your wife.'

" I looked at him with surprise and impatience, ' What do you mean, gentlemen ?'

" ' You are a clumsy fellow, Lanbardemont,' said Chavigny quickly.

" But the blow had been given, and I insisted on an explanation.

" ' Come, my dear Cossé, do not annoy yourself,' said Chavigny, mildly. ' We are all friends, and for my sake you will understand me aright.'

" My astonishment was at its height. I could not fathom the mysterious meaning of their remarks. A subdued passion laboured in my heart.

" ' Gentlemen, I beg you will explain yourselves clearly.'

" ' Can it be,' said Chavigny, ' that the marquis is not a confidante ?'

" ' Impossible,' replied Lanbardemont.

" ' Will you drive me mad with your double-meaning remarks?' shouted I, in a rage. ' Speak, gentlemen; I will listen.'

" Silence reigned on all sides. I had a presentiment of some dreadful revelation.

" ' Listen, M. le Marquis,' said Chavigny, ' and answer me honestly.'

" ' I am, as my friends here know, a man of honour.'

" Chavigny smiled.

" ' Can you deny that you have full influence over Orleans? Are you not his secretary and chief favourite?'

" ' Yes, and I glory in it.'

" ' The dispenser of favours?'

" ' Yes; conclude.'

" ' Have you not apartments next to his at the ducal palace?'

" ' All that is known.'

" ' And how long have you been attached to his highness's service?'

" ' Four years nearly.'

" ' That is a wonderful progress to make in four years.'

" I could not contain my anger, and indignantly said,

" ' Well, sir; and what inference do you draw from that?'

" ' Well,' said one of the party just aroused, ' that is enough. 'Tis a good understanding—health to it.'

" I fixed my eyes on the drunkard, whose head fell down on the table again. A thousand suspicions darted through my brain. I finally seized Lanbardemont's arm, and shook him violently.

" ' Is it also drunkenness which has caused you to speak, and which prevents a reply?'

" ' No; and I am about to be as clear and precise as if I sat at my tribunal. Monsieur loves you much; but why?'

" ' Why, because he knows he has in me a loyal and devoted servant.'

" My friends remained silent, but the cardinalists laughed outright.

" ' It was not your sword,' said one, ' that Gaston d'Orleans purchased so dearly.'

" ' Honour, M. de Cosse, makes men penetrating; but favours make a man blind.'

" A storm of sarcasms rung around me, and I wished that the whole of the guests had but one head and one heart, so that my sword might smite them at a single blow. All the courtiers had started up and half drew their swords. I said then in a broken voice to Chavigny—

" ' On your honour, sir, tell me the truth. Do not deceive me. My life depends upon your answer.'

" ' Well, marquis, I acknowledge that I am deceived; but I thought like all the rest of the court that you knew—'

" ' Finish, sir.'

" ' That Madame la Marquise de Cossé was the mistress of the Duke of Orleans.'

" At these dreadful words I staggered back and leaned on the table for support. I felt for my sword, but it had been snatched away by Villemore. Then by a violent effort I stood up, looked furiously round, and cried out,

" ' You are all liars, liars !'

" At the same moment a stranger who had recently arrived in the banquetting room without any one having remarked him amidst the din, approached Chavigny, and struck him in the face with his glove, The cardinalist started up; but when he saw the modest attire of the stranger, he said with contempt,

" ' Are you a gentleman ?'

" ' Petris d'Cossé will be at your service at any hour this very day on the plain of St. Jean.'

" I was struck with astonishment at the sight of my brother, who had so opportunely arrived at that terrible moment. M. de Chavigny saluted him courteously, and said he would have the honour to wait upon him with two seconds at six o'clock. In a short time all the guests had disappeared. Petris informed me that he wished to see me for the last time before he set out for South America. He accompanied me to the palace; but I begged him to leave me alone. I did not disguise my agitation, but suddenly entered my wife's apartments. There must have been some terrible expression in my countenance, for she started up and exclaimed,

" ' What has happened, my dear friend ?'

" ' Your friend ?' replied I with irony. ' It is to your judge to whom you speak, madam.'

" ' What is the meaning of these words, Bernard ?' said she, joining her hands in a supplicating manner.

" ' I have been insulted, madam, because I had a wife who did not know how to protect her honour ;—laughed at before all, and termed a coward and a hypocrite.'

" ' Bernard, in the name of God, what has happened ?'

" ' They have before me, madam, named your lover; and to protect your honour, which is mine, I have committed a crime. I provoked the man to combat, and when he refused I struck down your lover without mercy.'

" ' Gaston !' cried she.

" At this avowal, hatred seized upon my heart. I grasped her hand. ' It was then true !'

" ' Away, away, assassin ! Oh ! the faithful servant to kill his master.'

" ' Not yet assassin, madam. I merely sought to have the admission from your own mouth of the crime you have committed.'

" ' Oh ! Bernard, pardon me.'

" ' Pardon you ? No ! Embrace your child for the last time, madam.''

" She said not a word, but her eyes were directed towards your cot with a frightful look. She crawled towards her child. The remainder of this scene is effaced from my memory. It is like a horrible dream. I can only recal one circumstance—that of leaving, when I carried you away in my arms, the unfortunate creature stretched on the floor bathed in blood and apparently lifeless. I never saw Petris again. He wounded Chavigny, killed one of the seconds, and disabled the other. Through the assistance of Montresor and Frontrailles, he was enabled to fly and conceal himself until he embarked for America. I took refuge in Spain, whence I embarked under an assumed name for Hispaniola; and, after adverse circumstances having wasted all my resources, I was reduced to labour and gain a living by fishing and hunting. I have, in this condition, enjoyed some happy days, when excitement and fatigue have made me forget the past. I have never heard anything concerning your mother, nor have I ever inquired of any European passenger; and now, at the hour of death, I feel no regret, save one, and that is, to have been ungrateful towards my brother, Petris, and to have shown myself unworthy of his friendship."

" And if he pardon you, Bernard?" interrupted a voice much moved.

" What voice is that I heard ?" said Melchior, stretching out his arms.

Joaquin, surprised, turned round. The Leopard was advancing to the bedside.

" Is it a phantom, or a deception God has sent me in my last hour ?"

" No; but it is your brother himself, Petris de Cossé, who has never forgotten you, nor ceased to love you."

" My brother! my dear Petris !"

Melchior raised himself on his couch by a last effort, and stretched his arms to draw the buccanier nearer to him. But the emotion was too much, and the Leopard only embraced a corpse. At this moment, Vent-en-Panne reached the hut. With his assistance they interred Bernard de Cossé in a thicket, which they carefully felled as if some wild bull had rushed through it ; and then they rapidly directed their steps to the Port de la Paix. Joaquin was powerfully affected. He had left behind him all he loved on earth.

" Nephew," said the Leopard, sharply, " do not be feeble like a woman. We have now examined our ground, and in eight days you may again see Rancheria."

" In eight days ?" cried Joaquin, with a sparkling eye. " And for what purpose ?"

" Hush, my lad," said the buccanier, smiling mysteriously, " that is a state secret."

CHAPTER III.

THE LEOPARD.

THE " Brothers of the Coast" had adopted this singular name to testify the independence and formidable nature of their association.

At the period to which our tale has advanced, the Spaniards became more and more alarmed at the progress made by these adventurers. They confined themselves to the employment of several cruisers of small force, to scour the coasts, thereby permitting the buccaniers to acquire confidence and strength. Whilst, however, the Brothers were absent on the track of the Spanish gallions, they united their forces, and surprised the Isle de Tortuga, which the adventurers neglected to fortify. All its inhabitants who were captured were hanged, whilst a few escaped in their boats to the point of Hispaniola, where the buccaniers had established their rendezvous.

Such were the details given by the Leopard to Joaquin, previous to reaching the Port de la Paix.

At the present moment the Brothers were burning with a desire to reconquer the Isle de Tortuga. A deserter had just arrived, charged with most important information.

Cromwell, the Lord Protector of England, secretly made overtures to the adventurers, and sought an alliance with them, having sent out an expedition in their favour to the Spanish main, under the command of the celebrated Admiral Blake, the conqueror of Van Tromp and De Ruyter. This expedition, freighted with muskets, munitions of war, and merchandise, having a vast number of emigrants, and three hundred marines on board, had encountered a dreadful storm, and sought refuge in the Port Margot. It was thus placed between the shore batteries, and the Spanish fleet, and, to increase the evil, several of the British ships had parted company with the admiral.

Thus situated, and much disheartened, the British applied to the Spaniards for a supply of provisions, which they consented to furnish, if the British would go on shore ; but the latter declared they could only land by order of the admiral.

dreading, as they did, some ambuscade or treason. They promised, however, that if Sir Richard Blake did not appear in five weeks, they would set sail for England, under escort of a commanding Spanish force. Under these conditions, they were supplied with provisions. The Spaniards, on their parts, swore the admiral should never reach the fleet at Port Margot, and to prevent him doing so, they augmented their force at sea, and scattered along the coast a swarm of informers and spies. The deserter offered to conduct a party of trappers to the coast where the British were encamped on shore. They might have doubted the veracity of the deserter, had it not been for the arrival of a small vessel at Port de la Paix, manned by one British officer, and ten sailors. The adventurers held a grand council of war after the return of the Leopard. Joaquin was admitted a member under the name of Montbars, a celebrated character in their annals. It was decided by a majority, that twelve of the leaders should form a hunting party, and proceed in the direction of Port Margot, and if they could escape the vigilance of the Spaniards, they were to enter into negotiations with the British, with the view of joining their forces, and retaking Tortuga.

As for the deserter, his profound knowledge of a most difficult route through immense forests, across savannahs, and over unknown rivers, rendered his presence absolutely necessary. But he was sworn on the cross to be faithful, under the penalty of death.

During the progress of this party, the buccaniers were to harass the Spanish fleet on every occasion. The Leopard was pronounced chief of the expedition. No sooner was this decision proclaimed, than the governor, M. du Rossey, requested an interview with him, which lasted more than half an hour. Joaquin, according to his uncle's command, stood sentinel over the tent, so that the conversation might not be interrupted or overheard.

It was not long before the guide came sauntering along, and attempted to converse with him, so that he might approach insensibly towards the entrance of the tent; but the brief and reserved answers of the young man, discouraged him, and he moved on. Twice one of the English sailors elbowed him when passing in great haste, and threw an uneasy and anxious look towards the tent; but perceiving that he was watched, he hastened away.

Joaquin involuntarily reflected on the strange contrast presented by these two men, on whose countenances neither the jovial freedom nor the savage brutality of the Brothers, could be observed. The sailor had something blunt and hasty in his manner; but at times there shone a ray of intelligence in his blue eyes; his voice betrayed the accent of command, and the few gestures he made, clearly indicated that the man had been habituated to danger, and could subdue it by his coolness. Joaquin felt an involuntary respect for him.

The guide, on the other hand, concealed badly his pride and haughtiness. His forced smile before the Brothers, assumed, when at a distance, an expression of bitter sarcasm. His subtle and restless eyes were on every object; but at the first look of another, they were directed to the ground. When the Leopard quitted the governor, his brow was clouded, and Joaquin heard Du Rossey repeat to him, in a low voice, when on the threshold—

"I assure you, that the Spaniards have their spies here, and all the deliberations of the grand council are known to them."

"I cannot believe it, monsieur," replied the buccanier. "I have always been myself accustomed to treat matters openly. It is hard, at my age, to keep a secret, which, from my Brothers, is the first. But you have my word—I shall either perish, or him whom you know shall reach Port Margot, safe and sound."

"I trust more to your word than to the promises of the deserter."

"It is a terrible responsibility, however, you have thrown upon me, M. du Rossey."

"You alone are capable of undertaking it. Who does not know the Leopard to be the most heroic of the Brothers of the Coast?"

"May God grant, governor, that I may not have reason to repent me of having listened to you. It is, perhaps, my duty; but it is the first time in my life that I shall have sought to avoid the Spaniards." Then, having saluted the governor, the Leopard retired with Joaquin.

The latter then requested permission to accompany him, and share his dangers.

"No; it is too rough a trial for a novice. I wish you to remain here."

"But, uncle, have you not promised that I should revisit Rancheria?"

"I was wrong. You ought, on the other hand, to break

off all these ideas of servitude, and habituate yourself to a free and adventurous life."

" That is treating me like a woman, who is good for nothing but to bask in the sun, until the warriors return home again."

" You will have more glorious opportunities, nephew, to distinguish yourself against the Spaniards."

" But you expose me to the smiles and laughter of my new companions."

" Enough, sir," sharply replied the Leopard. " My will is not like a weather-cock, affected by every breeze. You remain here—that is settled."

Joaquin saw that it was useless to insist any longer, but he swore to be disobedient. The evening was spent in an entertainment to the adventurers, who composed the expedition, during which the guide sang and drank with the Brothers to the success of the enterprise. The next morning, at the very moment when the hunters were about to set out, amongst whom were the celebrated buccaniers, Grammont, Michel de Basque and Pitrians, the Leopard saw Vent-en-Panne running at full speed to join him with the true dogs, Gerondif and Caracas.

" It is a long time since we were separated before, but we shall see each other shortly," said the chief to his servants, with a melancholy air.

" What do you say ?" said Vent-en-Panne, in utter amazement.

" That you await my return this time at Port de la Paix. I have chosen another attendant."

" Impossible !" murmured Vent-en-Panne, who, during the space of six years, had never quitted his master, sleeping in the same tent, hunting with him, fighting with him, and sharing his good and bad fortune.

" This is the man I take in your place," replied the Leopard, pointing to a man who, as he limped a little in his left foot, was slowly advancing towards them.

Joaquin and Vent-en-Panne recognised, with surprise, the English sailor.

" You are joking, master ?" cried Vent-en-Panne. " Can you place any reliance in that rough sailor, who could not tell the difference between the track of a Spaniard, a Caribean, or a buccanier ?"

" Silence ! I tell you, if you value your skin. And now my lad," said he, addressing his new servant, " March ! You are now in training."

The Englishman hastened his pace to follow the buccanier, and they rejoined the troop, which was already in motion towards the mountains on the northern side of Hispaniola.

Vent-en-Panne remained immoveable, sad, and dejected, when he saw them depart. He started when he heard a voice behind him. It was Joaquin, who said, briefly—" To night, at sunset, we shall set out together, if you will; and should we overtake them half way they cannot send us back."

During the first two days of the march the buccaniers saw not a single enemy amidst the wilderness through which they passed; but towards the end of the third, Michel le Basque perceived smoke issuing from a thicket of the prickly palm. The guide requested permission to reconnoitre. The Leopard refused, and cautiously proceeded himself towards the wood; but what was their surprise on finding Joaquin and Vent-en-Panne tranquilly supping on a quarter of a wild boar, and who without speaking a word seized their arms on the approach of danger, as if by a motion quite natural and unconcerned. The old chief cried aloud; and he and Grammont advanced, Joaquin looking on the ground.

" Mad boy!" said the buccanier, with half tender, half angry accent, " is it thus you learn to obey? You deserve to be instantly sent back to the port; but in that case the danger would be greater than if you remained."

" Leopard," exclaimed Grammont, " look at these packages of bales and barrels," a pile of which were concealed under the palm.

" You see, uncle, I have lost no time on the way. We found the merchandise confided to the care of a few lancers, who sought to intermeddle with us; but, by my faith, we put them to flight, and the bales and barrels are ours."

" Well executed," said Grammont.

The Leopard frowned.

" Imprudent. You will draw down upon us the observation of the Spaniards, and perhaps cause us to lose our expedition."

He called a halt in this place, and during the repast he went, accompanied by the sailor, to examine the booty, so that he might, according to custom, render an exact account for general division.

The booty consisted of cochineal, indigo, jalap, and sarsaparilla. The sailor, who was examining one of the barrels, cried out suddenly,

" Here is something heavier—we must examine it." He

reversed the barrel, and poured a quantity of leaden ingots on the ground.

"That is strange," said the Leopard. Then pulling out one of his hunting knives, he began cutting the ingot. Under the leaden crust he soon saw the brilliant bars of massive silver. "Joaquin has commenced," said he, " by making a most valuable prize. These barrels contain, at least, three hundred bars of silver. But let us say nothing about it to our companions. Their anxiety to save this rich booty will deprive them of courage to advance. At the same moment he bent his ear, fancying he heard a footstep. He imagined he saw two shining eyes fixed upon him in the shade. But suddenly making a movement to advance his feet tripped over the heavy bars and he fell; as soon as he rose all was quiet. " I thought," said the buccanier, " that I recognised our guide."

" Bah ! you are too suspicious," said the sailor ; " as for me, I have neither seen nor heard anything; but I think it is time we had our supper. The guide is thinking more of that than at spying us. There he is emptying that leather bottle with considerable dexterity."

The Leopard shook his head, in doubt, but said nothing.

The following day our adventurers had to cross a stream, whose current was extremely rapid. The guide declared there was a ford near at hand, and wished to go in search of it. The chief consented, when the sailor remarked, in a low voice ; " What risk can we run, if you send with him two swift and strong swimmers?" Joaquin and Michel de Basque were entrusted with the duty of watching him. Once in the middle of the stream, the two adventurers suddenly found their necks compressed with an iron grasp, and whilst they were struggling hard, the guide dived and disappeared altogether. In vain the whole troop beat the bushes along one side of the river, whilst Joaquin and Michel searched the other; he could not be discovered.

This event began to excite many apprehensions, which were reduced to certainty, when, after two days' march, our adventurers found themselves wandering in an immense savannah. The azure sky began to assume a more sombre tint, whilst the prairie was still lighted up by the golden and purple fringe on the horizon. Not a single fleecy cloud spotted the blue firmament. The plain, scorched during the day by the rays of a burning sun, now swarmed with myriads of buzzing insects.

The buccaniers, worn out with fatigue, were seeking in vain

a rill of cold water, concealed by the sand or a knot of trees whose foliage might protect them, when their eyes were fascinated by the deceptive mirage. They imagined they saw in the distance great lakes, shining in the setting sun like polished steel; but the more rapidly they advanced, the further the illusion fled from their pursuit. Then the peaks of mountains arose, piercing the sky, which gigantic masses speedily rolled away in whirling vapour. Sometimes a buccanier would utter a cry of joy; in the distance he would see a town, he could distinguish the spire of the church, the ramparts, and the terraces covered with the orange tree; but presently the spire melted away, the ramparts became undefined, and all crumbled into vapour. The scent of the dogs was as useless as the sight of man, for the least breath of wind over the moving sand would efface the track of an army. The bravest of the adventurers became troubled, and their hearts began to sink by degrees. They would have considered it fortunate to have encountered an enemy; but what could courage effect against an ocean of wavy sand, which every instant gaped like opening sepulchres.

During this terrible journey the perfidious guide might be assembling bands of Spaniards; well, they would rather have been beset by an entire army than thus lost in the desert, where they ofttimes prayed for a whirlwind to overwhelm them. The twilight passed, and the stars shone out clear in the sky; the buccaniers then pitched their tents. The dogs laid down panting on the ground, with their tongues lolling out and their noses in the sand. The old chief retired after having posted sentinels, and shortly all, except they, were asleep, amidst the stillness of the desert.

In the Leopard's tent the sailor paced about slowly. But both had laid aside the parts they had played during the journey. The old chief stood uncovered before the British sailor, and in an anxious voice, said—

" Our provisions are exhausted—another day's march has ended like the past. We are lost, and I—my promise will have been broken."

" This infamous Catalan has deceived us, my good Leopard. Who can blame you? The fault rests with my foolish confidence."

" I was wrong," said the buccanier, " I should have watched him closer. I have been credulous myself. I am dishonoured."

"Be calm. To-morrow we shall find means, perhaps, to escape from this prairie."

"Perhaps never; but who comes here?" cried he, on hearing the crackle of footsteps in the sand. The curtain of the tent was raised, and Joaquin entered quickly.

"An alarm, uncle, we are sold!—we are surrounded by a whole troop."

"Ah!" cried the buccanier, raising his sun-burnt countenance proudly. "Now we have enemies. If we must die, we shall fall on the sand, red with the blood of Spaniards. Let us die like men, and not like sick dogs. Come here, my faithful companion," added he, grasping his musket; "you will render a last service to your master. You will not rust when buried in this desert!"

Joaquin was moved at the appearance of the old Leopard's enthusiasm. But the reflecting calmness of the pretended servant, and his saddened look, enraged him. He neither made a single gesture, nor uttered a word. Joaquin was about to address him with some biting reproach, when this extraordinary man turned towards the buccanier, who made two paces towards the entrance of the tent, and simply said,

"Remember!"

An instantaneous alteration was visible, the ardour of the chief was extinguished, the wrinkles of his brow contracted, and Joaquin imagined he saw his cheek turn pale. His emotion was so marked and profound, that had tears not been strangers to his eyes they would have flowed. He trembled like a leaf, then kicking his musket angrily into a corner, he said coldly to Joaquin,

"Put the camp into a state of defence, and send to demand of the Spaniards what they seek."

Joaquin was effectually prostrated by the Leopard's command. What magic could there be inclosed in that single word, which had so soon subdued his uncle's courage? What influence had this mysterious man over his judgment? He could not, in his first moment of surprise, avoid exclaiming,

"What do they want, uncle! Have we ever had occasion to ask? Do they not know that we seek to deliver the poor Indians from their yoke, and relieve them of their stolen treasures?" But his uncle interrupted him with an imperious and severe look,

"We are in a snare. The Catalan guide has betrayed us. How many are these hidalgo hunters? Fifty, to commence the ball; but let the dance once begin and we should draw an army on our backs."

" What signifies the number ?" cried Joaquin, impetuously. " We can only die, as you said, a short time ago, yourself."

" We must not die," said the Leopard, coolly.

" Has fear formed part of your calculations, uncle ?"

" Is it thus you address the Leopard ?" and his teeth ground together. " Do you think, young man, that my blood is frozen by age; and that I have any need of your lessons ? Obey—I order you." Joaquin stirred not. The Leopard, who felt his passion rise, with an effort said, calmly, " You seem to rely much on the fact of your being my brother's son; but, our laws give me the power to chastise disobedience, do not forget that. Ought I to be accountable to you for my conduct ? And did you take your uncle to be a coward, when he compelled Don Ramon to kneel before you ?"

This recollection moved Joaquin, and, bowing, he remarked, " I was wrong, uncle."

" Spanish balls may whistle past my ears, as often as they like, without discomposing a muscle; but, to day—I must convince this lad," said he, appealing to the sailor. " He is hot-headed, as you see, but he has a bold heart in the hour of danger." The pretended servant smiled and nodded. " You see, Joaquin, the Spaniards have spread this net before us, for a purpose easily understood. They seek to make us all prisoners, with the view of proving to the British that there is no hope of relief for them from the Brothers of the Coast. If we are either killed, or made prisoners, the object of our mission will be equally lost."

" You believe so, uncle ?"

" Yes, my lad, and I think it best to employ stratagem to escape them. If we give up the booty, and make them dread the effects of our desperation, we shall obtain honourable conditions."

" Honourable !—a retreat !" said Joaquin, bitterly.

" Now, sir, will you obey your chief ?" Joaquin retired hesitatingly. The Leopard and the sailor looked at each other. The latter held out his hand to the buccanier, and said, with emotion,

" My old friend, make all the sacrifices you can to avoid an engagement; but, if we must come to this extremity, my hand is acquainted with the sword, and you will find me at your side."

" I hope we may not be reduced to that extremity; but, I hear the war cry of our comrades. Let us sit down, and be as calm as if we were sitting in the great council, at the Port de la Paix." The Leopard lighted his cigar with the sailor's, and both sat down on mats, with the gravity of a pacha surrounded by his court, and attended by his executioner and favourite tiger.

In a short time Joaquin Montbars entered the tent, introducing a Spanish officer, and our old friend, Friar Eusebio Carral. The first had his hand on the pummel of his sword; the second on the ebony handle of his chaplet: both carried a high head. The buccanier regarded the visitors with indifference, and between two puffs of tobacco, demanded laconically—

" Why do you bring these prisoners here, sir?" At this singular reception, the friar looked with uneasiness at his companion; but the officer, bursting into a loud laugh, cried out,

" Prisoners? Ah! this incarnate fiend is always jesting; but it is you, most honest gallows-meat, who happens to be our prisoner."

" What does the fool mean, Joaquin?"

" The fool," replied the officer, angrily, " informs you that he now speaks in the name of Don Christoval de Figuera, who now surrounds you with 400 men, ready to exterminate every bandit who does not accept his full conditions."

To comprehend fully the sequel, it is necessary to transport the imagination to that period when the name of a buccanier inspired the Spaniards with terror; the greater number of whom regarded these adventurers as demons invulnerable, whose talisman protected them from sword or bullet. The audacity of these pirates surpassed the possible. The taking of Granada and Maracaibo appeared fictions. The Spaniards offered to these enemies, surprised for once and already conquered, those conditions which were considered unacceptable, but which were suggested by a secret fear of the desperate struggle which might ensue; and they judged that if by any cowardice hitherto unheard of, the buccaniers consented, their triumph would be more effectual, if several were left to carry the tale to their companions of the shameful disaster. A victory of this nature, secured without shedding a drop of blood, would tend powerfully to destroy the spell which the inflexible heroism of these men had established.

The Leopard made a sign to Joaquin to raise the screen and call his comrades. The buccaniers entered silently. When the Leopard perceived himself surrounded by the athletic and bronzed figures of the adventurers, all of whom look inquiringly upon him, he asked the astonished Spaniard, calmly, "Will you inform us, senor, what your conditions are?"

The officer could scarcely conceal his astonishment, and scrutinised the countenance of the Leopard before he answered.

"It is first necessary that you disgorge the whole of the booty which you have stolen since you left the Port de la Paix."

There followed a profound silence.

5   F

" 'Tis poor booty, we will restore it to you willingly, for it is rather a burden to us than otherwise, and embarrasses our march."

The buccaniers looked at each other. Then, retaining their breath, they listened with increasing attention. Joaquin felt a blush of shame on his brow.

" Of what description is this booty?" asked the officer, significantly.

" Cochineal, jalap, and indigo, I believe," replied the Leopard, carelessly.

" Is that all?"

" All."

" You lie!" said the Spaniard, in a thundering voice, which seemed not to be unknown to Joaquin.

" Ah! I lie, do I?" cried the Leopard, turning pale, and seizing his musket with a trembling hand, whilst a furious rage shone in his eyes. The friar shrunk from the chief with terror, but, turning round, the buccanier caught a sight of the impassable figure of the sailor. He dropped his arms, looked on the ground, and repeated, "So I lie, young man. There is not another man living besides yourself, who could boast of having said so."

The Brothers regarded each other once more with stupor. Then one of them murmured—

" The old Leopard jests. He is disposed to make game of him."

" Look how he bites the end of his gray moustache," whispered another.

" He shakes with laughter, the old fox, although he looks so calm."

" He is planning some devilish stratagem."

" He holds out the velvet paw. That is not often the case with him."

The monk became more and more uneasy, and glanced behind him. The officer preserved his scornful look. The circle of buccaniers narrowed around them, and several hunting knives began to glide from their sheathes. The Leopard resumed, in a jovial tone—

" And will your highness state in what respect I have lied?"

" In your statement you have forgotten three barrels, most virtuous chief," said he, in the same voice which struck as familiar on Joaquin's ear.

" The bars," cried the Leopard, greatly surprised, and throwing a piercing look at the Spaniard. "Ah! you know; but, what do you want with three hundred bars of lead?"

"You lie again." The buccanier shook like a wild bull, pierced by an arrow. "I speak of three hundred bars of silver."

"Silver!" repeated all the adventurers, whose cupidity was excited by this strange piece of news. "Impossible!"

"Ah! my good men, your worthy leader did not speak of this portion of his booty, and he knew its value well, for I saw him myself scrape one of the bars to be assured of its value."

The friar made a signal to him to remain silent, but it was too late.

"You saw me?" cried the Leopard in a voice of thunder. "I was not, then, deceived, wretch! You are the person who deceived us—betrayed us. You are the Catalan guide; answer me, are you not the guide?"

The officer turned pale, but answered, "Yes."

"In that case," said Joaquin with violence, "you are no longer under the protection of your mission. The traitor is out of the jurisdiction of honest envoys. It was you, then, who came, like a serpent, stealing under the grass? It was you who drank out of our cup, and sang our war song, and who designed, at the bottom of your heart, and under cover of your merriment, to plant a dagger in our breast, and turn upon us the muzzle of the Spanish guns? You have violated promise, oath, and conscience. Oh, infamy! Look you: not one of us—not one of those whom you designate brigands, would follow such an infamous trade—a spy—and yet you dared to enter the Leopard's tent, and you believed you would leave it with the haughty step you entered it. But we have your life in our hands; do you hear?"

"By one single word, one single cry, I could have you crushed by the Spaniards," proudly answered the officer.

"Yes, but justice would first be executed. If you had boldly followed our track, and by superior sagacity noted every sign and mark upon the leaves and soil, you would have honestly and fairly performed your duty, but treason like yours deserves a memorable punishment. Leopard," said he, turning quickly round, "who shall be the executioner of this man?"

"No one," replied the chief, calmly. "Senor, the three hundred bars will be restored to you. Is that all?"

"Never, uncle," cried Montbars, who had caused one of the

bars to be brought, and had cut it with his knife. "They are massive silver."

"I know that."

A murmur of surprise ran round the circle.

"They must be restored."

Several deep imprecations were uttered.

"Is that all?" asked the Leopard.

"No," said the officer, with a ferocious look.

"Speak, then," cried the old buccanier, whose heart pulsated with an undefinable emotion, although the same man had been carried off on the horns of a wild bull, which penetrated the sleeve of his coat, without uttering a single cry.

"You restore to us only that which we can take by force. That is no vengeance."

"You must be punished for the theft," said the friar.

"Punished! you are right," stammered the Leopard, who felt his throat contract, and a mist before his eyes.

"We must have three of your bandits given up for execution; one before the English encampment at Port Margot, the other two before the Hatto at Rancheria." So said the friar Eusebio, looking keenly at Joaquin.

The Brothers burst into a wild laugh. The monk's proposition appeared to them a piece of buffoonery. The Leopard allowed his head to fall in his cold hands, but the sailor uttered a few words in his ear. He instantly lifted his head, where there appeared marked an utter prostration of spirit. With a gesture he commanded silence.

"Do you leave me to choose the victims?" asked he, with anxiety, of the officer.

"Yes."

The adventurers did not comprehend the meaning of the question.

"Then your conditions are accepted. You can inform Don Christoval de Figuera."

The buccaniers understood this too well. What, then, was their confidence in the heroic chief in whom they confided? They remained stupified, silent, and terrified. At length, Grammont pronounced the single word—"Traitor."

The Leopard coldly said—"Step out of the ranks, Grammont; I forgive you the insult; but it deserves death. You shall be given up. 'Tis an honourable death, Grammont. You die for your brothers."

Grammont crossed his arms on his breast, with a saddened

air, and approached the Spaniards, without uttering a word; but another famous adventurer, Michel le Basque, influenced by his hot blood, sprung before the chief.

"You may deliver me also. I agree to it; but you shall not prevent me from speaking. By what right do you make merchandise of our blood, when we have arms in our hands? Do you think we have lost our accustomed vigour, and that the sword shakes in our hands? Is the Leopard, for the first time, afraid? Would it not be a thousand times better to die side by side, than to purchase a shameful safety through the tortures and agony of our companions? No—no, it cannot be; confess that you are only misleading the Spaniards, and that you are only waiting the moment when you will lead us into action against this rabble. Ah! I thought so. Your eye brightens. Now I recognise my brave old friend. I knew he did not want heart."

"Ay," said the Leopard, calmly stroking his beard. "I was wrong, and you, Michel, have given me a most fortunate idea. I shall perform my duty, and not a living man shall have it in his power to say, or to think for a moment, that I was guilty of a piece of cowardice."

"You retract, then?" said the friar, with anxiety.

"No, brothers. You know that, according to our agreement, I am your absolute master, until we reach Port de la Paix, and before that period, I owe you no account of my conduct. Is it not true?"

"It is true," replied all the hunters, with mournful accent.

"But," added he, "as it is not just to cause the association to lose the young and vigorous, whose hearts are full of life, so long as there are old and wrinkled heads amongst us, I shall accompany Grammont myself," and holding out his hands to the latter, as well as to Michel le Basque, he said—"Will you have it so, comrades?"

Grammont regarded him with admiration, whilst Michel exclaimed, "By my faith, it is going too far, old stupid head. Is that what you call a lucky idea?"

The adventurers cried out—

"No—no, he shall not go. We will not permit him to leave us."

The Leopard said sternly—"Silence!" They remained silent, then turning towards Joaquin, "You will supply my place in the command, Montbars," said he, looking with an eye of affection on the manly face of his nephew.

"No, sir, no—not in the command, but on the scaffold."

"Young fool, you must not think of that; ought the young oak to fall beneath the axe before the old moss-grown tree? Is it consistent with the laws of nature? Of what good am I now?" added he, with a melancholy smile, taking Joaquin's hand, "if it is not to die in the open air, as I have lived free in the forest of Hispaniola?"

"Never!" said Joaquin, "the Brothers have need of your experience. You alone know how to reach the end of this journey, and guide them from danger."

"Yes—yes," cried the troop, "any one of us, rather than the Leopard."

This reflection struck the old chief, who exchanged a look of despair with the sailor, and, striking his forehead, exclaimed—

"So I cannot even die!"

"I am ready to go," said Montbars, advancing to the Spaniards.

A profound silence reigned in the tent. The buccanier, who smiled at his own sacrifice, seemed to have no longer any thought or sensation, after the proposition of Joaquin. He permitted him to go; but when the young man reached the outlet of the tent, the Leopard heavily lifted his head, and regarded him with a saddened eye, as if some sad reminiscence had been awakened.

"Where are you going, Joaquin?"

His voice was so soft and tremulous, that Michel le Basque squeezed the officer's arm hard, and all the Brothers of the Coast looked upon the earth, as if, for the first time in their lives, they felt tears were about to flow. At this touching appeal, Montbars was rooted to the threshold. The Spaniard smiled.

"You are afraid—come, acknowledge it, and let the old man go with us."

"Go on," said Montbars, firmly, and he led the way.

The Leopard, with a sudden bound, was at his side.

"You do not hear me, sir, nor will you answer. What right have you to leave without my orders?"

"Good," said Michel. "He is of his own blood—the son of his brother."

"Yes, the son of my dearly beloved brother. I remember the days of our youth now. How you resemble him, Joaquin; you are his living picture: and yet I deliver you up to your executioners, although Bernard confided you to me. How shall I answer for it?" added he, bursting into a hysterical laugh. "No—no, you shall not go. Think of your father."

"Why speak of him at such a moment? You are cruel, uncle."

"The exemplary son," said the Spaniard, sarcastically. The young man pushed back his uncle, and moved on.

"Consider again. You cannot go, you so young—so brave. Your heart unacquainted with the cruelties which these monsters heap upon their victims. Think for a moment. They will give you a red-hot crucifix to kiss, and if you start, they will call you coward. Do they not see without remorse the Indian at the stake, who, when his bowels are smoking, look at them without a murmur. You are too young, Joaquin. You have not led, like me, a forest life, and felt all its hardships."

"We have no more time to lose," said the Spaniard, "make haste."

"Follow me," said Joaquin Montbars, "and you can judge whether my courage will fail before the torture, as my uncle fears."

"Stop, senors," cried the Leopard.

"One favour," cried Michel.

"Speak."

"Let me go in the place of this young gamecock. Forbid him to depart."

"I forbid you," said the buccanier.

"Uncle, take care, uncle. You are no longer the Leopard. Would you dishonour your blood? If neither you nor I will offer ourselves, who else can you ask?"

"True—dishonour. Well, then, go," cried the Leopard, making a gesture, as if he was afraid of his own firmness; then, turning to the adventurers—"Now, not a murmur. My life was nothing; but I have sacrificed the child of my heart."

The Spaniard then retired slowly, followed by Montbars, Grammont, and Michel le Basque.

When they reached the camp of Don Christoval, the monk demanded an escort to conduct his two prisoners to Rancheria, and observing Joaquin moved at the name, he put his hand on his shoulder, and said—

"A crime has been committed there, and there the assassin ought to expiate the murder. You perceive that my ven-

geance has even found you in the midst of the Brothers of the
Coast, and neither their arms nor their courage have been sufficient to protect you. Let the soul of Don Ramon Carral
be at rest. I have not lost much time in relieving the world
of his murderer."   Then he added, with a bitter smile—
" You have reason to thank me, Joaquin Requiem, for you
shall see your noble mistress for the last time on this earth."

Joaquin turned pale ; but the escort put itself in motion,
and Friar Eusebio had not long to enjoy the mental agony
which these remarks had created in Joaquin's mind.

After several hours of a forced march, the buccaniers left
the prairie. They ascended a gentle hill, covered with cocoa-
nut trees. The Leopard, who was at their head, uttered a
short guarded exclamation customary to them in the forest,
and his dark countenance brightened up at the same time.
When his companions rejoined him, he pointed with a triumphant gesture to the panorama which lay extended beneath.
It was Port Margot, where the Spaniards had shut in the
British fleet, the tents of whose crews were lined upon the
plain.

A crowd of soldiers and emigrants were gathered in confused
groups around a gallows, which could be but dimly perceived
through the morning vapours. Every eye of the buccaniers
was directed towards that one spot. By degrees the sky
cleared up—the morning breeze lifted up the sleepy mists, and
the gallows was more distinctly traced against the sky. The
Leopard became gloomy. The sun rose bright above the
horizon, and they saw a corpse suspended from the gallows.
It was Grammont. The sight lit up a menacing expression
on the burning countenance of the buccaniers. They threw
ferocious looks upon the brave Leopard and his companion.
Then they prepared to descend the hill, furious as a torrent let
loose for destruction. The sailor threw himself before them,
and, pulling off his coarse sail-cloth jacket and trousers, he
appeared in the uniform of a British admiral, and shouted—

" Now, my friends, we shall revenge Grammont's death in
floods of Spanish blood. I, Richard Blake, admiral in the
service of the British Commonwealth, swear it !"

At that name and these words the buccaniers stood petrified
with astonishment, and looked at the brave seaman with mingled admiration and curiosity. " But, after we have made so
many sacrifices, we must not compromise ourselves by a mad
attempt ; on the other hand, it will be absolutely necessary

for you to remain concealed in this wood ; whilst I, accompanied with your chief, penetrate in disguise the Spanish lines, and reach my soldiers and seamen. This very night I will join you at the head of the first, without noise or combat, and we shall reach the spot where L'Olonnais awaits us with shipping before the Spaniards can dream of our departure."

"And we shall retake Tortuga," cried the Leopard. "Do you now understand why I have sacrificed three of our Brothers. It was because I promised to Du Rossey that, at any sacrifice, I would bring Sir Richard Blake to Port Margot, where we should make Cromwell's force allies with us. Will you cast doubt again on your old companion ?"

All the buccaniers squeezed his hand, and Pitrians remarked—

"You are worth more than any of us, for not one would have allowed himself to be outraged and suspected of treason, even to have saved all the Brothers of the Coast."

"What of Montbars and Le Basque ?"

The Leopard remained motionless.

"Do you wish to make me regret what I have done ?"

"We may arrive yet in time to save them," said the admiral. "Follow me, master."

Entering the Leopard's tent, which had been hastily erected, they each took the costume of Spanish mountaineers, then, gliding into the thickets, they soon disappeared from the view of the buccaniers. On the day following this, Joaquin and Le Basque reached Rancheria under the conduct of Friar Eusebio, who watched over his prey with miserly anxiety. They were first confined in the slave prison—a horrible den, where the feet were covered with green and fetid water, and the head bent on the breast by the lowness of the roof. The two adventurers never exchanged a word. In a short time they were removed to the chapel, according to the usage amongst pious Spaniards, but a much more trying place, be-cause no one leaves it except to ascend the scaffold. Michel, however, smiled when he entered. The capilla consisted of two chambers, without windows. The first one was only fur-nished with a bench and a lantern, fastened to the roof. The second was about six feet by four, ornamented by an altar, on the white cloth of which arose a crucifix, and beside it, four wax candles. Mats covered the floor, and images were placed in the walls. As soon as the prisoners were alone Le Basque looked around with satisfaction, and said to Joaquin :

" All very well here, I see. At all events we will not be like frogs crouching in a marsh. This monk imagines we will wait his pleasure, and stretch out our necks for the rope like obedient children, but he has left us arms wherewith to avenge us, and God grant it, the vengeance will be ample."

" What is your project ?" demanded Joaquin, astonished.

" To celebrate our death by a magnificent conflagration, so that the worthy monk and a part of his attendants may perish with us."

At the same time Michel seized one of the wax candles, and continued, coolly—

" I am going to fire the chapel, and if, with the breeze we have to-day, the hatto is not in ashes before you could repeat a paternoster, the devil will have to be thanked."

At the same time he leaned the candle against the wooden crucifix.

" Stop !" cried Joaquin, who thought of the danger which threatened Donna Carmen, and his heart felt oppressed with agony.

" Are you afraid, then, to die ?" disdainfully asked Le Basque.

" No," replied Joaquin ; " but I would not give reason to the Spaniards to suppose that I was afraid of their torture, or feared my heart would fail before their outrages and indignities."

" Good ! You are the worthy nephew of the Leopard."

He replaced the wax candle on the altar, and preserved, as in the cell, a dead silence.

Donna Carmen knew that the friar had brought back two buccanier prisoners along with him, but she was to remain ignorant, until the moment of execution, that one of them was Joaquin Requiem, a remembrance of whom pursued her ever since that fatal night when they had their last interview.

The monk asked if she intended to be present at the execution. A nervous trembling seized her, and she hastened to reply—

" No, no. What ! witness the death of these unfortunates ? That pleasure may suit their judge or the executioner. When the presence of a female cannot save the condemned it is infamous and odious. I do not even intend to remain at Rancheria, during the execution, because I might hear their death-cry, and that one never forgets."

" In that case, senorita," replied Friar Eusebio, " you can

order the horses for an airing, for we shall not long delay the execution of justice. In an hour at most."

" In an hour ? So, then, these men, who even now talk of the past and the future, whose hearts may both love and hate, whose thoughts range over the world, will, in two hours, be only corpses, without life, or look, or thought !"

" God himself has said so, senorita. He who sheddeth blood, by man shall his blood be shed."

" Yes, yes. God has said it, and judged all those who have spilled human blood."

She remained plunged in a sorrowful dream before the astonished monk.

Finally he arose and said, softly—

" Time passes."

" Yes. I had forgotten that I ought to fly this execution. I shall soon be ready."

When her toilet was finished she descended to the court of the hatto, mounted her horse, and, followed by a dozen of her slaves, she spurred the animal and set off at a gallop, but at the gate the horse stopped before a melancholy spectacle. The gallows was erected, and towards it, between two lines of lancers, the two buccaniers advanced, concealed by a black veil. They were followed by a crowd of fishers, slaves, and Indians almost naked, who covered them with imprecations and groans. The monk, standing at the foot of the scaffold, sang with a strong voice the consecrated words—

" Merciful Virgin, have pity upon these miserable sinners who are about to die, and pray your well-beloved Son to pardon their sins in the world to come."

The first of the condemned shortly passed before Donna Carmen. As he approached, the young girl experienced an instinctive alarm. The buccanier, who held down his head, had not as yet observed her ; but when he found himself before the gates of the hatto the monk interrupted his psalmody to exclaim—

" Assassin of my brother, you forget that I promised you should once more behold Donna Carmen de Larates."

The unhappy girl uttered a cry of alarm at those terrible words, which revealed to her the truth. The condemned stopped and quickly lifted his head.

Donna Carmen, the noble Spaniard, so lovely in her corset of velvet and gold, with diamond buttons, remained pale and trembling before the buccanier, covered already with his winding sheet, and who was about to perish before her eyes. The condemned had cast his veil backwards. His countenance was lighted up with a joyful expression. Then he bowed respectfully, and calmly resumed his firm tread as if he did not know that every step brought him nearer the grave. Neither uttered a single word, but she, motionless, followed Joaquin with a look, feeling in her heart all the agonies of death. But Michel de Basque, who came next, stopped before her to admire the exquisite beauty of the poor girl. At this moment Donna Carmen allowed the reins to drop, and the horse plunged furiously. Le Basque sprang forward, with one hand he seized the reins, and with the other he encircled the slender and elastic figure of the young girl, raised her quickly, and, with the brutal hardihood to which he was habituated, he kissed the cold cheek of her whom he had saved. This outrage recalled her to her senses. At the moment two lancers seized the audacious buccanier, Donna Carmen struck him in the face with the silver handle of her riding whip.

" Wretch ! am I arrived at a point so low as to be insulted by a bandit about to mount the scaffold ? Am I not the daughter of Don Juan de Larates ? What, then, has thus altered my destiny ?"

Her eyes were then directed towards the fatal tree. An athletic negro, naked to the waist, his limbs being only covered by light red drawers, was slowly mounting the ladder for the purpose of acting the part of executioner. Joaquin ascended after him. When both had reached the summit they looked at each other. During every step of their ascent Donna Carmen suffered as much as if the executioner had trodden on her heart. Some terrible struggle was racking her mind, and twice she moved towards the scaffold. Without doubt she wished to reveal the truth, to brave public shame and humiliate herself before her slaves, by one single word break down the barrier existing between her high condition and the lowly one of the condemned, slip off the brilliant garments and assume the accursed sackcloth. But when she saw the dark hand of the negro planted on the young man's shoulder like a living brand of shame and humiliation, woman's weakness subdued her, fear took possession of her soul, praying forgiveness from God, and seeking to fly from the tumultuous ideas which rushed burning through her brain, she sprang into the saddle and set off at full speed, followed by her attendants.

When Michel le Basque, whose countenance was pale from

the affront he had received, arrived near to the monk, the latter said—

" Very well struck : was it not, brave Brother of the Coast ? Cowards who yield themselves up to men without a blow, and who insult females who cannot fight, deserve it."

" One may revenge themselves on a woman as well as a monk," said Michel, ascending the ladder with great coolness. The negro prepared his cords, and having put the noose around Joaquin's neck, he did the same for Michel, and awaited the commencement of the psalmody by the monk.

" Do you still hope for vengeance ?" demanded the friar.

" Between the cup and the lip there is life and death," said Michel, very tranquilly, who imagined he heard a distant cry of dogs.

" For thee it is death," said the monk, and he thundered out the terrible service : " Merciful Virgin have pity upon these miserable sinners who are about to die—." But he was interrupted by the cry, which became full and distinct, and which the Spaniards began to notice.

The executioner seized upon Joaquin.

The monk continued :

" And pray your well-beloved Son to pardon them in the life to come."

At this moment an Indian ran up breathless, and exclaimed—

" The buccaniers have landed in the Bay de la Hache, and all along the shore. In a few minutes they will be here. Sound the alarm !"

" What does it signify ?" cried the monk, seeing Michel smile, " provided we have time to perform this duty."

These words were lost in the tumult. The executioner fled. The lancers hurried into the hatto, the Indians and pearl-fishers into the woods, the slaves alone stood stupidly insensible, perfectly careless of the change of masters. The friar hesitated several minutes, considering what part he had best take. Finally, he decided on following the route of Donna Carmen, so as to inform her of the danger, and endeavour to save her from the buccaniers.

The British and buccaniers soon arrived, and cut the cords which bound the condemned, amidst shouts of triumph and joy. Michel le Basque was no sooner free than he looked wildly around him in search of some object. The Leopard pressed Joaquin to his breast, and the admiral declared aloud—

" What recompense will you have, my friends, for your noble

devotion ? Speak. I pledge my word you shall receive whatever you ask for."

Joaquin, who then thought only of Donna Carmen, and who guessed the designs of Michel, replied in a calm and proud voice—

" We only ask in return for our conduct permission to be the first to convey the news of this enterprise to our Brothers at Port de la Paix."

Michel looked at his companion with surprise, but he was obliged to concede on hearing the hurrah, which greeted Joaquin's response.

" Sooner or later," said he, " I will encounter this noble Spaniard ; and then I shall not be the criminal whom they were leading to the gallows. I shall then, perhaps, be absolute master in turn."

The buccaniers pillaged Rancheria, and ranged over the whole neighbourhood. They conveyed on board an immense booty, and a vast number of prisoners, amongst whom was Friar Eusebio Carral. He scarcely ever aroused from his prostration, except to speak to a young negress of rare beauty, over whom he watched with uneasy care, and whom he sought to conceal from the attention of the adventurers.

At this moment, the worthy Brothers of the Coast occupied themselves very little with their captives ; and except one or two heretical English sailors who made some broad remarks on the monk and his companion, whom they called ebony skin ; none of the others took much notice of them. They left them to dream of the miserable fate which awaited them. The monk recalled the prophetic menaces of Michel de Basque, and the young girl trembled on thinking that death alone could free her from the shameful slavery to which she was now doomed.

The adventurers set sail, and in eight hours they triumphantly entered the Port de la Paix, with Admiral Sir Richard Blake and upwards of six hundred Englishmen.

The disembarkation was most agonising to the monk's companion, who was dragged along as part of the booty, for she was a marketable commodity. There are evils so great, misfortunes so complete, that they subdue for a time the most resolute minds. The young girl listened no longer to the monk's consolations. She looked around her as if struggling through a fearful dream. The sight before her was frightful, for the adventurers were as brutal as they were brave. They celebrated their orgies of victory on the beach, calcined by the sun. When the prisoners had arrived before the tent of M. du Rossey, under the conduct of the Leopard, the old buccanier turned towards the young girl and said sharply—

" Here you must stop, ebony skin ;" but the unfortunate girl moved on. " Hollo! do you hear me ?" she stopped. " The child is tractable," said the Leopard, " she is no doubt dreaming of her native country, which she will never see again."

" Beautiful country !" said another.

" Where the bride," remarked Michel le Basque, " receives a glass ring one day, and is sold to the merchant the next: the honeymoon does not last long in Guinea."

At this moment the negress uttered a suppressed cry, and shrunk as if she had touched a venomous serpent. The terrible Michel had seized her, by the hand, to drag her into a dance ; which a number of the Brothers had commenced with the women of colour. The young woman threw such a suppli-cating look, one so full of despair, at the Leopard, that the latter said to his comrade,

" Leave this conceited piece of stuff, Michel, she is not yet adjudged."

" Since you wish it," replied Le Basque, with unusual resig-nation ; " and, instead of wearying my legs, I shall go and drink." And he stalked off to join a bevy of adventurers ranged around a mountain of wine barrels. A bung was drawn, and the sparkling liquor ran into the large drinking utensils of all kinds, which were eagerly stretched out from all sides. Those that were near enough put their mouths to the wine, and when any one fell down insensible, shouts of laughter arose at his discomfiture. These bacchanalian exploits soon began to produce the usual wild and ungovernable passions for which the adventurers were celebrated. Here excess of friendship ; there violent quarrels for nothing, and everywhere tumult, noise, and brutality.

The poor captive trembled in every limb. She saw that no pity need be expected from these men, and that a miracle alone could save her. She turned towards the monk and briefly said,

" Friar Eusebio, have you your poniard ?"

" No," said he, heavily.

" The sea is a vast sepulchre !"

" You like sea bathing then ?" said Michel, who had left

the topers; "do not think of it, we have subdued prouder hearts than yours;" and he looked on her with a curious and insolent eye.

"The monk was right," murmured she, looking sadly around her; "there is not one true manly heart in the breast of any of these ruffians. They are indeed demons." All at once her eye became fascinated by the appearance of one of the buccaniers, indolently leaning on his musket, and contemplating the scene before him. A cry escaped her lips. She recognised Joaquin, and from that moment her heart was relieved of an oppressive burden. Her destiny appeared to her less terrible. A short time ago she was less than a woman, a slave—a body without the soul. She now felt herself Donna Carmen again. She was no longer alone amidst the banditti. She believed herself saved.

But when she perceived Montbars, attracted by her exclamation, look at her and his countenance brighten up, as if by recognition, she felt troubled anew. The young man loved her, and if the humble fisherman dared to speak of love, what might the buccanier not do? Whilst these reflections were passing through her mind, Joaquin, pale, silent, and ashamed of his emotion, advanced towards the prisoners. He looked at the trembling Guinea girl, but such stratagems could not deceive him, either as to voice or figure. That which Le Basque only vaguely supposed, Joaquin was convinced of, besides there was nothing in the countenance typical of the African race; on the contrary the hands were small, the hair long and beautiful, and the feet so little and well formed, that a Grecian sculptor might have envied them. He drew near and in a voice of emotion, said,

"Senorita, do you not recognise me?" The young girl still hesitated. She cast a humiliating look at her humble attire; the grand lady had disappeared to supply a place for the poor slave, and she blushed to see herself thus degraded before her late servant. "Speak, do speak!" continued Joaquin, "I do not require to pronounce your name: my heart has recognised you."

"I must then recognise one friend amongst these brigands."

"The reproach is unjust. These brigands," said he, in a low voice, so that the monk should not hear him; "are my brothers. Have you forgotten already that I spilled precious Spanish blood, and that our association alone offers a refuge to criminals who are not cowards?"

"You revenge yourself cruelly, Joaquin; but, I think you will take pity upon me; besides, you are young and cannot yet have renounced every sentiment of humanity."

"I have already suffered much for you, but this time the sacrifice of my life would be unavailing to you. Yes, I could save you; but, alas! there is only one method."

"What is it?" said Donna Carmen, in agony.

"The wife of Montbars will be respected by all!" murmured the buccanier softly. The Spaniard smiled with disdain, but Joaquin, without perceiving it, continued—"It would be the realisation of a beautiful dream, senorita. In this free country every one is his own king. We have no prejudices.

rank, nor pride. Every one is master of his own heart and life. Your existence is not chained down by old habits. You do not pass your days in denial of God's mercies, the air, liberty and nature, merely to pursue the crochets, or subdue the obstacles which have been created by the vanity or folly of men who lived before us. In your life every natural inclination, every secret wish, all the desires of the mind are constrained and imprisoned. Here we need only conceal our happiness in the depths of the forest. You are accustomed to every luxury. Here we coin money with our carabines; and I should search for you, even in the middle of Vera Cruz, everything which caprice could dictate to you."

"It would be caprice, indeed; but I did not wait for the pearl-fisher to make such an offer, on condition that he would save me."

"The pearl-fisher exists no longer, senorita. Now, I am a free man. On this spot in the midst of my bold brothers, who throw into the sea or burn the richest stuffs of India for amusement, and sleep naked on the ground, I am prouder than the Spanish planter, who depends on his slaves, his confessor, and his king."

"You are free," said the friar, "but you have not the power to save a woman."

"We are all equal here. I must submit to the common law. I can do nothing of my own accord. Believe me, had it been otherwise, I should not have offered Donna Carmen such a mode of escape. Think only, senorita, that nothing in this world can prevent the division which is about to take place."

"I will await it," said she, firmly. They were then interrupted by loud cries from all parts.

"The bond! the bond! the oath! the oath!"

These clamours gave force to Joaquin's last words, and Donna Carmen saw in despair the adventurers shortly about to decide her fate. The captives were brought behind the troop of buccaniers, all of whom were leaning on their arms; savage-looking, grave and silent. On the right the pirates were more miserably accoutred. These adventurers, who owe their name to the English word corsair, were active, fierce, fiery men; their appearance being less gloomy than the more solitary buccaniers, and their hearts more unrelenting and blood-thirsty. When they set out on an expedition, all the individuals associated themselves two and two, and being bound by mutual oath they assisted each other in case of wounds, making over their booty to the survivors. In no instance was such a bond ever broken, and sometimes it lasted for a voyage only, or during life itself. The term by which such compact was known, was "matelot," and the compact itself matelotage.

Around the corsairs were gathered the inhabitants, cultivators, and traders, men who were little adventurers, but extremely cunning and selfish. These colonists were present apparently from curiosity, but they knew that all the plunder must eventually fall into their possession, the adventurers never putting out to sea until all their booty was expended. Finally, in front the ground was occupied by the hired servants or slaves, who crouched on the sand silent, inert and almost naked.

A profound silence soon succeeded the tumult. M. du Rossey, the Governor of La Tortuga, the Leopard, and L'Olonnais appeared standing before the barrels, bales, and booty, piled together on the sand. The governor had a book in his hand.

"You all know," exclaimed he, in a loud voice, "that before anything is divided you ought all to bring here everything you may have procured, even to the value of one penny."

"Yes," cried all.

"Very well, Leopard, call the roll."

"Montbars, draw near," ordered the old chief. Joaquin advanced.

"Are you about to denounce me?" murmured the young girl with contempt.

"Fear nothing. I will not betray you."

He endeavoured in vain to discover some means of avoiding the catastrophe, perceiving a rival in every Brother of the Coast. When he stood before Du Rossey, the governor seemed surprised at his agitation, nevertheless, he said to him, kindly, pointing to the book—

"Put your hand on the new testament, Montbars."

Joaquin obeyed.

"Now swear you have reserved nothing from the booty."

"I do swear it," said he loudly.

"Farther: that you have not concealed the value of any object in the name of any prisoner."

"Dare you purjure yourself," said a voice behind him. It was Michel le Basque.

Divining a rival in him from the very instinct of love, he looked at him with defiance, and replied once more, "I swear."

"You are aware that the brother who swears falsely," said

Michel, "loses his share, which goes to his brothers, or some chapel."

"I know that," said Montbars, proceeding towards the prisoners, followed by Michel, whilst the call proceeded.

"Do you hope, then, to save this woman who despises you?"

At this remark he regarded Le Basque in the manner an adversary would do in some deadly combat before slaying him. They had then reached the friar and Donna Carmen.

"I also have recognised this woman, and I have to revenge myself of an outrage."

"Silence!" said Montbars. "If you seek a quarrel you will speedily find it; but the division must first take place."

"You are a fool," replied Michel. "You do not know what consequences would result, if you snatched this Spaniard from us and permitted her to escape."

"That which awaits him is glory," said the monk, "in having mercy on the victims, and saving them from the executioner."

"No," cried Michel, imperiously, silencing the monk; "but the opprobrium and disgrace of being considered guilty of treason and perjury."

"Let him come to Hispaniola with us, and he may be rich without becoming a chief."

"Let him leave us, and we will pursue him like a cowardly deserter. He will become a *Maroon*." [So called when a servant, slave, or dog, deserts.]

"Silence, both of you," murmured Montbars, turning pale, and unable to turn his eyes from the captive.

"It is never too late to desert from crime," continued the monk. "Joaquin, save Donna Carmen."

"No kind of duty can excuse treason," said Michel. "Montbars, be faithful to your oath."

"God has inspired you, Joaquin, with this excellent idea. Come, you will be praised by all, and your name separated from all connection with these bandits."

"Only hearken to him," said Michel, sneeringly. "And this man would be the first to mock you. The very children at Rancheria would throw stones and hoot at the lion that allowed its talons to be cut."

Montbars trembled and looked to the Leopard, who continued calling the names, and to whom all the adventurers addressed themselves with a kind of veneration.

"Your uncle will renounce you. He will never recover your disgrace."

The monk perceived he lost ground. "Think, only think, Joaquin, that all these brigands are damned, and if you now abandon them you may hope for absolution from your sins."

"Absolution!" shouted Michel. "There is a recompence, Montbars! It is economical, too, on the priests' part. You can aspire to more, Joaquin."

"Hear not the heretic. You will purchase safety in the world to come. A good action effaces all sins."

"And humility and degradation will be part payment. The rich planters will shrug their shoulders when they meet you, and if you do not hasten out of their road, the whip will make you. Yes, yes; I remember that myself," added Michel, with a ferocious laugh.

Joaquin, with his arms crossed, looked on with a bitter smile, pale and indignant.

"You must suppose me either to be very feeble or notoriously vile, when you dispute thus about my soul and will. You have spoken long enough, methinks. It is my turn now, I now know you. In a few seconds you have revealed your dispositions, and, had it not been that I sought to know them, I should have long ere this imposed silence upon you. So you, monk, thought that cupidity and folly would lead me to rescue Donna Carmen; and you, Michel, believed me such a coward that I would resign the task of thwarting your vengeance through puerile fear. Ah! if the dangers of such an attempt only menaced me, the greater they were, the more I should thank heaven for the trial."

"Well, Montbars, what do you intend to do? Speak; I shall soon be called to take the oath."

The young man trembled violently. The call continued rapidly. He studied some method of relieving the young girl from the terrible lot she had to undergo, but wild and insane projects alone filled his brain. He was like a dreamer, flying from a ravenous animal.

"If Donna Carmen's name is uttered," said the monk, in a low voice, "there is no earthly hope of safety."

"If," said Michel, in his turn, "you will promise on your honour not to make any attempt of violence or stratagem to deliver the Spaniard, but leave her to undergo her fate, I shall not name her."

Montbars was lost in conjecture before this terrible alternative. In vain he consulted Donna Carmen's look. Her countenance was calmly resigned, and showed not one fugitive expression.

At this moment the Leopard called Michel le Basque.

" Decide," said he, rapidly.

" Promise, always promise," said the monk. " It will afford us time."

" But it does not now concern a light promise, but my word of honour, which is sacred."

" I have perfect faith in it. Be quick."

" Michel le Basque!" shouted the Leopard anew, and all eyes were turned upon the group of prisoners.

Joaquin looked again at Donna Carmen. He discovered the same impassability ; not a gesture, not a look, not a sigh, nothing but concentrated disdain.

Michel retired from them.

" A vulgar slave might easily escape," said the monk, bit-t erly, " but the Brothers will watch with a gaoler's anxiety over the mistress of Rancheria."

Joaquin briskly lifted his head. Le Basque advanced slowly towards the three chiefs. The young man no longer hesitated. Hurried on by an instinctive impulse of the heart, he rejoined the buccanier, and said, in a voice almost extinct—

" Neither stratagem nor violence ; I give you my word."

Michel took the oath without denouncing Donna Carmen.

When the call was finished, the governor turned towards the Leopard, and delivered to him a packet, trebly sealed, saying—

" Before we proceed to the division, read aloud the bond of agreement, signed by the leaders before their departure, the clauses of which must be rigorously enforced."

The buccaniers applauded, and drew nearer, so as to hear more distinctly.

The Leopard broke the seals, and, unfolding the parchment, commenced reading amidst profound silence—

" Art. 1.—The Buccanier Chief of the expedition to Port Margot shall have, independent of the common share, all the slaves of condition."

Michel le Basque smiled ; Joaquin understood it.

" I have allowed myself to be deceived like a child. If Donna Carmen had been denounced, she would have fallen to my uncle's lot, and then I might have hoped. In seeking to save her, have I then lost her ?"

" Listen, listen," said the friar.

" Art. 2.—The Captain of the shipping shall have the first boat captured, and two shares.

" Art. 3.—He who first descried the prize shall receive one hundred crowns.

" Art. 4.—For the loss of an eye, one hundred crowns, or a slave. For the loss of both, double.

" Art. 5.—For the loss of a right arm or hand, 200 crowns, or two slaves."

" Alas !" said Montbars, " I have not even been wounded."

The Leopard continued—

" Art. 6.—The adventurer who shall signalise himself by his devotedness, whether in being the first to board, or whether in accepting any mission which shall expose him to almost certain death, may demand a recompense."

Montbars listened to this article with deep attention. His countenance brightened up, and he uttered a cry of joy.

" My God !—thanks." He rushed beside the Leopard. " Uncle, I have the right to make a demand. Is it not so ? It is but just and fair. You will admit it yourself. You do not answer me."

Murmurs arose in the crowd, " The reading of the bond ought not to be interrupted."

" Art. 7.—For the loss of a leg or a foot 200 crowns."

The Leopard went on as if he had never heard Joaquin.

" Will you kill me, uncle ?" impetuously demanded Joaquin. " I ask you, in the name of your own statutes. You cannot refuse my demand—nor you, governor—nor you, brave L'Olonnias. Speak. Have you heard me ?"

The Leopard's voice resumed in a cold and impassable tone.

" Art. 8.—If any one not having actually lost a member, shall have been deprived of its use, he shall be recompensed equally as in the other cases."

" Uncle, are you deaf or blind ?" cried Montbars, amidst the laughter of several.

" Art. 9.—It will remain for the choice of the maimed to take money or slaves."

" And now, when our duty is done, what demand has Joaquin Montbars to make, who seems in such haste to receive the price of his devotion to his duty ?"

Attention increased.

" I demand two slaves. Is not my life worth such a price ?" and he pointed to the monk and Donna Carmen.

Surprise was expressed on every countenance. Every one expected some exorbitant demand. After a moment's silence, M. du Rossey, said—

" It appears to me that there is nothing to prevent it."

" Before that," said Michel le Basque, " will you listen to me ?"

The crowd preserved a dead silence, foreseeing some interesting incident.

" Spead, then," said Du Rossey.

" All this, Brothers, is deceit and falsehood," and grasping the young woman by the arm, he brought her, trembling, before the governor. The poor girl let her head drop on her bosom.

" What does my matelot mean ?" asked the Leopard.

Michel hesitated on seeing the agony of his old friend ; but Joaquin had scarcely recovered from his surprise, when he pushed Le Basque violently aside, and planted his body before Donna Carmen. Michel became furious.

" This negress, whom you are about to give to Montbars, is a powerful lady—a noble Spaniard."

Imprecations and cries burst out on all sides.

" Name her !" said the governor.

" Would you infuriate yourself thus, for the ruin of a woman ?" demanded Montbars. Michel shrugged his shoulders.

" Montbars has demanded a negress for a slave. I demand Donna Carmen de Larates, mistress of Rancheria."

" Treason ! treason !" cried several of the adventurers.

" Is it thus you deceive your Brothers," said the Leopard to his nephew, thunderstruck at the revelation.

Joaquin, feeling that all was lost, if he trembled like a culprit, resolved to face the danger, and replied—

" Yes, uncle, and I appeal to you all, if you have aught human about you. There is this terrible enemy before you. She is alone, feeble, defenceless. Is it brave or fair to make a woman tremble before you ?"

" She is a Spaniard," said the Leopard.

" Give her to Michel le Basque," cried several voices.

" Well," cried Joaquin, " what crime has she committed ? Let us hear it. Do not be so cruel towards her. Would you punish her for crimes of which she is ignorant ? Do you know that, with her own fair hands, she has dressed the wounds of her slaves ? If you had seen her, like me, raising her voice in behalf of offenders, you would not remain silent. If you were to canvass the inhabitants of Rancheria, a thousand voices would bless her. Not one would accuse her."

" It is useless," interrupted the Leopard, " to endeavour to soften us towards this young girl. Our statutes cannot be infringed, and they do not listen to pity."

"Go on with the division," cried many voices, with impatience. Not a voice or gesture was shown in behalf of Montbars.

Joaquin began to bemoan the cruel fate of Donna Carmen; but his uncle exclaimed—

"Silence, boy."

"Oh!" remarked Joaquin, "to think these men's hearts will not be moved, when they see this young and frail girl dropping on the sand, worn out with fatigue and cruelty. If she says 'I am thirsty—I am hungry—I can work no more:' they will reply, brutally, 'Get up, and go to work;' perhaps, even the rod may be applied to her—to Donna Carmen. No; I will never suffer that. Who, then," said he, advancing towards the three chiefs, "who gave you authority to act thus?"

This time an explosion of fury was excited amongst the adventurers. By a gesture, the Leopard restrained them; but seizing his nephew's hands in his, as if in a vice, he said, passionately—

"Do not sport too much with our patience, boy. This is our final decision. The adventurers of La Tortuga will not throw to the wind those statutes which form the basis of their association, to suit the folly of a young madman. Mark me well: this girl is one of an accursed nation. She must abide by her destiny. I swore, when I became a buccanier, that I would show no mercy to the Spaniards. In their eyes we are savage beasts. Why, then, should we show clemency and generosity for our implacable foes? They have caused their dogs to devour young Indian girls, and why should not Spanish women become slaves and labour?"

"But she—" murmured Montbars, in a low and convulsive voice. "Do you not know that I love her?"

"You love her? You?" said the Leopard shuddering. "You love a woman of that tyrannical race? You; the son of my brother, Melchior, whom they slew. Do not repeat that to me, nor admit that you have so far laid aside the mourning of your heart. As for me, I have never loved, Joaquin: and you ought to know what your father gained by that terrible passion. Michel, you have demanded this woman for a slave. I assign her to you."

"So," cried Le Basque, who until then remained calm and tranquil. "The senoras of the great isle are proud and haughty, but we know here how to bend them to our will."

The adventurers loudly applauded the Leopard's decision. It was like a thunderbolt to Joaquin. The superstructure of all his dreams was overthrown. A mortal chill ran through his veins when he saw this child, accustomed to respect from her infancy, handed over to the ferocious adventurer. Her whom he worshipped like a deity. He repeated to himself, " A heart so proud and lofty can never endure servitude ; the infamy will never be accomplished." When he felt himself powerless against the brutality of the Brothers of the Coast, the young man could not restrain two big tears which rolled down his sunburnt cheeks.

Donna Carmen saw him weep. She then looked at Joaquin with a melancholy smile, in which resignation was painted, and said softly to him—

" Recover yourself, Joaquin. You have predicted the truth to these men. I shall have ceased to live before this ruffian, who is my master, shall have been able to offer an indignity to the daughter of Juan de Larates. Misfortune can alone prostrate timid minds. My hands are bound, but the immortal spirit is free. Donna Carmen will never bend the knee to the scourge of an adventurer."

" As for thee, Montbars," said the governor, " choose from the booty whatever you desire as a recompense."

A smile of disdain curled Joaquin's lips. He thought of a final attempt upon his rival. " Michel, choose if you will in my place. I offer you the whole of my share as a ransom for Donna Carmen."

" You are a fool, my lad. Do you think all that is worth the revenge I shall have ?"

" Fool ! Well, as for me," said he with an insulting accent, " I regard every man as a coward who dares to revenge himself upon a woman."

A cold perspiration damped the brow of Michel le Basque.

" You are the nephew of my matelot ; but when you have recovered your reason, if you are not afraid to repeat the insult, we will settle our quarrel according to our customs."

Montbars retired totally disheartened. He cast himself down by the side of a rock, his eyes haggard, and his arms convulsively crossed. The division was about to begin.

M. du Rossey divided the troop of buccaniers into parties of ten men each, every one having its distinctive sign, such as a poniard, a bonnet, &c. A boy blindfolded threw one of these emblems at random upon each lot, all of which were then parcelled out into ten divisions, so that each man had his share.

Donna Carmen took no notice of these strange proceedings. She remained immoveable, awaiting the conclusion of the affair, and a stranger might have supposed her a veritable Guinea woman, perfectly indifferent as to her fate. The monk, too, seemed completely prostrated.

At this moment Montbars seemed aroused by some sudden thought. He started up and mingled with the group of buccaniers. He heard the rough voice of Michel shouting, "Come, let us be going." He spoke to his hired servant, who was piling the booty on the shoulders of the slaves. Joaquin did not look at Donna Carmen, but stretching out his goblet to Pitrians, he said, "Come, Pitrians, let us drink. Do not forget old friends."

Donna Carmen seeing herself abandoned by him on whom her last hope depended, shuddered and murmured,

" I am now afraid."

Montbars never turned his head, but gaily emptied his goblet. Michel's servant unbound the hands of Donna Carmen and those of the other slaves. The young girl raised her eyes to heaven with a triumphant and bitter smile, and leaning towards Le Basque, she snatched his knife hastily. Already it had touched her breast, when the buccanier caught her hand, and taking away the weapon, said—

" You may prick yourself with that, my little queen."

Montbars involuntarily stretched his arms towards her, but he had command enough over himself not to move or utter a cry.

" I am lost!" exclaimed the young girl, in despair.

" Not yet," said Joaquin, who drew near when the buccanier retired to give some orders. " This man loves vengeance, but it is not the only vile passion God has planted in his breast."

" Come along, senorita," cried Michel, who had just sent off his slaves with the booty.

" Follow him," said Montbars, in an under tone; " offer no resistance. I am sure he will not go with you." At the same time Du Rossey called upon Le Basque, who joined him.

" What is your intention, Joaquin? A crime?—it will be your ruin."

" No," said Joaquin, exultingly; " a crime cannot save you. This is my last hope. Le Basque is one of our most inveterate gamblers. God be thanked for that part of the

booty which I a short time ago despised, because it may afford
me the means of securing your liberty. Do you hear the sound
of the dice on those barrels? That sound rejoices my heart, like
the sound of your voice, senorita, when you demand a service
of Joaquin. The rattle of the dice possesses a magic power;
it excites a burning fever, takes away reason, and maddens the
intrepid Brothers of the Coast, who would not even wink in a
shower of balls. Those dice are worth more to you than gold,
or steel; may they be lucky for me in the hazardous duel
which shall ensue between me and your master."

"That I believe is but a frivolous hope."

"Frivolous?—ah! you do not know Michel le Basque. He
would laugh at a drawn sword—menaces are of no avail. I
have offered him my share of the prizes; he despised it; but
when he loses his booty, bale by bale, piastre by piastre—when
every throw ruins him, when his heart will be oppressed and
sad, then I shall conquer him, and be master of his life, his
courage, honour and vengeance. This brave fellow will play
for his revenge like an infant, and weep over his last jacobus;
but, hush! he is here." As Michel approached his slave,
Joachin turned carelessly towards Pitrians.

"Well, old satrap, now that we have drunk enough, will
you play?"

"Play?" yawned Pitrians, "I should only rob you of your
money. After the commotion you made, you are not calm
enough."

"Bah!" replied Montbars. "You know the old proverb—
'unlucky in love, lucky at play.'"

Le Basque heard them.

"You may do with me as you please," said Pitrians, "let
us play." They established themselves at a barrel. Pitrians
pulled out the dice, and the game began. The latter was not
in the humour, and when he had lost a hundred crowns he
retired. The eyes of Michel le Basque remained fascinated
upon the players.

"Who takes his place?" cried Montbars.

"I have," thought Michel, "declined the young man's
share; but if I could keep the slave, and secure the money, also,
of this amorous swain—" He approached with a hesitating
step. "Are you man enough to play with me without a
grudge?"

Joaquin raised his eyes coldly, and replied—

"I was a fool, as you told me a short time ago. Now, I
would play with the devil."

"I thank you, Brother," said Le Basque, laughing, and deceived by this apparent candour.

They had presently a crowd of adventurers around them. Gambling was the predominent passion of the adventurers. They devoted themselves to it with desperation and frenzy. A short time ago, they might have equipped a fleet. Now, many were compelled to borrow their supper. Every eye was fixed on the two gamblers, as if drawn by a powerful magnet.

"What stake?" asked Le Basque.

"What you like," replied Montbars, whose lips were parched.

"Five hundred crowns?"

"Be it so."

Montbars' hand shook when he threw. He dare not look.

"*Eleven*," cried the lookers on.

With the facility of a fortunate player, he recovered himself. He saw fortune smiling upon him. He believed her chained to him.

Michel then threw, and Montbars breathed freely, as the spectators called *seven*.

"The remainder of my share," proposed the loser.

"Against all mine? I consent," said Joaquin, and again the dice rattled in the box. This time the young man had confidence. It seemed to him as if the dice ought to obey him, and in truth he repeated the same figure, *eleven*. Michel threw *six*.

Le Basque caused two goblets of Xeres to be filled by his servant, kicked his dog until it howled, and looked fiercely around him. He sought for some smile, some gesture, some look that might provoke him, but perceived nothing. There was a profound silence. Finally, he looked at the cold and passionless face of Montbars, and said, in a gloomy voice, "If I propose to stake my slaves," laying emphasis on the word, "against all I have lost?"

If Joaquin had exhibited the least sign of hope or joy Michel would have retired, not to be the dupe of the young man; but, Montbars had decided on his part. He heard the offer made calmly, and, by an extraordinary effort, he smiled.

"Your slaves against what you have lost? They are not worth one hundred crowns."

Le Basque hesitated. Joaquin turned towards the spectators, and exclaimed—

"Come, who will take Michel's place. I have no time to lose."

Le Basque recovered himself.

" Well, that amuses me."

" 'Tis lucky. Go on then."

" My slaves against six hundred crowns."

Donna Carmen felt hope returning to her heart. She approached Montbars. He stirred not. He only saw the dice-box shook by Michel, who rattled well, and threw—

" *Eight!* " cried the buccanier.

The young man grew pale. Fortune had turned. He threw *five*. Joaquin's eyes were covered with a veil. He tried to be calm; played; lost again; lost repeatedly. His money slid through his hands. He played for his share of the prize; his arms; his dogs. Le Basque still won, until, at length, the unfortunate young man had nothing.

" You have no more," said Michel. " Let us be going."

Carmen felt her limbs petrified. A tear, not of rage, but of profound grief, rolled down Joaquin's cheeks. All at once an idea struck him.

" Sit down again," cried he, furiously, pressing Michel's arm. " Play on; play on." His countenance bore an expression of wildness.

" But, what can we play for? " said Le Basque, jeering. " You are ruined; do you not know it? "

" Yes, but I am free. Do you not know that? "

" True! Well? "

" Do you consider me a man, skilful and brave? Have you ever doubted my courage? "

" Never," answered Le Basque, who thought Joaquin sought a quarrel with him.

" Are not my limbs sufficiently robust? Do I not know well how to mark the game? In short, am I worthy of being a valet? "

" What do you mean? " cried Le Basque, who believed Joaquin was a fool.

" What I mean," replied he, with force, " is to offer you a hazardous but magnificent game. Against your share, my share, silver and slaves, I stake three years of my life, during which I shall be your servant."

Carmen did not comprehend the meaning of this desperate proposition, but she divined its horrible nature on perceiving a shudder run round the circle of spectators. The stoical Leopard was even alarmed, and said to his nephew—

" Joaquin, take care."

But Montbars, pale as death, impatient and disturbed, answered, in a broken voice—

" You have willed it to be so. No other name but yours could have saved me from the abyss before me."

The silence became solemn. Every one awaited Michel's answer. After he had reflected for an instant, he observed—

" Bah! you are jesting, lad. I am sleepy; besides, it is a folly. Ought I to risk the loss of—"

" I take you all to witness," interrupted Joaquin, "that Michel dare not take up this stake. He is afraid of the turn of the game. Have I refused him his revenge, or does he think I am not worth some lacs of crowns and a few slaves?"

Michel le Basque looked around him. This odd and hardy offer had delighted the adventurers, simply because the chance was desperate and unheard-of. All seemed to admire Montbars, and several encouraged him with both word and gesture. Michel remained sitting.

" You have clearly understood me?" resumed the young man. " If I lose, my hand and head are at your service. I will obey you faithfully. My booty shall be yours. You shall have power over me of life and death."

Michel dared not retreat.

" I take it," said he, then seizing the dice-box, he shook it.

Montbars' heart was heard to beat. His powers were stretched to the utmost.

" *Three!*" cried Michel, with an uneasy and ferocious smile.

The Leopard shuddered. Joaquin breathed freer; but his cold icy hands shook as if he had had an ague.

" May God protect me!" murmured he. The dice fell on the barrel. He turned away his head, and was silent, like the rest of the adventurers.

" What singular luck," cried Michel.

" Come, Joaquin, follow me."

" It cannot be possible," stammered Joaquin. He looked. He had only thrown the *aces!*

He made no remark, but arose unsteadily amidst the general stupor, and rejoined the troop of slaves, whom Michel's servant was preparing to lead to his master's tent.

" You see, Joaquin," said Donna Carmen, " that I am fatal to all who love me."

" Fortune has betrayed us to the very last, senorita," replied Joaquin, sadly. " But your master is now mine, and his servant may be of more service to his slave than the free buccanier could have been. Thanks to the loss of liberty we are not separated, and you can still calculate upon a protector."

"But such an agreement, can it be, in reality, enforced?"

"It is an agreement, voluntary on my part, from which death, or the expiration of the term, can alone free me. For the future, I am the valet of my old companion, and must carry his gun and his game. He has a right to punish my laziness, my disobedience, a word or a look, without any right of complaint on my part, or pity or defence from any one."

"Poor Joaquin!" murmured Donna Carmen; "but Le Basque will not dare——"

"To scourge me—perhaps deprive me of nourishment and sleep, or throw me, as others do, into some infectious hole to torture me. It is possible. An imperious order or commanding gesture will be the most cruel to me. Therein will consist my punishment."

Donna Carmen made no reply. Whilst they retired, the Leopard said to Michel le Basque, who followed with a joyous look——

"The lad required such a lesson, but do not carry it too far, my matelot. Do not forget that he is the son of my brother."

"Do not disturb yourself, old carabine. You know that I have no malice towards Joaquin; but as for the damsel, I shall never forget the manner in which we first made our acquaintance; and when the devil is mixed up with it, I must have my revenge."

Michel pursued his way to his tent, whistling as he went along. Michel le Basque was not one whom they would ordinarily call a bad man. He even passed amongst his companions as a good fellow, but he had a violent and rancorous disposition, like most of the common people of the meridian. His pride, of a vindictive nature, could even push him to gross cruelty. He had that profound hatred common to all the southern peasants towards the master class—a hatred which was unpitiable when it found an opportunity of crushing by brutal force those before whom they ordinarily uncovered their heads. He could not then forego the mean delight which he felt in being obeyed by a noble Spaniard. But he was much discontented when he saw the dignified resignation of Donna Carmen, who, having pledged as it were the life of Joaquin, did not consider herself justified in evading slavery by death. Le Basque instinctively conceived that the only way he could make her suffer was through the person of his rival; and every day, without himself designing it, he became more and more severe towards Joaquin. Every master has always sufficient opportunity to express his rage. His tyranny neither requires the aid of logic, nor any pretext. But Joaquin, who did not wish to quit Donna Carmen, remained insensible to all. It

was then a constant struggle between defiance, provocation and resignation.

In the meantime, however, Joaquin had never been more happy. It was under this jealous surveillance that his affection grew, and the young girl herself could not prevent the natural impulse of her heart being felt.

Joaquin was bent down with toil, but in the midst of his

7   H

labour his mind brooded over Donna Carmen; and when at times he saw her white robe in one of the woody vistas, he derived new courage from the vision. Influenced by pity and gratitude, the young girl showed at times proofs of innocent sympathy for the valet, feelings which never would have been divulged to the buccanier. These little kindnesses, so natural and yet so timid, so unstudied and sweet, were preserved in Joaquin's recollection with tenacity and care. The fact of their forced equality had produced in their relations towards each other a charming familiarity. When the noble slave returned from the cistern, during the heat of noon-day, bearing the jar of water gracefully on her shoulder, she would pause before Joaquin, who was panting at his labour, and advance the brim of the vessel to his parched lips. Sweet child's-play of love—misfortune thus united them. Each softened under the suffering of the other. They scarcely felt the burden of slavery—affection blunted every coming evil. The more Michel multiplied their chains, the faster he bound them to each other.

Every fresh difficulty supplied an additional reason for their love. Nature in all things became their accomplice, and the instrument of their secret communion. A few verses sung by Donna Carmen, though meaningless to others, had their mysterious language to Joaquin. He read a gesture, interpreted a flower, whilst a broken twig in the forest, a piece of ribbon encircling a shell on the beach, all contributed to uphold their secret intelligence. Both were faithful to the rendezvous which these signs indicated, without their master even guessing at their existence. Every evening they concerted twenty different schemes of flight, each of which were chimerical. Michel le Basque at length perceived that he had failed to debase Joaquin in the eyes of the young girl by incessant humiliation. Donna Carmen never forgot that it was for her that the young man had become what he was. In the mean time the vengeance of the buccanier had insensibly been converted into love; but it was that species of rough jealous affection which men of his age experience, who know that the feeling cannot be reciprocal. He then resolved that the young girl should no longer leave his smoky tent. He questioned her concerning her sadness, her silence, her dreaminess. He dare not allude to the change which had been operated upon himself, but at times he was furious when he looked upon her, and thought he never could be loved in return. One day, on returning from the chase, he found her standing at the door of the tent watching the ocean.

" What are you doing there, ebony-skin?" said he, sharply.

" I am admiring the sea, so calm, and smooth as a mirror."

" Oh! I know well what thoughts are passing through your foolish head. You were thinking if a bark could be found on the beach some fine evening, like this, for example, perhaps, one might reach some love-sick swain who would have pity on a young girl—"

" Master—Michel!"

" Oh! that master was absent for a few days. All these ideas have been trotting through your little head. You look involuntarily to see if the horizon is pure, and you hope. If master would only stay late a hunting, you would still hope, or better if some accident befel him. If some valet should pass and smile, and the wind be favourable, you would then have nothing more to do than wish and fly."

" Truly, you are an excellent diviner of one's thoughts, since you can read the hearts of slaves who yearn for liberty."

" You avow it then?—so, you endure much here? You find me an heartless monster, who is a sort of wild beast to you— that is it." She made no reply. " Truly, we know how to fight, but we do not know how to play the flaunting, perfumed dandy of Cuba and Hispaniola, with their feathers in their hats, rings on their fingers, and perfumes in their hair, dancing attendance all day with comfits and bouquets for the ladies. What miserable fellows we are." Donna Carmen's sarcastic smile, just visible at the corner of her mouth, recalled the buccanier to the past. " Ah! these fellows do not receive the blow of a whip," added Michel, clenching his fists; " but, if we do not know, as adventurers, how to pay compliments to ladies, we know how to give orders to slaves. I am hungry, ebony-skin, get ready my supper;" said he, brutally, and turning into the tent he elbowed Joaquin, and ordered him to turn the grindstone and sharpen the axe. In a moment afterwards he enjoyed his triumph, in seeing the noble girl carry in her white hands a portion of smoked boar's meat, and place it on a barrel, which served for a table, the viands being rolled in banana leaves. She then stood before him, with her eyes cast down and a beating heart. A large tear rolled down her cheek. Le Basque repented his rudeness, and said more softly—" Come, sit down, senorita;" and he pointed to three or four velvet cushions, which contrasted strangely with the

dirty smoked tent. " Sit beside your master.—I allow you."
She stood still, and he gathered his bushy eyebrows. " I
command you." She stirred not. " What means this disobedience ?" cried he, in a rage.

" Chance has made me your slave; but God has not willed
that I should be your equal. I must submit to the evils of my
destiny, but I should despise myself if, by my voluntary act, I
accepted such favours."

" Sit down peaceably; or forcibly—" and he advanced towards her.

" You may kill me, I know it !"

A prey to a most furious passion, but hesitating between
rage and love, Michel cast his eyes around him. He noticed
Joaquin, who, greatly excited at the scene, had suspended his
occupation so as to hear and contemplate what passed. A
frightful smile of sarcasm and vengeance lighted up the
buccanier's face.

" Coward ! idler !" roared he : with a bound forward he
seized the axe, and whirling it round his head, he drove it with
all his might, and with the speed of lightning, at Joaquin ;
most fortunately rage had altered the direction, and the axe was
buried in the trunk of one of the trees against which the tent
was erected. Joaquin did not even wink. He had not ceased
to watch Donna Carmen, who uttered a cry of horror, and fell
on her knees, supplicating the buccanier. Then Michel was
ashamed of his conduct, but he would not allow them to see
his repentance, and said, rudely—" Resume your work, miserable, you did well not to move, or else—"

" Oh !" said Joaquin, with disdain; " you only struck me,
or else—"

" A threat ?" and le Basque reddened, and seized his
scourge.

" What are you going to do ?" muttered Carmen.

" I can slay him like a dog. Petrians compelled his sick
valets to work. They resisted, and he flogged them at the
triangles. He got off, by declaring they died of laziness."

" Horror ! You would not dare to imitate such a monster."

" Let him cease to browbeat me, or I shall not answer
or it."

" How long is it," said a voice, " since Michel le Basque
became an executioner ?"

All three were surprised, and turned towards the entrance
of the tent, where they perceived a woman singularly attired,

who became a spectator of the scene. She seemed more like a phantom than a human being. Her great height contrasted with her extreme thinness. She spoke slowly, and in a reprimanding tone. Her appearance was rather wild, and her face assumed an expression of solemnity and extraordinary haughtiness. Her garments were both sordid and sumptuous. A Capuchin mantle of white linen entirely enveloped her; but when half opened, black satin and lace appeared in profusion. Strings of pearls were interwoven with her hair; on one of her emaciated fingers sparkled a diamond ring. On her breast was suspended a gold locket, enclosing two curls of fair hair, which she frequently carried to her lips by a mechanical and convulsive movement.

"The seigneuresse! (her ladyship)" cried Michel, with stupefaction, after hearing the reprimand of this singular woman.

Joaquin and Carmen regarded her with interest, because both had often heard of her. She was a sort of witch to the buccaniers. As if this creature required constant activity to escape from herself, she wandered everywhere, unceasingly bestowing aid upon any of the Brothers in distress. She dressed their wounds, nursed the sick, prayed by the side of the dying, was ready for every duty, fatigue or danger; and in these charitable duties she seemed to expiate some terrible fault which was concealed within her own bosom. She was never seen to smile. She never joined their revels, or took part in the division of the spoil. But she entered every tent from which escaped a cry of suffering, and was often left alone on the scene of action, where the mutilated were mingled with the dead. Everything about her bespoke a distinguished origin. She abhorred all vulgarity, and when any new comer talked to her too freely, the blood was seen to mantle on her cheek. An imposing dignity of manner characterised her, and the proud lady became suddenly unfolded to the adventurer, who imagined he had to do with a fool. It was this haughty and dignified manner which gave rise to her title of ladyship. All these ferocious men, inaccessible to all fear, loved Margaret as a mother; but a superstitious dread was mingled with their affection. They believed her to be unsettled in her mind, because they often noticed her, after being plunged in deep thought the whole of the day, suddenly start up and, amidst loud bursts of laughter, imperiously demand—

" Have you seen my son?—tell me, have you seen aught of him?"

They, however, attributed to Margaret's folly divine privileges; and, instead of despising her weakness, they venerated it as a gift from Heaven, and consulted her on futurity, tempests, and the probable result of their hunting and plundering expeditions.   Michel le Basque was one of the most superstitious partisans of Margaret.   The seigneuresse advanced towards Joaquin, and regarded him with a kind of tender and melancholy curiosity.   Then she murmured whilst kissing her locket—

" He, too, would have been about this age.   He would have been strong and beautiful, like this young man.   He would have been brave, like him—like his father; but, he would not recognise me.   He has never been nursed on his mother's knee, or prattled her name."

She remained plunged in her recollections, which no one disturbed.   Finally, she placed her dry and wrinkled hand on the shoulder of the valet, and said softly to him—

" Be docile, my child, and Margaret will watch over you; never resist your master."

Joaquin felt himself involuntarily moved by the tone of authority in which the seigneuresse addressed him, and which seemed to indicate some real and mysterious interest which she took in his fate: one is seldom deceived by the language of the heart.   The young man found an expression imposing and tender, in the look of this extraordinary woman, which seemed fixed upon him.

" Be wise!   I tell you, the future will be great for you."

These prophetic words reanimated the valet, although Margaret did not seem in a condition to free him from the servitude he had chosen for himself.   Then turning towards Donna Carmen she could not conceal a shudder of emotion, and said, imperiously, to the buccanier:

" As for thee, Michel le Basque, respect this child as if she was blood of my blood, if you do not wish us to be at variance ; and you know what Margaret's anger is."

" This voice," thought Carmen, " is not unknown to me." She had, for several instants, examined the features of the seigneuresse, trying to recal confused and dim recollections. Michel, who had twice owed his life to Margaret, replied to this strange woman :

" Be calm, dear mother.   We shall treat ebony-skin in the best manner we can, and we will not touch this fopling any more, provided he applies himself to his work."

" Hear me, Michel, and do not forget a single word I utter: the life of every one is at the disposal of him who wishes to take it whilst his own is safe. Do not rely always on brutal force. The servant's hand is better than the master's arm."

" But, how does it happen that you take such a lively interest in a young stripling whom you never saw before?"

" What reason have I?" replied she, in an altered voice, whilst she pressed her forehead in her hands, and her eyes became brilliant and uplifted. " It is because this young man resembles my child! who, perhaps, now lives, and who would be about his age and appearance—sweet and yet manly."

" Nonsense!" grumbled Michel. " There she has struck upon her madness, and her folly will take the bit in its teeth."

" Who calls it folly?" interrupted Margaret, with a fierce accent. " Who uttered that word? Do I not see the infant every night? Folly! Did I not hear him, last night, cry— ' Mother, why have you abandoned me? You are very cruel to your son. What are you doing whilst he suffers—eh! mother? If you knew that they make me work unceasingly, that I cannot sleep, and that my black bread is mingled with tears.' Folly! that has made my hair white, and forced me to wander like a sorcerer and a vagabond through the solitudes of the forest."

" Oh! it is indeed her," said Donna Carmen, to herself, taking, at the same time, the seigneuresse's hand. She was about to speak to her, but the former returning to her reason, looked at the young girl with tenderness, put her finger on her lips to silence her, and said:

" Do not despair, daughter, we shall see each other again."

" Adelaide," murmured Donna Carmen.

" Silence!" interrupted the seigneuresse; " Margaret will bid you all adieu for some days. But you, Michel, shall answer for these unfortunates."

This singular woman rapidly disappeared, without turning her head; whilst the spectators of this scene remained silent and absorbed by the various thoughts which it suggested.

CHAPTER IV.

THE DUEL.

IN the meantime the Leopard was not indifferent to the fate of Joaquin. A little after the departure of Margaret he entered the tent of his matelot, and sat down on the ground as if he had come with a friendly intention. According to their custom of borrowing from each other whatever they wanted he took from Michel's trunk some powder and shot. Michel le Basque remained, at first, silent, on observing the old adventurer act so coolly, and without even looking at his nephew, who was turning the grindstone. At the expiration of a quarter of an hour only, the Leopard spoke:

"You are a free buccanier, Michel. You have not for-gotten our friendship. You remember, also, that you yourself demanded once a favour from Joaquin. You know, also, how much I love the son of my brother."

"What do you mean to draw from that?" asked Le Basque.

"I should have expected that my matelot would not have treated like a Guinea slave or a Spaniard a brave young fellow who was once his comrade."

"I am master of my servants," said Michel, sharply; "and I owe no one an account of my conduct."

"It is true there is no law to compel you to be humane and generous; but if you are neither, I see nothing to prevent me telling you, Michel le Basque, that I thoroughly despise you."

Le Basque grew pale, and started up, exclaiming—

"Well, be it so, since you will have it so. I hate that youth now because he braves me so often to my face. He is my servant, and certainly I will not free him."

"Very good," replied the Leopard, coolly. "In that case, Michel, we must fight, because you cannot strike my nephew without causing me to feel the blow in my own person. My blood

flows in the veins of that young man, and through him you
have insulted me."

" Uncle—" interrupted Joaquin, much moved, and endeavouring to catch his hand.

" Silence !" said the Leopard, with severity, biting his lip.
" Valet, attend to your duty, and leave the buccanier to perform his."

Michel le Basque, however, hesitated to accept his old
friend's proposition.

The buccanier uncorked his calabash, and taking the powder, scattered it upon the ground in renunciation of friendship
and matelotage, which is one of the most cruel injuries one
buccanier can render to another.

" No, no, not so, my matelot, not so," murmured Michel.

The action required a most powerful act of self-command on
the part of the Leopard.

" You will agree, then, Michel, that I employ your powder
and lead against yourself ? Well, I consent to it, also, on my
part ; and in return I expect you will fight without feebleness or
hesitation, as if you had to do with a Spanish lancer."

Le Baque assembled his faithful dogs, who devoured his
hand with caresses.   He trembled, too, in loading his musket ;
but when he saw Carmen and Joaquin exchange a look—a look
of hope, perhaps, his jealous rage prevailed, and he cried :

" No, no ; no weakness.   Leopard, your matelot's hand will
not tremble, nor his eye fail.   Oh ! I am not buried yet, my
faithful servants."

A duel occurring amongst the Brothers of the Coast was
always regulated by special statute.   All differences were settled by musket or rifle shots.   The two buccaniers buried
themselves in the forest, attended by Joaquin, Vent-en-Panne,
and the surgeon to the corsairs.   Having found a clearing
sufficiently convenient, they planted themselves face to face, at
about forty paces distant.

The Leopard being the aggressor, Michel had the right to
fire first.   If he missed, his adversary was then entitled to his
shot when he thought proper.   The surgeon was present to
examine the wounds.   If the ball was found to have entered
from behind or too much towards the side, treachery was
necessarily implied, and the witnesses were justified in tying
the conqueror to a tree and dashing out his brains.

Michel le Basque was a very celebrated shot.   He took a
long aim at the old chief, who stood perfectly calm and composed.

" Send me that sugar-plum of yours without any more ceremony," cried the Leopard.

" You know that I have no deadly intention." At the same
moment he fired, and instantly uttered a cry of triumph. He
had hit the Leopard in the wrist of the right hand, desiring
only to disable him, and in that he had succeeded.

" My poor nephew," was all the Leopard uttered.

Michel, leaving him in the care of the surgeon and Vent-en-
Panne, ordered Joaquin to attend him to the tent. Irritated
by the numerous obstacles which opposed his passion, and for-
getful of his promise to Margaret, he was no sooner at home
than he cried—

" Off to the hunt, now ; off to the hunt for the whole day.
Senorita, you will follow us."

Joaquin and Donna Carmen grew pale at this order, but
there was no refusal. Michel imposed a heavy task upon his
valet, and ordered him to take care of the tent. The young
man resolved not to obey, but to follow the hunters at a distance, at every risk. Joaquin perceived with joy that Le Basque
led away with him the two dogs, Gerondif and Curaçoa, which
his uncle had given him. He then set to work vigorously, and by
no external sign showed his secret intention. Donna Carmen,
perceiving such an expression of confidence in Joaquin's countenance, offered no resistance to the will of Le Basque.

Michel, preceded by Curaçoa, set out, followed by the valets
and a pack of hounds. He protected his slave with an awkward
solicitude, but very pressing in his attention. He broke down
the branches which in the narrow path might wound or annoy
her. He spoke not to her ; he seemed pre-occupied. Once
when she lingered behind, he approached her saying, with un-
accustomed sweetness—

" Are you wearied, senorita ?"

" Have I any right to be fatigued ?" said she, with a bitter
smile. " The slave follows the master."

She endeavoured to pursue her journey, but her small feet
were soon tired, and Le Basque stood still, regarding her.

" I am indeed cruel," murmured he. " But only say one
kind word to me ; I shall be so pleased to satisfy the least of
your wishes. Do you wish us to rest here ? You have only
to speak."

" Master, go on," replied the slave, coldly.

" Always this implacable Spanish pride !" cried Le Basque,
in a rage. " She would rather die than ask me a favour. It

does not matter ; I shall be generous, as I promised the seigneuresse." And he said to his valets, " Go ahead ; I will overtake you. I will keep two dogs besides Curaçoa, so as not to lose your track."

" I am no longer fatigued," replied Donna Carmen, alarmed at remaining alone with the buccanier. The valets and the pack soon disappeared, and a profound silence reigned in the forest. Donna Carmen felt herself become drowsy from the fatigues of her journey and the sleepy influence of solitude. The mocking birds were silent ; the monkeys had ceased to play amongst the branches ; everything was asleep at that hour. A few jets of sunshine penetrated here and there through the leafy canopy, quivering like golden arrows, and lighting up the twilight shade where the two were seated. The occasional flutter of wings and buzzing of insects mingled with the monotonous bubbling of a rill of water, concealed by plants and vegetation. In the depths of the forest confused sounds now and then rumbled, distant grumblings from the clearings, barking of dogs, shouts of men, and growlings of wild beasts.

Donna Carmen felt her heart oppressed as if she had been confined within the walls of some gigantic prison. She hid her face in her hands on seeing the sparkling look of Michel fixed upon her.

" I always frighten you," said he, sadly. " Now, however, that we are alone, you must listen to me. I have many things to say to you, senorita. But when I see you trembling before me I forget all my good thoughts, and become gross and brutal, for I cannot comprehend how you can hate a man so heartily who would sacrifice his life for you."

Curaçoa now began to show much uneasiness, and leaping over the brook, he ran into a thicket, but soon returned to his master, howling furiously.

" The dog has scented game of a high order," cried Michel, who listened with profound attention after having made a sign to the two dogs to set off.

Instantly, Donna Carmen heard a rapid and singular noise approaching nearer and nearer to the tree against which she was leaning. She heard the branches cracking, and saw the leaves shake.

" It is a wild boar rushing this way," said the buccanier, placing himself quick before her. In fact, a tremendous wild boar with a bloody head appeared with the speed of lightning, received the dogs on his tusks, who had rushed at him, and fixed his red eyes on Donna Carmen. Michel grew pale, feeling his musket shake in his hand, and said, furiously—

"I have exposed you to this." He fired, but the ball scarcely marked the tough, bristled hide of the brute. Curaçoa, contrary to the habits of setters, threw itself between Donna Carmen and the wild boar, but the terrible beast gnashed his tusks together, and at the sight of the foaming mouth and teeth, the dog slunk away, howling. The young girl cried, in a feeble voice, "Joaquin!" and fainted at the foot of the tree.

Fortunately, after the shot, the wild boar turned upon Michel. The buccanier threw down his musket, and drawing his hunting knife, awaited firmly the approaching shock. He buried the knife in the animal's throat, whose haste and precipitation hastened his fate so speedily that his last bite did not even scratch the hunter. The latter measured coolly the length of the animal, then tying Curaçoa with a cord to a tree, he gave it a share of the prey. Turning to Donna Carmen, he said, with an accent of ferocious satisfaction:

"This time, at least, I alone have saved you."

At that bitter expression, which implied a terrible jealousy, Donna Carmen comprehended the extent of the passion which troubled the mind of the buccanier, and she thanked him with one of those sweet but saddened looks which one throws on a madman whom they pity. Alas! that look lost her, and excited once more the violence of Michel.

"I am not a child to be led by a smile," said he, striking the ground with his foot. "I will not be pitied. On your account I hate Joaquin. For you I have broken up all friendship for my matelot. No, I would rather be feared or abhorred; but I shall never be duped by the grimaces of a woman," and he tried to seize Donna Carmen's hand, who cried:

"Wretch!" repelling him with contempt.

"Ah, the same gesture as at Rancheria?" said Michel, gloomily, whilst his face grew pale. "Good; you do me a service, senorita. A short time ago I was moved—confounded by your terror. Now I become Michel le Basque again, your master, notwithstanding your pride and hatred. We shall see whether the noble Spaniard will always lord it over the poor buccanier.

Frightened on hearing these words, and the look of the buccanier, Donna Carmen drew back, and instinctively attempted to fly, but he rudely grasped her arm, and said, in a brief and reprimanding tone :

" Hear me. It is vain that I try to hate or forget you. It is impossible to avoid thinking of you continually. Ever since you have slept under my tent my heart has seemed changed, and everything around me. Why, I know not. Can you tell me ?" She made no reply. He continued : " Formerly I was happy when I had been successful in hunting, or obtained a large share of booty. I loved my comrades. Sometimes before falling asleep I thought of my native land—that was all. Now I forget the chase, and dream of you whilst awake. I am like a man intoxicated by some philter, which affects my reason. My companions seem gross and disagreeable to me, and if I must admit my last weakness, I am jealous of every one who is not old like myself. I envy Joaquin his look, his voice, and his appearance. I feel ashamed of loving, for the first time, at my age ; and I am troubled that this love, which has made my heart young again, should not also have removed the wrinkles from my brow."

" Why have I consented to live," said the young Spaniard.

" Since you hate me," said Michel, bitterly, " although my chief crime is that of asking your pity for that blind passion which I cannot subdue, I want to have you always near me. I suffer when you are absent. My thoughts pursue you. All this is, perhaps, folly ; but it is a folly of which I feel myself dying."

" Oh ! God, you punish me cruelly for my faults in compelling me to listen to such language."

" Oh ! it is too much to brave me thus. You jest with a master who trembles and sighs before you like a schoolboy ; but I long for a termination to such a game."

He looked around him uneasily, fancing he had heard a crackling near to where they were. But shortly, convinced of the contrary, he turned towards the young creole, who cried out in agony :

" Come, Joaquin, come !"

" You depend upon him. You then love him, senorita ; but he will not come."

A deeper shade began to invade the forest, and through a glade the edge of the moon began to arise.

" We are alone, you see," said the buccanier, with a bitter accent, and he squeezed the young girl's hand, who shuddered at the contact.

" Joaquin !" she again cried.

" He is here !" said a voice, trembling with rage, and the young man rushed out of the thicket, where he had silently observed the scene for some time. Friar Eusebio accompanied him in his robes. Michel, at first, regarded them with stupor. Then an expression of joy shone on his countenance.

" Treachery !" cried he. " It is a plot. You have designed it. I ought to have expected it. Well, so much the better. This time, at all events, we shall put an end to it. Go behind me, slave," said he, marching up to Joaquin. " Have you forgot who I am ?"

The young man remained motionless, but boldly replied :

" If your axe had wounded me this morning you would not have seen me lift my hand against you, nor would an insult have passed my lips ; but since you address your outrages to a defenceless woman, she will find a protector, not in the valet of Michel le Basque, but in Joaquin Montbars."

" Be it so," said the buccanier, shaking with passion. " But defend yourself well, for I will not spare the traitor who has violated his oath."

" I respect my master," said Joaquin, with an ironical smile. " It is not a question whether we are to fight a duel. I merely want to put it out of your power to do mischief."

At the same moment, and before Le Basque recovered his surprise, Joaquin, with a rapid movement, took a lasso from his shoulder. The buccanier rushed at him, but the young man made two steps backwards, and threw the noose skilfully over his body, which he tightened around him. Michel made the most furious efforts to free himself, turning and twisting like a serpent, but they all terminated in his finding himself stretched on the ground, totally unable to move.

" You see, Michel, that I do not wish to do you any mischief."

" Begone, begone !" said the vanquished Le Basque, grinding his teeth. " It is disgraceful, Joaquin. Do you mean to insult me thus—the old comrade of your uncle, too ? Kill me if you like, but do not treat me like a wild beast. It is cowardly and disgraceful. Even a Spaniard would not have done so," and Le Basque could not restrain his tears, which rolled down his cheeks. He continued, in a fury : " You may boast that you have seen me shed tears, and make sport of me amongst my Brothers. Youth is arrogant and presumptuous, but God knows how to chastise it."

"We shall, perhaps, never see each other again," said the young man.

"What!" cried the buccanier, twisting in the cords. "Then I cannot revenge myself. Think first, Joaquin, if you become a maroon, what fate is reserved for you."

The valet interrupted him.

"Master, you have made sport of my sufferings. You have scorched my heart without pity. My vengeance is mild, and you are wrong to complain of it. Adieu."

"Help! help!" cried Michel le Basque, with all his might.

"We must fly," said Joaquin to Donna Carmen, and the monk, who remained stupified by the unexpected *denouement*, said—

"The cries of the poor devil may attract the hunters, when we shall be pursued. We must make haste."

He took the musket and calabash of powder from the buccanier, gave one of the hunting knives to the friar, and grasping the hand of the young girl, who trembled much, he led her in an opposite direction to that from which he came. They proceeded onwards during the space of a quarter of an hour, and soon were out of hearing of Michel le Basque's desperate cries. But all at once Joaquin slackened his pace, and striking his forehead, cried:

"My God! what forgetfulness. I never thought of untying Curaçoa and bring her with us. It is a setter which my uncle gave me, and which I lost to the accursed Michel."

"Well, how can that increase our danger?" asked the monk.

"What, do you not understand that they will put her on the scent, and that she never loses?"

Donna Carmen was completely exhausted, and could proceed no farther.

"I can go no farther. Leave me, leave me."

"Make one last attempt," said the monk.

The young girl sadly made a sign in the negative.

"In that case," said Joaquin, "let us wait here the approach of the hunters. We shall not have long to wait," and he leaned with folded arms against a tree."

"You do not understand me," said Donna Carmen, with energy. "I will remain, but you, Joaquin, fly with the friar. I can wait the arrival of the buccaniers without fear. What harm can they do to a poor girl? You are alone culpable, and Le Basque will be satisfied to have found his slave. They will stop here, and pursue you no farther, Joaquin."

At this moment they believed they heard Curaçoa bark.

"Poor dog," said Montbars, whose brow became suffused. "You see, senorita, he rejoices to overtake his master."

"If it is thus I will try to move on. I will follow you until I drop from exhaustion."

"Listen, Donna Carmen, and do not reject the request of your servant. I have strength enough. Allow me to carry you, and I will answer for it that we will shortly reach the Great River. I know a ford. They will lose our track there; besides, it is our only chance of safety."

"Carry me," said Donna Carmen.

Joaquin took her in his arms and carried her, like an infant asleep, feeling his strength augment instead of failing under his precious burden.

The progress of our adventurers became rapid and breathless, for they comprehended the value of every moment, and the barking of the dogs became more distinct every minute. At times they cast behind them alarmed looks, conceiving the hunters were about to overtake them on the path they themselves had opened for them. Once the monk, who made tremendous efforts to pass over the irregular ground, turned and said to Joaquin:

"Let us face these brigands; we have arms in our hands, and can, at least, die bravely."

But the young man, without pausing, replied—

"By dying we leave Donna Carmen the slave of Michel le Basque."

They reached, at length, a hill which crowned the skirt of the forest; and, from which, they rapidly descended to the Great River. There a new misfortune awaited them, and Joaquin could not restrain a cry of despair, as he showed by a gesture to the friar, the yellow, boiling, and rapid flood which rose far above the banks.

"It is impossible to cross," said he, sadly; "the river is up at least fifteen feet."

"We are lost then," said the monk, falling on his knees, together with Donna Carmen, upon the sandy bank.

"Perhaps saved, who knows?" said Joaquin, examining the sky, the horizon narrowing and the gloom increasing, whilst the wind blew in gusts, sweeping along the earth. They all trembled on hearing joyous barkings in the forest, and shortly Curaçoa bounded towards them. The keen setter rolled over at Joaquin's feet, his tongue lolling out, and his sides panting.

" So soon ?" murmured Joaquin, and he held out his hand to
it to lick. " Poor Curaçoa, you do not imagine that your
zeal has betrayed your master." The dog raised its paws
to his master's knees, and looked with intelligence in his face.
Joaquin seized his arms with a trembling hand, whilst Donna

Carmen patted the dog's neck. " Retire, senorita," said
Joaquin, softly.
" Why ?" asked she, with surprise ; " What are you about
to do ?"
" My duty," answered Joaquin, with a sigh. The dog
whined to attract his master's attention. " Those who are
8   I

pursuing us cannot be more than a quarter of an hour behind us. The dog guides them, and will sacrifice us."

" I understand you, but it is frightful." Joaquin made a sign to the dog to retire. " Do not do it. I will not suffer it."

" Make haste," said the friar, coldly.

" It is absurd—is it not ? I tremble in spite of myself. What can I do ?—but away with weakness. It concerns our safety." He fired, Curaçoa fell without a cry, shot through the head. The monk kicked the body into the river, whilst Donna Carmen turned away her eyes with horror. The atmosphere now became more and more gloomy and threatening.

" I do not know," said the friar, " how I feel ; but it seems to me as if my legs were unsteady, and my sight disturbed."

" And I," said Carmen, " feel in my ears strange sounds, like those we experience in a fever."

" I was not, then, deceived," cried Joaquin. " We shall shortly witness a terrible scene, to which, perhaps, we may owe our safety ; for man's vengeance cannot struggle against the wrath of Heaven."

" What do you mean ?" asked the monk.

" Prepare yourself and pray, may God will us to be saved from the earthquake which now approaches."

" An earthquake !" exclaimed Donna Carmen, " Let us rather bid a final adieu to each other."

" You are safer here than in the centre of your hatto ; but take my advice : you must lie down among those herbs and await, as calmly as you can, the lot which God may send us."

At one glance the fugitives perceived their imminent danger. The trees groaned and rocked, although the wind had entirely ceased. The river boiled up as if its bed was a hot furnace. The clouds seemed piled on each other, and falling, like a veil, over the earth. Several wild beasts began to prowl about in terror. At this moment the buccanier appeared with the hunters on the top of the hill they had left. He uttered a cry of joy on seeing Joaquin.

" Yield !" shouted he, " your lives will be spared."

" We are waiting for you," answered Joaquin, coldly.

" You cannot now escape. You are at our mercy."

" And you at the mercy of Heaven !"

" Forward !" shouted Michel. But the dogs trembled with terror and refused to advance. " Flog them !" roared the buccanier.

" Madman ! instead of chastising these animals rather

admire their instinct; do not advance a step, the hill has already shook, and vacillates to its basis now."

" You are afraid, boy, with your child's stories." He moved a step forward, but drew back with terror. The hill opened before him, and presented an insurmountable barrier to his progress.

Joaquin leaned towards the young creole.

" Donna Carmen, you are free."

The adventurer seemed furious and desperate. He twisted his musket convulsively, and cried, jeeringly—

" You think you have triumphed over Michel le Basque—" but he could not accomplish what he designed to say. The sky became obscured entirely by fleeting vapour, through which the lightning belched forth its vivid streams. Twice by its aid Joaquin saw the buccanier still rooted to the place where he stood, leaning on his arms, and watching an occasion to fire.

The trees fell here and there, uprooted with a tremendous noise, and the earth shook, tossing up hills or forming chasms in their place at random. Our fugitives remained prostrate and overwhelmed amidst the terrors of the scene, for no human courage can withstand the awful convulsions of nature. Once or twice the waters of the river drove up into their faces and covered their limbs, which they scarcely observed, the night being passed in terrible agony. When the day dawned a new landscape was displayed. Here the river, turned from its course, had turned a prairie into a lake. There the hills had blocked up the bed of the stream, forming foaming rapids and cascades.

Joaquin could discover no trace of Michel le Basque or his companions. The edge of the forest only presented a line of bent and uprooted trees, blasted here and there by the lightning. The plain seemed like an immense brazier, whose fires were scarcely extinct.

The fugitives contemplated the scene of overthrow with different sentiments.

" God has punished violence," said the friar, "and protected the feeble."

" Poor Michel!" remarked Joaquin. " He was a rude companion, but he carried a good heart under his grossness."

" Let us pray for him," said Carmen, " and may Heaven still protect us."

Joaquin regarded her with emotion; then directed his steps

towards the Great River, and after having examined the bank with anxiety, he returned with a joyous air, saying—

" Senorita, I have discovered the ford, thanks to which we can reach a retreat, the secret of which I alone am acquainted with, and where, for some days, we may put all pursuit at defiance."

Donna Carmen and the monk, without hesitation, followed their generous guide, and, after three hours walk, they reached a grotto, hollowed by nature in a rock, which stood isolated like a sheep on the opposite bank of the river.

CHAPTER V.

THE RETREAT.

HE grotto, at the entrance of which we left our three fugitives, was of extraordinary beauty, owing to the innumerable stalactites with which it was adorned.

As we have before said, it was hollowed out of the rock, the base of which was worn away by the constant action of the stream. A cascade descended from an eminence behind the rock, and poured its spray over it, which, acting as a prism in the sun's rays, rendered the scene at times extremely beautiful. A fissure formed the entrance to the grotto, under a low vault, which was still more effectually screened by a curtain of creeping plants, the tendrils of which danced on the stream.

When our fugitives had entered, Joaquin said—

" Let us now thank God, for we have nothing more to fear."

" From the buccaniers, perhaps," said the monk. " But, are you sure we shall escape another danger, equally formidable ?"

" To what new danger do you allude, father ?" asked Donna Carmen.

" Hunger, hunger, which paralyses courage and strength, and the progress of whose agony may be counted, moment by moment."

" Let us have no more of these chimerical fears," said Joaquin, joyfully. " We know well that courage is not the predominating feature in the character of your order." The monk looked obliquely at him, with condensed hatred. " Don't alarm yourself, friar. Wherever the waters roll or space extends, there are resources for the adventurers. God has supplied the stream with fish and the air with birds, whilst he has created the herds that roam over mountain and forest."

" Very good," replied the monk, gravely. " But if the hunter deceives the fugitive, what shall we gain by following your advice ?"

" Trust to me, father, and do not yield to such puerile fears. Forget, if you can, that you wear a monk's habit, and try to remember that you are a man. Imitate Donna Carmen : you see how fatigued she is, yet she does not tremble at imaginary dangers, as you do."

The monk started, but replied in a calm, soft voice—

" What do you mean, Joaquin, when you say that courage is not our predominating quality ? But, at least," added he, in a low murmur, " vengeance is."

" You must understand that the rock is surrounded with lagoons, where the best turtles of Hispaniola come to feed, and at nightfall you may procure yourself an excellent supper, by means of the harpoons concealed under those dried leaves."

" Why did you not at first make these explanations, Joaquin ?"

" We must now, father, think of lighting a good fire with these dried sticks, so as to reanimate the benumbed limbs of the senorita. We have passed a rough night, and I must confess that at times I feel a strong temptation to sleep."

A strange smile passed across the monk's face, like a sudden flash of light.

" Let us return thanks to Providence, Joaquin. I have, most fortunately, preserved a phial of the best of all cordials in the world to prevent sleep. You know that my profession renders it necessary for me to know something of medicine. A few drops will restore to you your entire strength."

" With all my heart, father ; although we are safe here, I do not mind keeping company with the fire whilst you take some repose."

Whilst Montbars piled up a heap of dried sticks and withered leaves, the monk took out of a little skin bag which hung at his belt, a phial, which he regarded with mysterious interest.

The young creole, overcome by fatigue, had been asleep some time.

The monk poured five or six drops of his pretended cordial into a leathern cup, and handed it to Joaquin; after which he retired to the bottom of the grotto, for the purpose of coolly watching the effect.

The adventurer lighted a good fire, and regarded Donna Carmen with emotion as she lay pale in its rays, which were reflected in a singular manner again by the diamond-fronted stalactites. There was a profound silence. The soft and regular breathing of the young Spaniard was alone heard; together with the cheerful crackling of the blazing twigs.

All at once, Joaquin, who was leaning over the fire, stirring it up continually, felt a strange shiver all over his back. His eyelids closed, weighed down by an irresistible desire to sleep. His ideas became confused and fleeting, like the vague images of a dream. In vain he tried to overcome this torpor, accustomed as he had been to resist the most violent fatigue. In vain he fixed his gaze on the young girl whom he had saved, and whom he had still to protect. In spite of all he felt a chillness benumb his limbs. Finally, his hands allowed the cup to fall, and then he recollected the cordial, that the friar was Don Ramon's brother, and that some horrible vengeance might be attempted. He made a desperate effort to reach the fanatical monk, who advanced towards Joaquin, whose limbs began to fail him. The monk looked at him steadily. Joaquin's sight grew dim. He tried to utter a cry, so as to awaken Donna Carmen; but the sound died away in his throat. He comprehended that he was lost; and when the monk approached him, he fell motionless at his feet. But what was most singular, his body alone presented the appearance of death. His perception, however, remained active. He heard the monk's voice—

" Now, I have him at my mercy. Madman, to suppose he had subdued his enemy. When your look and voice insulted me, I remained impassable."

Joaquin attempted to rise. He felt his heart beat violently, but that was all.

" You love Donna Carmen. You are now speechless, without strength to protect yourself from the least danger. Let her now summon you to her assistance, and you will remain cold and motionless. Of what use, then, is your courage and fidelity. You thought to extinguish in my mind all memory of my brother's death; but vengeance is the only resource of those whom you have injured, and who are without courage. Do you hear, Joaquin?"

He put his hand on the heart of the young man, who moved not at the contact.

"Well, Joaquin, how calmly you listen to me; yet you curse me in your mind. You would give the best part of your life to be revenged on me; and yet your lips move not. Your heart beats under my hand, but you cannot repel it. Oh! how you hate me now."

He was silent a moment, to allow his insults to sink deeper in Joaquin's heart.

"However, all is not yet terminated between us. I keep you in the most cruel torture. You comprehend me, for your heart beats more violently. Be calm, Joaquin: control your emotion, if you do not wish to die too soon. You think, no doubt, that this proud Spaniard, Donna Carmen, is not insensible to you. You will soon know that."

The monk approached the young girl, and called her softly.

"Senorita! senorita!"

The creole did not awaken. Joaquin heard her tranquil breathing.

"She is beautiful," said the monk aloud.

The young girl started as if under an electric shock.

"Is there any danger, father?"

"See how well we are guarded. The adventurer is asleep."

"Oh! my God," thought Montbars; "only one moment of life and of strength, face to face, with this monster."

"Poor Joaquin," said the young girl, softly; "what fatigue he has undergone to save us. So much the better, if he can sleep a few hours. God be praised, he will forget many sufferings in sleep."

"Yes; God be praised: for he has now put him in our power, senorita."

"A little lower, a little lower, or you will arouse him, father. Surely I did not rightly understand you," continued she, regarding the friar with astonishment.

"Oh! what would not the Spaniards give for this man, who has inherited the accursed name of Montbars, the exterminator."

"You frighten me, father."

"Hear me, Donna Carmen. We must now take a most decisive resolution. If you visit Rancheria in company with this adventurer, on whose head a price is set, and whose name is a living reproach to Spain, your character will be ruined in the eyes of all Hispaniola. They will not believe that he has saved you from slavery at the risk of his life, without some secret motive, some ambitious end."

" Father, you are very cruel," cried Donna Carmen, blushing.

" In their opinion, you will have purchased your freedom by tolerating the addresses of a Brother of the Coast. Such all will think to be the case ; and do you not think that calumny and lies will do the rest ?"

The young girl became pale, and trembled. Joaquin felt his life depended on Donna Carmen's lips.

"Can you, then, brave the disgraceful reports which will spread on your return ; subdued it will be at first, but these rumours will spread. Will you consent to encounter one half of the hatred which surrounds this brigand ?"

" Brigand !" repeated she, with stupor. " Do you really speak of this generous young man, who has been so devoted to us ?"

Joaquin thanked heaven. How he could have wished to have cast himself at her feet.

" Yes, brigand ; never forget that to the Spaniards he is a pirate, who has pillaged and burned their property—that he is Montbars. Amongst the Brothers of the Coast the name is a war-cry ; ay, a name which forces the strongest rampart, and shakes the soldier beside his cannon."

" What would you, then, advise me to do ? What do you aim at ?"

The monk smiled, and pointed again to Joaquin.

" Do you not see, senorita, that at present the wretch sleeps, without power of resistance."

" Well ?"

" Well ; a child could bind his strong and valiant arms."

Donna Carmen threw back with a trembling hand the long hair floating over her shoulders in profusion, and looked in the monk's face, not believing what she heard. After a moment's silence, the young creole arose, and standing before the friar, exclaimed, with a bitter smile, full of doubt and alarm—

" So, then, it is not a trial to which you subject me ? You are not jesting ? You advise me. You even thought I would consent. Without doubt you know how such an action is termed ; and you have supposed me capable of committing it."

She could not conclude ; her voice trembled with emotion.

" It concerns your honour," said the monk.

"In truth," said Donna Carmen, appearing to reflect, "no one would suppose that I loved the man I betrayed. Calumny itself would be silent before such a proof. Who, then, could ask for more? Where could there be a higher virtue than to sell to his executioners the very man who has sacrificed for us not only his blood and life, but his pride and oaths. We should, then, in return for his fidelity and confidence, recompense him with death. You will at least, father, promise me to preserve a profound silence for ever on the subject of this brigand's mad affection?"

Joaquin's heart bounded as if it would burst from his breast.

"She will consent," thought the monk. "I shall be silent, senorita. This folly shall remain unknown. You will become the noble and rich mistress of Rancheria. The courage you have shown in your escape will astonish all. You will be honoured, and the bandit once delivered up, you need not fear that any future audacious look will make you start, nor any insulting voice recal your days of slavery, whilst demanding the price of your deliverance."

"But, if, in spite of honours and riches, I despise myself, and my own heart condemns me, pronouncing me cowardly and treacherous without excuse? It will be in vain to hide the terrors of conscience beneath my diamonds, or remorse under false smiles."

"What does it signify, if both dazzle the eyes of man?"

"But God, at least, cannot be deceived," cried she, with agony. "He looks under the mask of hypocrisy, and reads the heart itself."

"God will be silent like the world, I tell you, senorita, and the church will bless you."

"Spare me, father, a whole life of repentance could not expiate such an offence."

"Offence? It is an action which will cause your name to be honoured throughout all Spanish America!"

"Rather say, Friar Eusebio, that it would cause me to be despised all over the world."

"Senorita, every mother would kiss the hands of her who had delivered up Montbars, the exterminater."

"But Joaquin merely inherits the fatal name. You know that as well as me. He never wished to carry out the likeness further."

"You know, senorita, that the name must never die amongst the buccaniers. It is full of terror to our countrymen, and the magic power of the buccaniers is contained within it. Let him who now bears the title become our prisoner, and be hanged from a Spanish gibbet, and the spell will be broken."

"So, father, you have no other motives for instigating me to this treachery?"

"She will consent," thought the friar; and he continued in a low voice—"I need not allude to the magnificent recompense which awaits us from the Governor of the Island."

"True, the treachery will be rewarded. One need not hesitate. The gold, father, will not bear the stain of blood; and when your brow is calm, and your smile joyful, who will think of inquiring whether the mind be at rest. Besides, have you not promised me peace of mind?—and I ought to believe you, for you are a holy man of God."

"Unfortunate being," thought Joaquin, filled with horror, on hearing her cede bit by bit to the persuasions of the monk. "Will she vilify herself thus. Is her heart made of brass?"

"I have triumphed," said the monk, seizing the hands of the young girl. "Yes, we have everything with us, God and men, riches and honours."

Donna Carmen looked at him without anger or uneasiness, and remarked in a soft voice, singularly calm—

"Hear me, father. Do you think he loves me?"

"No," said Eusebio, after a moment of silent surprise.

"A short time since, however, you thought otherwise."

"If he truly loved you, would he sleep so tranquilly when he ought to watch over you?"

"Infamy—infamy," thought Joaquin, who, in vain, tried to open his eyes, which were heavy and cold.

Donna Carmen listened to the friar, with a melancholy smile.

"Why, then, has this brigand saved us?"

"What he loves in you is the difference of rank. The pearl-fisher aspires to the lady. Can you be duped by such an affection, senorita, and can you feel any pity for the vanity and ambition of this madman?"

"You want, then, father, a decisive reply. Here it is. Your proposition is that of a coward and traitor. Do not interrupt me. That which I esteem more than the world's consideration is nobility of heart. When my honour and safety were in that man's power, who now lies at our feet, I treated him with disdain and harshness. Nothing has discouraged him. He could not then divine, by word or look, that I appreciated his unbounded fidelity. But now that he sleeps defenceless, calumniated in his affection, and menaced in liberty and life, it is my turn to protect him, as he has protected me—to love him as he has loved me."

Joaquin thought he should have died on hearing these words, without being able to testify the fullness of his joy.

"Take care, senorita," cried the friar, in a stupor. "You seemed just now to assent. You have spread a snare for me."

"How is it possible," said Donna Carmen, indignantly, "that you misunderstood me, and concerning Joaquin above all others?"

"Tremble, then, yourself, noble heiress, for in spite of you, he shall be given up. Ay, both of you shall suffer; he on the gallows, and you from shame."

"These are vain menaces," said she, leaning towards Joaquin. "Beware, friar, lest I arouse him, and lest his rage make you repent your criminal designs."

The monk smiled with disdain. The young girl shook Joaquin by the arm, and muttered his name. The unfortunate young man heard her, the blood circulated more rapidly, but not a muscle moved on his pale countenance. Donna Carmen looked at him earnestly, and alarmed at his awful immobility, she cried twice in his ear—"Joaquin, Joaquin!" Tears flowed to the adventurer's eyes, but he stirred not. Donna Carmen remained on her knees beside him. Stupified, annihilated, contemplating, with haggard eyes, the scene before her. The monk still smiled. In a few minutes, she cried in a sad and broken voice—

"Wretch! have you committed this horrible crime? Are these cold hands already those of a corpse? For mercy's sake answer me."

"Compose yourself. Joaquin lives."

"Thanks be to God!"

"Joaquin hears you. He knows that you love him." Donna Carmen let the adventurer's hand fall, which she had taken in her own. "No human power can restore, before twelve hours, heat and life, strength, or vengeance. I tell you he is lost, for we are not far from Spanish dwellings."

He put a whistle to his mouth, which was concealed under his robe, and gave a shrill and prolonged sound, like that of the macaw. Instantly, a savage growl replied to the friar's summons.

"Wretch!" cried Donna Carmen. But the monk heard not; he seemed uneasy, and listened anxiously. During several minutes all was quiet ; but at their expiration, the curtain of plants, at the entrance of the grotto, was lifted up, and the fugitives saw a singular and unexpected apparition, at the sight of whom, the monk quickly resumed his whistle, but let it fall on a menacing gesture from the stranger. "A Carribean!" exclaimed Donna Carmen. "He will, perhaps, be more merciful than you." The Indian calmly regarded the affrighted monk. His savage look would have intimidated bolder people.

"Who are you? What do you seek here?" asked the friar.

"I am Oby, the Indian bravo," said he, coldly, in bad Spanish.

"Oby?" repeated the monk, with consternation, which our readers can easily comprehend, if they recollect the conversation he had with Don Ramon. Oby was the sorcerer of the Indians, on whom the friar had imposed the tribute and the sacrament, and whose daughter had been sold as a slave to chastise the rebellion of the father, through the sufferings of the child. Donna Carmen had not forgotten the cruel statement, and far from being alarmed, she depended on him for protection.

She paid a marked attention to the struggle between the two enemies, who hated each other as rival fanatics. Oby regarded the monk with that calm dignity which characterises the Indians, when they are unaffected by fire-water. He enjoyed his savage delight in thus having his enemy completely in his power, and to have spoken would have diminished his pleasure. Finally, he spoke in a guttural accent.

"The servant of the white man's God has wandered from his path ; why has not the crucifix pointed him out his danger? Is his God silent?"

"Sage Oby," said the monk, pretending not to comprehend the irony of the savage, "you will be merciful, and be our guide to the habitations of our people."

Oby shook his head, and replied jeeringly—"I do not know how to preach mercy and forgiveness. I am no servant of the crucified God of the white man. Our Fetiche requires blood. He tells us to kill our enemies."

"But I am not your enemy. If you agree to what I ask, you shall name your own reward."

"Restore to my nation what you have stolen. Do you not remember that you have burned our Fetiches, and made our tribes wretched?"

"Be generous to a defenceless man, and a feeble innocent girl."

Oby looked curiously at Donna Carmen, and continued in a solemn and inflexible tone—

"My child was also innocent. You sold her as a slave. She escaped, and joined her father. We were concealed many days in the marshes, crouching like reptiles. She remained senseless in my arms. The spirit returned; but her words were wild. She would have perished, but for a white angel who discovered our retreat, and saved us."

"In the name of this unknown benefactor, do not be merciless."

"Why have you and yours pursued our tribes to the depths of the forest, and forcibly imposed upon us a strange God? Have not the graves of our fathers been defiled by the white man, and have we not been driven under a different sun than that which shone on the homes of our infancy? What have you given us instead of these?"

"Another and a better God—a God of mercy and of peace," said Eusebio, hurried away by his fanaticism, and forgetting that he thus aroused all the hatred of the Indian sorcerer.

"And what has this God done for us? When we prayed to our Fetiches we had a good fishing, a fortunate hunt, and many scalps; but in the name of your God you impose tribute, you make us slaves, you subject us to torture. Then, when we chance to be the stronger, in His name, again, you invoke us to be merciful. No, no; the Fetiche has sent me here; you shall die. It is justice. The white angel would say so; it is only justice."

At these words the monk felt, nevertheless, a ray of hope. Oby proceeded to the entrance of the cave, and in a short time returned with the mysterious creature whom he called the white angel, and who was no other than the seigneuresse.

Margaret could not restrain an exclamation of surprise on recognising the monk and Donna Carmen, who ran to her and threw herself in her arms.

"Ah! you never abandon us!" cried the young girl.

"No; you shall not die," said Margaret; and, turning to Oby, with a dignified expression, she added—"In return for your daughter's life, grant me the lives of these unfortunates."

The Indian looked at her, confounded, and then, with an intelligent glance, he replied—

"You do not know this Spaniard. He is my enemy. He burned my lodge, sold my daughter into slavery—I have sworn to my Fetiche that he shall die. You understand me?"

" Margaret, you are a Christian," cried the monk, terrified. " Save us from the hands of the idolators."

The seigneuresse shrugged her shoulders, and said, forcibly, to the Carribean—

" Listen. If you refuse, I abandon you to the Fetiches, who are angry with you."

Oby started, but advanced so resolutely to the monk, that the latter turned pale as death. Margaret, without any visible emotion, coldly continued—

" If you refuse, your child will become lethargic, as she was when I found her." Oby became more attentive. " She is about the same age as this young Spaniard. Their destiny is the same. They will undergo the same trials ; and the death of the one will be the signal for that of the other."

These words, pronounced with an inspired accent, appeared to make a forcible impression on the superstitious mind of the Carribean. After a moment's silence, he replied, gravely—

" This young woman is yours, Margaret ; but do you believe that my destiny is united to that of the monk's ?"

The seigneuresse addressed the monk in a low voice—

" Is falsehood, father, sometimes pardonable ?"

" Every word which gives life is blessed."

" I await your answer," said the Indian.

" You have both of you the same destiny," replied she.

" Good !" said the impassable Oby, with a strange smile.

Eusebio was not satisfied, although the Indian appeared to have extinguished all hatred and ideas of vengeance, so blind was his confidence in the prophetic intelligence of the white angel.

" How did you escape from the Port de la Paix ?" asked Margaret, from Donna Carmen. The young creole pointed to Montbars, asleep beside the expiring flame.

" There is our liberator, mother !"

" Noble young man !" said Margaret, regarding him with a melancholy interest ; " but, what means this profound sleep ?" Donna Carmen replied in a low voice. The seigneuresse could not repress a movement of horror, whilst she threw a look of concentrated contempt on the monk.

" We must now," said she, " think of departing. We can descend the river to the sea in Oby's bark-canoe, and we shall doubtless find at the Cape some Spanish vessel to convey us to Rancheria. As for Joaquin I shall leave him in Oby's care until my return."

Donna Carmen kissed her hands, and casting a look of tender interest on our heroic adventurer, she followed the seigneuresse, who left the grotto and entered the canoe which was dancing on the stream at the foot of the rock. The monk followed her, and was about to imitate her example, when he uttered a frightful cry which alarmed the two females. On turning they beheld an awful spectacle. Oby had seized the friar in his nervous grasp. Certain, after Margaret's prophecy, that the monk would perish at the same instant with himself, he had devoted himself to death, so as to accomplish his vengeance.

He wanted to cast himself into the stream with his enemy; but, from his rapid motion, his feet slipped on the moist stone and he remained bound to a point of the rock which caught his dress. He twisted round, like a wounded serpent, making tremendous efforts to roll into the river before his strength was exhausted. He could not free himself, and the more he grasped the monk the more his strength failed. Finally, he allowed him to fall into the river. The Carribean looked after him. The monk swam to the boat and got in.

"Falsehood, falsehood!" cried he, throwing a glance of reproach towards Margaret; at the same time he writhed himself free and fell into the river, whose waters closed over him, just as the bark-canoe broke loose from the bank and rapidly whirled down the stream.

What contributed more to the affright of the fugitives was the loss of one of the paddles, owing to the efforts of the monk to save himself. The canoe thus sped down the stream without direction and with frightful rapidity.

"Wretch, what have you done?" said Margaret, looking to the banks, and perceiving that they proceeded with the speed of an arrow, everything seeming to be in rapid motion on either of the banks, whose picturesque scenes were gilded by the rays of the sun.

The seigneuresse, who knew that the least jutting rock would crush the frail bark, was then silent. With an imperious gesture she commanded her companions to sit motionless whilst with the remaining paddle she directed the boat towards the left bank, where a beautiful prairie extended. Three or four times she was successful, so far as to allow Eusebio to catch the branches and plants, but they were instantly swept onwards. Finally, the two banks widened, forming a bay, the canoe was no longer hurried on with the same rapidity; whilst before them extended the boundless waters. Margaret arose, and pointing to the horizon said, in a hollow voice:

" There is the sea, Eusebio."

" The sea! can it be possible? It is fortunately calm as a mirror, not a single ruffle."

" Not a cloud," added Donna Carmen, " or a breath of wind." The canoe still progressed.

" Now that the current has joined the sea," said the monk, " we shall not be carried far."

" We are only about two leagues from the coast—is it not so Margaret?"

" Four already, child, my feeble sight cannot now perceive it."

" If they do not perceive us," said the monk, " from the isle—it is impossible; but some boat must pass—even a pirate, Margaret."

" Perhaps," answered she, coldly.

" Thus," said Carmen, " we run no other risk than that of remaining several hours under this burning sun, rocked on the wave as if in a cradle."

" May God so will it, poor child, that this canoe may not become a coffin for all of us."

" That is impossible, is it not?" said the young girl, smiling, although troubled.

" Alas, alas! the calm is terrible," replied Margaret; " would that some cloud would arise on the pure sky, or that the smooth surface became ruffled. I should not then fear so much for you."

" Do you mean then to say," interrupted the monk, "in your prophetic language, that you desire some tempest to swallow up this frail bark?"

" With God's will, if it only contained you; but I don't wish Carmen to die. Do you hear me? I do not wish this child dead, whom I have reared with so much care, until your worthy brother, Don Ramon, drove me away from Rancheria. Nor is my hour yet come. I do not wish to die, as I have yet another duty to perform."

The canoe moved slowly, rolling on the swell. The sun blazed continually, and the heat became almost insupportable. There was no shelter for the fugitives. The monk began to comprehend Margaret's apprehension concerning this calm. He looked around, and often with a scrutinising uneasy glance. Not a sail whitened on the horizon. The young girl at this moment closed her eyes before the dazzling rays of the sun.

" Poor Carmen, she dare not utter a complaint; but she would now wish a breath of air to fan her burning brow."

Margaret then took off her mantle, and making the young creole sit on her knees, she covered her over, singing one of those plaintive, monotonous chaunts familiar to the negroes.

Donna Carmen had no longer strength to speak or act.   So

many shocks during the last few days had exhausted her strength.   She sank into a half slumber, dreamy visions boiling in her brain.   Margaret touched her hands; they were hot and burning.

" The fever is racing through her veins.   She cannot resist the fatigues to which, thanks to you, Eusebio, we are yet reserved."

9   K

The monk watched steadily the sheet of water, still calm and unruffled.

Donna Carmen in the meantime in her delirious dream, reviewed all the events of the past, the phantom of Don Ramon being prominent in her visions. She heard his cry of agony again, and felt his icy hand on her shoulder. She screamed out; and opening her eyes, she looked at the monk fixedly, he having turned towards her, and believing her dream realised, she cried—

"It is him—it is him; this vision will pursue me always."

"What do you say, senorita?" said the monk, moving nearer.

The seigneuresse stretched her hand towards him.

"I forbid you to approach." Then addressing Carmen—"Calm yourself, child. You are suffering. You have had some horrible dream."

But Donna Carmen, as if she did not understand her, looked with alarm at the monk; and grasping Margaret, she trembled violently. The monk, on the other hand, had his curiosity violently excited by her vague remark; and although undecided for a moment, he finally moved nearer and nearer.

"Oh! mother, do not let him come near me. See, he demands satisfaction—satisfaction in my blood. Do not give me up to him. Must I always have this bloody shade clinging to my dreams, and now present a reality."

Eusebio grasped the mantle.

"Do you see him, Margaret? Do you see him there before me, gloomy and enraged as he was on that fatal night."

"That night!" repeated the monk.

She could not conclude, but turned away her head with horror.

"Unfortunate girl," said the seigneuresse; "she is delirious. Why will you cruelly deprive her of the repose she needs?"

"Woman, Donna Carmen is a penitent—my penitent. Do not place yourself between her and one who answers for her conscience to God."

"But should a priest be a spy and an executioner?"

"Neither; but a judge."

"Your sight is torture to this girl. Will you kill her?"

"If she dies," cried the monk in a voice of thunder, "would you have her perish, cursed and damned?"

"Are you not afraid still further to unsettle her reason, addressing yourself thus to her fears?"

The monk's countenance suddenly cleared up. He breathed more freely, and his eyes shone brightly. The seigneuresse did not perceive the change. Had she turned round, she would perhaps have observed in the horizon, just where sea and sky seemed united, a white speck. That speck brought hope, life and vengeance back to the friar. He guessed it was a sail; and that was worth the universe to a man condemned to death, to a death slow, unnoticed and agonising. He resumed, with more mildness—

" Abuse the confidence of Donna Carmen during a moment when we ought to resign ourselves to death, and prepare to meet the Judge everlasting ? No, Margaret ; you do not know me. I wish to prepare her soul for death ; it is my duty."

" Yes," said Carmen, " it is time to die."

In her wandering visions she heard the friar mechanically; and falling on her knees, she added—

" This secret was indeed a terrible weight on my mind ; and I ought to humiliate myself in avowing my crime."

The seigneuresse seized her hand—" What do you say, un-happy child ? Your crime, dear innocent ?—to pronounce such a word with angelic sweetness. Not another word, Carmen, and you, Eusebio, do you not see that the fever puts such wild language in her mouth ?"

" Woman, let her speak on."

" I am guilty," murmured Carmen, in a broken voice.

" No—no," exclaimed Margaret, pressing her in her arms and trying to raise her. " Had you have committed a crime whose remorse remained for ever like an open wound in the memory, your countenance would become furrowed like mine —your hair would be white—your thoughts would wander as mine do, when they term me mad. My God !"

" I am guilty," repeated Carmen.

" Guilty ?" said Margaret. " Have you no tears—are your nights sleepless ?—recover yourself, child, and do not play with such words."

" I hear you," said the friar, looking keenly out to sea, where the sail rose rapidly to view.

" Pardon me—pardon me," said Carmen, who, in her burn-ing fever, still thought Don Ramon stood before her. " Yes, I have deceived you all. You believed me innocent; but I will speak the truth—horrify you—perhaps you will not be-lieve me."

" Carmen, recover yourself."

" I, mother, whom you call a child, I have shed blood !"
and she hid her face, shuddering.

" Do not hear her, Eusebio—do not hear her."

" Silence, woman !" said he, fiercely. " Let the horrible truth
be revealed ;" and snatching Carmen from Margaret, he cried—
" What blood have you shed, Donna Carmen de Larates ?"

She looked at him wildly, then subdued by his eye, replied—

" I allowed an innocent person to be accused. I was afraid
—pardon me. I was afraid of disgrace and death."

" The name—the name of him whom you slew ?"

" Silence, Carmen—silence."

" But he whom I believed dead, is here, mother ; his countenance is terribly menacing. He comes now to curse me, and
reveal all ; hide me—hide me !"

" It is the blood of my brother which calls for vengeance,"
cried the friar, darting at the females a deep look of hatred.
" Donna Carmen, on you shall descend the full punishment
due for the death of Don Ramon Carral."

At these words, the young girl started, and recoiled, terrified and motionless ; she then repeated—

" Ramon Carral—Ramon Carral !" and fainted away.

The seigneuresse then raised her, and indignantly said to
the monk—

" And you, Friar Eusebio, are a minister of our Divine
Saviour !" The monk gazed seaward. " But God is just ;
this secret will perish with us ; we, who alone have heard her
avowal, will soon be silent to all eternity."

The monk smiled, and pointed to the waves which were just
beginning to be affected by a gentle breeze.

" We must not all despair in Providence," said he, with
bitter irony. " Human justice knows how to aid us. It comes
even in search of us in the middle of the ocean."

The seigneuresse, alarmed, turned round, and gave a cry of
terror. She saw approaching a large Indian pirogue pro-
pelled by sails and long sweeps, invented by the Spaniards
for their special service on the American coast against the
pirates.

" Oh !" exclaimed Margaret, like a lioness aroused, " will
you dare to abuse the confidence of this child betrayed to you
by her delirium ?" The monk made answer by seizing the
mantle from Carmen, and agitating it in the air. " Answer
me—answer, or in a moment I upset the boat !" At this
menace, the monk grew pale. He knew Margaret well enough

to know, that the deed would quickly follow her threat. "You hesitate," and she put one foot on the edge of bark.

"No. I promise you not to denounce her as the assassin of my brother."

"If you deceive me—" added the seigneuresse, reflecting. The monk proceeded to wave the mantle above his head. The signal was perceived on board, a boat was lowered, and the monk watched its approach. Margaret scrutinised his countenance, but not a sign appeared to betray the inward thoughts. When the boat came alongside, the monk and the seigneuresse climbed the pirogue. The sailors knelt to receive the friar's blessing, and then carefully removed Donna Carmen on board. The breeze increased and the sea gradually became rough. The friar could not contain his joy when he recognised on the quarterdeck the Captain l'Alferez, who had accompanied him to the Leopard's tent by order of Don Christoval, and who, as a reward for his hardihood, had received the command of the pirogue to protect the galleons against the pirates. The monk, who knew the young captain's hatred for the buccaniers, went gravely to him and held out his hand, which the other pressed cordially, glancing curiously at the two females. Donna Carmen looked so innocent in her immobility that all seemed to rest their eyes upon her with lively interest.

"Who are these women, father?"

"The elder is a kind of sorceress, who acts as a spy to the buccaniers."

A cry of horror escaped all who heard this, and the attentions shown on all sides to the seigneuresse instantly ceased, the most pressing recoiling several paces. A smile of singular meaning, unperceived in the tumult, lighted up the captain's visage.

"And the young one, father?"

Margaret regarded the monk keenly, to ascertain if he would keep his promise, or if he was going to decide the fate of Donna Carmen. He answered, indifferently—

"I do not know her; I have been a prisoner amongst the pirates, since the pillage of Rancheria. To assure my flight I had to set off with these two women; that is all."

"Good!" said the captain, coolly giving his orders.

The seigneuresse breathed again, and in a low voice said—

"Thank you, friar, for your generosity; now I can die tranquilly."

The monk pointed to the captain, who advanced.

" I have kept my word, but you have thanked me too soon, Margaret."

" In fact," the captain said, sharply, " so Friar Eusebio is right : you are the buccaniers' spy ?"

" Why should I contradict the word of a man which is sacred?"

" You, then, make no defence ?"

" None."

" You know your fate ?"

" Yes.   The same that would await you at Port de la Paix or Tortuga."

" So, then, you do not fear death ?"

" Death ! I have awaited its approach a long time, sought it often amidst dangers, sought it amidst contagion and death. What, then, do I care for your menaces ? My hour must come."

" Truly.   You have, then, no regret to leave behind ; you have burst all the ties of life ?"

Margaret heard him attentively ; then her mind plunged into an abyss of thought.   She muttered—" I hoped to see him before I died—Oh ! how happy I should have been to have embraced him— to have heard his voice, even had he addressed me as a wandering beggar.   But, I have not merited that.   I shall see him later, but on high only," added she, with an uplifted countenance.

" You see how patient I am," said the captain.

Margaret recovered her ideas, and said, coldly—

" I am ready, captain."

" We are about to treat you as a pirate, taken with arms in your hand."

" I await my fate, captain."

" Since we have no executioner on board you must execute the sentence yourself.   Will these waves form a sufficiently good winding-sheet for a spy ?"

Having given a last kiss to Donna Carmen, Margaret advanced, without the least emotion, to the side of the pirogue. The friar whispered in the captain's ear—

" I do not understand you ; what use will such sterile vengeance be to us ?"

" What would you do, father ? We can get nothing from this singular woman ; still there is something imposing in her conduct and language."

" With a word you could crush her courage ;" and the monk spoke in a low voice, with his habitual smile. The captain nodded his head in sign of approval, and cried, to one of the sailors—

" Bring hither that woman, and get ready four cannon balls."

" Four !" repeated the seigneuresse.

" Worthy mother, I am more humane than you believe. We do not wish to enjoy your struggles as a savage amusement. I will do more : I will give you a companion."

" A companion ?" said she stupified.

" Yes. We will throw both of you into the sea."

" Both ? I do not understand you."

" By our lady you seem to love this pretty fainting lady too much to allow us to separate you. You will make the voyage in company. You should thank me."

At this menace even the sailors were terrified ; as for Margaret, she restrained a cry of agony, but the trembling of her lips showed the captain he had struck home to her heart. She however stammered—

" Oh ! you amuse yourself, my good captain. It is a joke. People do not kill their own. I am your enemy ; it is just to condemn me : it is the fate of war. But this child is a Spaniard ; you owe her assistance and protection. You smile, captain, but when I say she is a Spaniard I tell no lie."

" A Spaniard," said the monk, " whom you love and protect ; you, our enemy, who have so proclaimed yourself. She has denied her country to deserve your affection, and must share your punishment."

" I swear, captain, that she is of your nation, and hates the Brothers of the Coast."

" But the friar says he does not know her, and you have confirmed his statement."

Finding herself taken in a snare, she turned to the monk, and, in a low reprimanding voice, remarked—

" It would be a most infamous vengeance, father ; proclaim the truth."

" The truth ! do you believe that would be the means of saving this young girl. I cannot reclaim her, except as a murderer, nor take her out of the captain's hand, except to give her up to justice."

The sailors brought the cannon balls, and the chains which were to attach them to the feet of the unfortunate women. Margaret regarded them with a bitter expression, and observing their enormous size, she pointed to the small feet of Donna Carmen, and laughed hysterically.

" The captain cannot be serious. Who would load such feet
with these enormous weights? But I am not so credulous.
Sleep on, Carmen. Fear nothing. They will do you no harm."

" Begin with the young woman," ordered the captain.

The seigneuresse sprung up, exclaiming, in a menacing
voice—

" Back! back! you cowards!" Then said in a lower tone—
" Fear nothing, Carmen; I am near to defend you."

" Does the old fortune-teller frighten you?" said the captain,
sharply—

The sailors advanced resolutely. Margaret threw a look of
despair around, but seeing no friendly face, her energy forsook
her. She cast herself down beside Carmen, who then only
recovered and opened her eyes in astonishment.

" You will curse me, child. It is I who am about to be the
cause of your sacrifice. I have dragged you into this misfortune—you, so young, so beautiful, so beloved, to be thus
reserved for a shocking death." The sailors endeavoured to
detach her from the young woman, whom she convulsively embraced. " What!" said she, with a savage accent; " nothing
can, then, move you, captain?"

" Nothing."

" Will my death not be enough? What difference will it
make to the King of Spain, if you permit a young girl to live,
whose only crime is that of being beloved by me?" The
captain struck the deck angrily with his foot. " But I have
reared her, and as her mother was dead, and I had no child of
my own, how could I avoid loving her? It was natural, and
for that she is to die! I am then doomed, it would seem,
to do evil to all whom I love."

" What stuff—come, make haste, there!"

The sailors succeeded in tearing Carmen from Margaret's
arms. Perceiving the inutility of resistance, she said, in an
almost extinct voice :

" I must, then, renounce all hope. We must pray to God
and die! Is there no means of saving her?"

" None."

She let her hands fall down by her side, and staggered as if
struck by some nervous affection, which prostrated the mind
and its faculties. When Don Esteban observed this stupefaction he was moved at the sight, and murmured :

" Does not this poor woman move you to pity, Friar
Eusebio?"

Margaret suddenly aroused herself, her eyes sparkling with hope :

" You have found the means, my good captain. You are generous, one may read it in you. Speak—nothing shall be too great a sacrifice, if I can only save her life ?"

" I am, perhaps, wrong to be so indulgent; but I wish to give this old sorceress a chance of saving her companion."

" You are not deceiving me—no—then tell me what sacrifice can purchase her freedom ?"

" I will name it," said the friar, " it is only, old buccanier spy, for you to return to the Port de la Paix."

" It is a dream—a raillery."

" And announce to the Brothers that you have seen a Spanish vessel doubling the Cape Gracias à Dios. It is the truth."

" My God ! and is that all you exact ? Is it not another snare ?"

" What necessity exists for me to spread a snare for you ?— come, do you consent ?"

She looked keenly at him, as if she still entertained some doubt, and wished to penetrate his thoughts.

" Make haste and answer," said the captain. " You will tell them, that you encountered, in these latitudes, a Spanish vessel, a galleon, freighted with ingots and piastres. Tell them only that, not another word—repeat my words."

The seigneuresse cast a rapid and sagacious glance at the pirogue, and replied :

" Yes, I will tell them, captain, that I have seen a powerful pirogue, carrying two hundred brave sailors, and working seventy sweeps, doubling the Cape Gracias à Dios."

" No, no ; but a galleon bound for Cadiz," interrupted Esteban.

" A galleon ?" continued she, nodding her head with an incredulous look. " A galleon bristling with arms, and loaded with powder and shot ?—a galleon carrying twelve carronades and three long swivels ?"

" No, no—a galleon, I tell you, freighted with ingots and piastres. Do you understand me, cursed sorceress ?"

" However," said she, pointing to the guns, " I am not blind, I only mention what I see."

" But you should see nothing," said the captain. " This is only a galleon. The scurvy has reduced our crew two thirds. We cannot defend ourselves against a handful of pirates ; no danger for them; but, on the other hand, an immense gain; that is what you must say.   Do you understand me now?"

" It is a falsehood—it is treachery; you ask that from me?" cried Margaret, falling on her knees before him.   "Think a moment, good captain, that if the buccaniers have confidence in me, they will be lost—they will fall into an abominable snare."

" That does not concern you, fool.   We want to engage these terrible Brothers, to revenge ourselves of our defeats, or to furnish them with an opportunity of exhibiting their courage. Will you assist us—yes or no?"

" In such an ambuscade, never, never," replied she, rising indignantly.   " It would be a crime which God would never pardon ; and I should be for ever separated from him whom I await on high."

" Attach the shot to the young woman's feet," said the captain, coolly.

A sailor again put his hands on Carmen's shoulder to prevent resistance.   She arose, shuddering at the rude contact, and sighed pitifully.

" Help, help! Adelaide, help!"

The seigneuresse was about to rush towards her, when two iron hands held her firmly where she stood.   She could not resist the appeal, and cried to the captain—

" I will say all you order me, Senor Esteban."

And she trembled in every limb.

" You promise it in the name of the Gospel—of your patron saint—and of all you love?"

She stammered out in a weak voice—" In the name of my patron, of the Gospel, and of those whom I have loved."

" You perceive," said the friar, " that we have confidence in you."

" Oh! God, who reads the bottom of our hearts—pardon me!" exclaimed the wretched seigneuresse.

" Lower away a boat there," ordered the captain.   " You will be put ashore as near as possible to the Port de la Paix, by four comical black fellows, who cannot speak a word of Spanish, and who cannot betray us in case of surprise."

" Come, then, Carmen, come.   You are saved ; do you hear ?   We are to return to the Port de la Paix."

" Never, never," said Carmen, in a low voice; " I have not forgotten Michel le Basque.   We are free ; is it not so ?—then let us return to Rancheria."

"You are a fool, Margaret," said the captain. "This young woman remains with us. Embrace her, and bid her adieu. You know that it will rest with you whether you see her again."

" She stops with you ?" said the seigneuresse, terrified.

" Certainly," replied Don Esteban. " If she is Spanish, as you say, it is much more natural for her to remain amongst her countrymen, than return amongst her enemies."

" But, good captain—"

" But, worthy seigneuresse—If you deceive us, or alter a single word of the message I have entrusted to you—if you hesitate the least, or inspire us with the smallest suspicion, we shall instantly attach the shot to your companion's feet."

" A demon must have conveyed to you the idea," cried Margaret, in despair. " Chance, however, may destroy the best arranged schemes. This snare may be guessed at, and counterplotted, through some hypocrisy in my tone or look. The pirates may not believe me ; and have I not said that I love this young woman as my own child ?"

" She is, therefore, the better hostage, and can answer for your fidelity. Prove your tenderness for her by serving us faithfully. I repeat, by a sign or a word, you may lose or save her."

Margaret stood motionless and as if dead, allowing them to bear her to the boat, where she remained in a state of mental prostration, repeating, as if in a state of delirium—

" Oh ! my God, have I then merited such suffering ; and must the expiation of my fault only end with my last breath ? Oh ! God, your justice is rigorous."

The four negroes rowed lustily away, rapidly increasing the distance between the pirogue and the boat, the latter being followed by the gaze of the ambitious captain, and the vindictive Friar Eusebio.

CHAPTER VI.

THE SNARE.

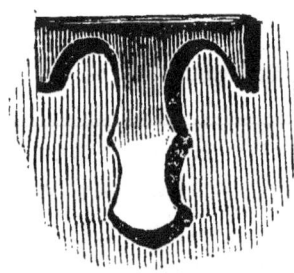HE morning seemed fresh and charming. The sun tinged the summits of the distant hills, with their groups of palms. As the adventurers, assisted by Admiral Blake, had retaken the Isle de la Tortuga, there only remained at the Port de la Paix a small number of pirates and buccaniers. The fires lighted, here and there, to roast their meat, indicated their habitations, which were mostly concealed behind clumps of trees.

When Margaret found herself on the well-known shore, and saw the Spanish boat depart, she could scarce believe the reality. She breathed with avidity the perfumed air—walked at random to assure herself she was free, and asked herself if she had indeed taken the oath, the recollection of which tortured her mind. A thousand mad projects passed through her brain. She would avow all to the Brothers, lead them against the Spaniards, and return triumphantly with her well-beloved Carmen. But that was a project impossible to be realised. On the first suspicion, would not Don Esteban sentence the unfortunate girl to death. Margaret clasped her hands with rage and terror. Time was pressing. She remained, however, watching the fires of the adventurers glowing in the last mists of the morning, and listening to the songs of the hired slaves.

"To think," murmured she, " that, if I obey this Spaniard, all will be silent and deserted there to-morrow; the smoke will not curl joyously over the tree tops, nor will the song echo in the woods. All will be silent as the grave."

She approached slowly, and perceived a troop of adventurers leaving their huts, and drinking their morning glass of Geneva. Their light-hearted joviality saddened her spirit. She started on recognising them, and whether it was a deception of vision through the morning mist, or a wandering of the imagination, it seemed to her as if she was separated from them by a transparent veil, an imaginary barrier she could not pass through. Her feet were nailed to the spot. Her voice sank away, and she pressed her brow with her icy hands, imagining that the jovial buccaniers were about to penetrate her treason. At this moment, Pitrians saw her, and exclaimed—

"Hurrah! here is Margaret! Our mother is come! Ah! there is always room for you at the fire."

"And at the table, too," said Jean David.

The seigneuresse stirred not. She felt as if she could burst into tears, but suppressed the sensation.

"She is gay as night," said Pitrians.

"Where could she come from with such a gloomy countenance?"

Margaret shuddered, and repeated in a husky voice—"Where do I come from—where do I come from? They have already guessed."

"One might think it a phantom." cried Pitrians.

"She is in one of her dark humours," said the Leopard, sharply. "Leave her alone. You know she does not like jokes."

"Come, seigneuresse," continued Pitrians, "join us in a thimbleful of Geneva. It will warm your heart," and advancing towards her, he touched her lips with his goblet. But she looked at him with such a sad and melancholy expression, that he drew back, saying—"So, so. You are angry with us, mother."

"Have you reason, Margaret, to complain of any of us?" said the Leopard.

"I only accuse fate," said she, with bitterness. "I am sad, because I feel a presentiment that shortly many of your Brothers will perish." These words escaped her, unconsciously; but yet from irresistible impulse. The adventurers heard her amidst a profound silence.

"Let us have no gloomy prophecies, Margaret," said the Leopard. "They enervate the spirit. Rather foretell us a good prize. For a long time the galleons have evaded us, and we cannot find another hatto to surprise."

"Two days will not pass, Leopard, without blood being shed."

"Speak more clearly, Margaret."

"I have learned good news during my journey," said she, growing pale.

"Good news!"

With a shout, all the adventurers arose, and surrounded Margaret. Before she continued her narration, she threw a disordered look upon them. She had, all at once, present in her imagination, Joaquin Montbars, that brave young man, so devoted, and so generous, towards whom she felt herself drawn by an inexplicable sympathy. She pictured him pale, bleeding, and dying, and without knowing why, her heart beat, and she threw aside the plaintive image of Donna Carmen, saying to herself—" Never—never, if Joaquin must be delivered up to them with the rest." The young man was not yet returned to the Port de la Paix. They were waiting his return, as well as that of Michel le Basque. Margaret breathed again, and resumed—" Yes, children, last night a galleon doubled the Cape Gracias à Dios, and now it is coasting along timidly, on account of its damage, to regain San Fernando."

" A galleon? You are not deceived," cried Pitrians; " a galleon? *Tonnerre!* Is it, indeed, so?"

" That is to say," replied Margaret, hesitating, " to escape you more easily, believing you all to be engaged at La Tortuga, the Spaniards have freighted one of their pirogues with ingots."

" A pirogue?" repeated Pitrians. " Then we are not sufficiently numerous to attack her."

These words inspired the seigneuresse with a doubt as to the success of her enterprise; and thinking of Carmen, she continued coldly, but with an accent of irony—

" Not sufficiently numerous, Pitrians? This is the first time I ever heard you speak thus. Recover yourself; this terrible vessel is damaged. It has encountered a dreadful storm, and is disabled so much as to require to be brought into port. The scurvy has diminished the strength of the crew by one-third. They have lost their sails, and depend upon their sweeps alone. They have thrown many of their guns overboard to save their silver; and they cannot well defend themselves unless they charge their cannon with ingots. Do you now think yourselves strong enough to take her?"

She concluded, exhausted and tremulous.

" We'll board her," cried the Brothers, with excitement.

" You are cold, good mother," said the Leopard, affectionately pressing her hands in his; " you shall have your share in the prize."

" My share," repeated she in a broken voice, " my share?"

The word struck her like an electric shock. Her share. She had indeed purchased it dearly. Her treason then flashed more vividly on her mind. She thought of the rigorous account God would demand of the lives of all these men whom she so unmercifully condemned, and whom she, notwithstanding, loved. These fierce adventurers had so much confidence in her; they were credulous enough to regard her as their guardian angel—as their mother; and this very confidence was about to consign them to a snare in which they would be lost. She said again, with a savage but forced smile—

" Yes, I shall have my share."

She then remained silent and immoveable.

In the meantime, the Brothers of the Coast separated, to busy themselves with preparations for their expedition. In about an hour later they embarked in four boats, all that remained since du Rossy's departure for the Isle de la Tortuga. Forty men composed the crew of this little fleet, but they were the best men in the association, forming the troop commanded by the Leopard and Pitrians. Three of the boats were sent out to sea as if fishing, with orders to form a circle around the pirogue, and surprise her on all sides, so that she could not escape. The fourth, commanded by Pitrians, was to join them later. The Leopard ordered his companions to lie down flat in the bottom of the boats, for success depended on the rapidity and audacity of boarding.

The pirogue, on the other hand, after having recruited its strength by taking on board fifty soldiers at the Cape Gracias à Dios, sailed during the whole of the night. In about two hours the Leopard, whose boat coasted along, half concealed by the trees which stretched into the sea, discovered the Spanish vessel by aid of his telescope. He examined it attentively, whilst Margaret, standing by his side, watched the expression of his countenance with agony. Finally, he turned to her, and said, with a satisfied air—

" Mother, you are not deceived. The pirogue has parted with her sheets, and crawls along like a slug. Not a soul is on deck; it is a floating hospital. We will make a good market of her. You shall have a golden cross, Margaret."

Her heart felt overcharged. Remorse almost forced a revelation from her lips. She felt proud in thinking there was still time to speak. Like a queen, by a single word, she could prevent the shedding of the blood of so many men, previously condemned, as a horrible ransom for one single life.

But the Leopard, having again examined the pirogue, suddenly exclaimed, with passion—

" If I am not deceived, Margaret, I see something like a woman's dress on board. Have we to do with amazons ? What can these Spaniards be thinking about ? Are they so safe from all danger that their decks must become a promenade for ladies ?"

"A woman's robe ?" said the seigneuresse in a hollow voice, clasping her hands.

"You did not tell me of this reinforcement to the crew." He smiled.

"He smiles," thought Margaret; "unfortunate man. You may well smile," she replied. "I had forgot. Yes, it is, I believe, the captain's daughter—Don Esteban."

"Come, come, what folly. Don Esteban is a young man."

"A young man ? Pardon me, Leopard," said she, comprehending that her troubled mind betrayed her, and that she had committed a gross error. "You know that at times my memory is confused. The captain's daughter; I was truly a fool. It is his sister returning to Spain—to Cadiz."

"That is curious," interrupted the Leopard. "She has for her companion two seamen who watch her like a prisoner."

"Two sailors ?"

"Rather funny cavaliers, mother. Is it not so ? They look more like gaolers."

The seigneuresse shuddered. From that moment, the fate of the adventurers was sealed. She examined Carmen through the glass, and recalled her days of infancy, when she nursed her on her knee, and shared with her all her joys and sorrows. She remained mute and inflexible. The voice of remorse was silent, and she made not the slightest effort to alter the course of events.

The Leopard declared his intention to board the vessel, and requested her to land, so as not to run unnecessary risk.

Margaret silently pressed his hand and went ashore. Once there, she fell on her knees murmuring prayers, interrupted only by wild looks, which she cast upon the sea, and convulsive sobbing.

The Leopard's boat soon advanced towards the pirogue. The latter took no notice of his approach. She seemed dismasted, the Spaniards having lowered their spars on deck. Don Esteban had not even sent up a boy to act as a look-out.

"Lazy rabble," cried the Leopard. "Mordieu! the pirogue is taking her siesta."

"You will see," said Vent-en-Panne, "these Spaniards shortly lowering a ladder and opening the gangway for us."

"This calm is not natural, my lad," said the Leopard; and his countenance became gloomy.

"What are you thinking about, master?" said his servant.

"Did you not remark the sad and embarrassed air of the seigneuresse? What fear could such a combat cause in her?"

"Bah! the old witch loves us so well, it is natural, master. She has shown to most of us the care of a mother. We are good Margaret's family, and it moves her heart to think that

perhaps we may never return. There is not one of us who would not risk his neck to save her."

The old buccanier still looked at the great pirogue with attention.

"To the devil, with all presentiments," cried he, at length. "You are right, Vent-en-Panne. It is old wives' trust, after all. Let us do our duty, more especially as the pirogue has

10 L

the appearance of wakening up, and seems about to say a few words to us."

In fact, several sailors had collected on the deck; the captain gave a few rapid orders, and presently a couple of shots were fired at the boat to intimate that she must sheer off. The balls danced across the waves at a short distance from the boat. The pirates preserved silence, lying in the bottom of the boat. Vent-en-Panne guided the helm; the boat rapidly neared the pirogue, whose progress seemed exceedingly dubious. The other boats belonging to the Brothers neared at the same time. The Leopard, forgetting his inquietude and thinking of the fight, was no sooner alongside of the Spaniard than he uttered a terrible cry.

" Boarders, away !"

His companions started up, repeating the cry, cutlass in hand. The buccaniers soon grappled with the enemy, and opened a terrific fire on the rowers, driving them and the sailors below, several of whom, however, took refuge beneath the cannon.

The Leopard, who would have considered it cowardice not to have been the first to board, seeing the other boats alongside, leaped on deck, followed by his companions, brandishing their cutlasses and pistols. They believed themselves already masters of the ship, and several threw down their arms so as more easily to commence the pillage. What was their astonishment, however, to see a hundred soldiers suddenly start up from behind a slight barrier amidships, and a vast body of seamen rush from below, in the midst of whom was the Captain Esteban, who, ordering several carronades to be manned against the pirates, waved his sword and shouted—

" Surrender, pirates !"

" Never !"

Truly the Leopard did not know fear; he, however, drew back and stood still, overcome by the surprise. Joaquin, at least, is not here, thought he, amidst the terrible scene.

" Down with the Spaniards !" cried he, in a voice of thunder, throwing himself forward against the barricade, his cutlass in one hand and a pistol in the other. The Spaniards fired their muskets and discharged grape along the decks, killing eight of the pirates.

Two of the boats' crews at this moment boarded the pirogue, and still the Spaniards were being reinforced from the main hatch.

" It is not a question," said the Leopard, " how we must conquer, but how we must die." A shot at that moment killed Vent-en-Panne, and he himself was wounded in the arm. He dropped down beside his Brothers, and feigned to be dead. The Spaniards gained the action, although several of the adventurers still fought on the deck, attracting the principal attention of the conquerors.

The Leopard profited by this circumstance, and crawled, little by little, towards the gun-room, without being observed. In a few minutes, creeping from corpse to corpse, he reached it. He then started up with a gloomy smile and looked around for an enemy. Two paces from him, at the cabin entrance, he saw a young girl, pale and trembling and drenched in tears. She was like a beautiful vision in the midst of blood, smoke, and battle. The poor girl uttered a cry of terror on seeing the bloody and threatening aspect of the Leopard, in the very place where she had sought refuge. The Leopard recognised her.

" Donna Carmen here !" murmured he. " I now understand it all. We have been betrayed. Margaret, Margaret ! what have you done to those who called you mother !"

He grasped the young girl's hand, and said—

" It is for you, then, wretched girl, that so many brave men have been sacrificed. But, thanks be to God, treason will not save you."

Donna Carmen lost all recollection, thought, or sight. She listened, without understanding the implacable buccanier. In the meantime, the sailor charged to guard her, and who had gone off to see the issue of the fight, returned on hearing her cry. He came forward boldly, and was much surprised to see a pirate still on his feet. A bullet from the Leopard soon stretched him dead. Donna Carmen's eyes closed, her head fell backwards, and her body shook with convulsive force. The Leopard's knife already touched her breast, when, all at once, a well-known voice uttered a cry of horror, and unnerved the arm of the fierce buccanier.

" Mercy !—have mercy on her !"

The Leopard, with a glance, perceived that Pitrian's boat had boarded, and recognised, with the latter, Joaquin, the son of his brother Bernard. He was startled at the sight, and then shook with wrath.

" Joaquin, too ! Has he fallen likewise into this snare ? Oh ! Margaret, this is the worst blow of all." A sudden idea crossed his mind as the only method of forcing him to return,

He raised in his robust arms the young Spaniard, who had fainted, and shouted to Joaquin—

" Behold!—here is the beauty for whom you became a slave."

" Have mercy on her," cried Joaquin, dismayed.

" Here is the Spaniard, for whose sake the best buccaniers of La Tortuga are entangled in a snare;" and, without any emotion, he threw her into the sea, exclaiming, " Let this be an expiation."

Joaquin threw himself into the sea after her.

" The sea will save both of them ; whilst the planks of this ship will soon be scattered like ashes to the sport of the breeze."

The Leopard rushed from below, and left behind him a slow match burning in the magazine. He instantly appeared on deck, exclaiming—

" Save himself who can, the ship will blow up instantly!"

At the same moment a tremendous explosion ensued, which the imagination may conceive, but which the pen cannot easily describe. The fragments of the ship rose to a prodigious height, amidst the confused noise of shattering timber, rushing waters, clamour, groans, and cries. The most astonishing incident in this frightful scene was the miraculous escape of the Leopard—an incident which might be considered impossible if it was not authenticated by Vexmelin in his history of the adventurers. The valiant buccanier was thrown so far above the deck that that alone, according to his own admission, saved him from being powdered amidst the wreck. He fell into the sea completely stunned, where instinct forced him to contend with the waves. He mechanically seized a piece of the wreck, and looked around him. He saw two Spaniards, one of whom was the Captain Esteban, who had lost both legs, raising themselves three or four times above the waves, dying them with their blood. The Leopard swam ashore. There his first thought was devoted to his nephew. He threw an uneasy look upon the sea, and became shortly convinced that Joaquin and Donna Carmen must have been picked up, as well as Pitrians and his companions, by the crew of a Spanish sloop, which followed astern of the pirogue. He dived into the wood, saying—

" Now for the seigneuresse. We shall have an explanation of this affair. As for my Brothers, they ought to be contented with the funeral I have given them."

The seigneuresse remained in prayer during the horrible combat. Each cannon shot made her start as if she had been hit. Her cold hands pressed the locket, and her prayers became mechanical. When the explosion occurred, she arose and cried, " My God! my God! how am I punished!" Then horrified at the profound silence which followed the terrific shock, she attempted to fly; but after a few paces, she fell exhausted over the root of a tree. There she remained for some time, her eyes lifted to the blue and purple sky, horrified at herself, and listening with agony to the least sound that broke on the sea, or in the forest, as if it menaced her existence. After she had recovered a little, she murmured—" All is over now; but where is Carmen? Can she have sunk with all the others—all the others? Oh! if I had only saved her! It seems as if I should suffer less. I must see her again. I must seek her out, and feel her arm around me once more. Then, perhaps, I should not see the livid spectres of the others passing before me." She uttered a loud cry. The leaves shook, and she saw a scowling look through the trees. She recognised the Leopard, feeble, bleeding, and crawling on his knees. She stretched out her two hands as if to repel him, turned her face away, and sought again to fly, but the buccanier arrested her.

" Margaret!" She had never disobeyed his call. She stopped involuntarily. He said, softly—" Margaret, I am thirsty."

Margaret forgot the past. Her fears departed. He suspected nothing. She would become again the sorceress of the Brothers. She uncorked the gourd she always carried with her. Pity overcame her alarm. She approached with slow steps, and placed the mouth of the gourd to the buccanier's lips. The Leopard drank long and deep. He was reanimated. One of his hands played with the handle of his hunting knife. The blood still flowed from his wounds.

" Margaret! I fear I shall lose my strength, and I wish to live another hour," said he.

The seigneuresse felt frozen to her very heart. Without answering, she tore away the handkerchief which covered her neck, and her scarf, tore them in pieces, and bound up the buccanier's wounds.

" I must live, for I have to revenge myself," continued he, in a calm voice. " Why do you tremble, Margaret? You are a bold and courageous woman."

The seigneuresse breathed, and inquired:

" The fight has, then, been terrible ?"

" Dreadful.   I am the only one left."

" Alone.   Is it possible ?"

" Alone of all the Brothers and all the Spaniards," added the Leopard, with a ferocious smile.

She thought of Carmen.   Her lips trembled, and she joined her hands in a supplicating manner.

" Yes, all the brave fellows whom I loved. Did not you love them, Margaret ?" and he looked keenly at her.

" Dead !   Oh ! my God, whilst I prayed."

" For them—is it not so ? You were right, Margaret. They were hardy, gay, loyal, and fearless men.   You remember the time when my brave Vent-en-Panne found you asleep beneath a palm.   A serpent had twined round the trunk, and its flat head was hissing close to you, when, with a stroke of his steel ramrod, he disabled it.   Had he failed, he must have been the sufferer.   Do not sleep again, Margaret, in such a place ; for Vent-en-Panne can no longer render you such a service.   He fell at my side."

" Dead !" said she, mechanically.

" Do you remember the hunting party, Margaret, when we were lost in a forest on the Spanish territory ? The Spaniards fired the wood to destroy us : what a sea of flame and ashes above and around us, and branches crackling before us. Every one then thought of himself ; you alone lingered behind. When we stopped and counted our numbers, Pitrians perceived your absence. 'It shall never be said,' cried he, 'that the Brothers of the Coast left their mother behind, because they were afraid of scorching their skins.' He returned, and rushed through the flames, bearing you away half dead on his shoulders. Do not lose yourself again in a Spanish forest, Margaret, for Pitrians is dead, like the rest.   Why do you tremble so, seigneuresse ?"

" You are composed, Leopard, in relating such a calamity."

" A judge should never allow himself to be carried away by his passion or indignation, Margaret.   There are crimes so infamous as only to deserve cold contempt.   Our brave companions have perished only because they were taken in a snare : because they were shamefully betrayed."

" Betrayed ! do you believe so ?   My God !" cried she, her limbs shaking.

" Weep for them, Margaret, in tears of blood.   You will see these brave Brothers no more sleeping on a bed of Spanish piastres ; nor taking towns by storm ; nor succouring each other as matelots, sharing honestly their booty. You will never hear more their song of battle—you will never more fill their goblets when they return from the chase. But, why do you tremble so, Margaret ?"

The unfortunate woman was overwhelmed. The Leopard's bitter remarks brought the full horrors of her crime before her. Her teeth chattered ; she dare not answer the old buccanier, before whose look she bent her eyes. All at once, the latter changed his tone, and asked quickly—

" Margaret, have you ever had reason to complain of a Bro-ther of the Coast ? Has any of them outraged you, by accident or design ?" She made no answer. " Avow it freely," continued he. " Sometimes words may cut to the heart sharp as a sword, and bring the blood to the face ; then a deep hatred sleeps and grows in the mind until the moment arrives for some signal vengeance ; subterraneous fires light up volcanoes. Let us see. Have you ever been insulted by a drunken brother ? Answer me, Margaret ; answer me."

" Never," murmured she.

" You know that on the first complaint justice would have been rendered you, with the utmost rigour."

" I know it, master ; but why all these questions ?"

" What does it concern you ? Let me drink, Margaret."

The seigneuresse handed him the gourd, which he emptied. She took it again with a trembling hand.

" Why do you tremble so, Margaret ?"

" Master," answered she, seeking to dissemble her uneasiness, " time marches quickly ; you ought to fly or conceal yourself. The Spaniards may have seen you swimming. They may come here, and you will be lost. You are alone and wounded ; you cannot defend yourself."

" Good, Margaret. It is for me you are afraid," said the Leopard, in a strange accent. " Compose yourself ; I do not care about surviving my brethren ; and if I have dragged myself here, it is because here it concerns me to be."

" Here, in this desert ?" said she, confounded.

" Even in this deserted wood. Tell me, Margaret, what chastisement the treachery to which we have fallen victims ought to merit ? Your counsel is good—speak."

" Treason similar to that. Oh ! it is horrible ! horrible ! But why ask me the question ? It does not concern me. I am an old woman, considered at times mad. I am no judge. Do not ask me."

" You have lived long enough amongst the adventurers to have a firm mind and ready decision. I speak to you, then, as if you were a man. Hear me, Margaret. Do you desire a few minutes to pray to God? In remembrance of our ancient friend- ship, I accord them to you."

" Pray to God?" replied she, turning pale.

" Yes; make haste," said he, harshly.

" Pray to God! What do you mean, Leopard? I do not understand you. Your looks alarm me."

" You have understood me well, Margaret. No cowardice. You know well why I have rejoined you. You know the fate you deserve—the fate of traitors."

" My God! my God! What would you do with me?" exclaimed she, kneeling before him.

" You must die. Blood for blood."

The seigneuresse saw from the buccanier's accent that all was decided. However, she felt such a powerful desire to see Donna Carmen again that she wished to dispute her life with the Leopard, but without hope or confidence, like the wild beast who bites his chain.

" I must die, then ?—die by your hand ? Who could have predicted this ? A few days ago we should have looked upon it as madness ? God, however, guides men's actions. In a short time I shall exist no more. Horrible idea! All that affection which still exists in my withered heart, my remorse, the secret of my life and sufferings—all will be shortly covered over by earth and brushwood. But," added she, sneeringly, " the sun will not cease to shine, the birds to sing, or the hunters to drink and laugh. If any think of me, it will be to curse me. Oh! what a funeral oration. However, you are right, Leopard. The dead yonder beneath the waters—the dead there claim me. One corpse is wanted to make up the number. There is an empty place for me. I shall fill it up."

She looked at the buccanier, and imagined she saw a softer, and almost tender, expression on his countenance.

" Master, you will accord to me a signal favour, if you allow me one day—only one day more—to live. I do not want to escape; you know that well. But I should die tranquilly if I could only once more see—"

" Donna Carmen. Is it not so ?" interrupted the Leopard. "Impossible, Margaret. Your punishment shall be to remain ignorant, even to your last breath, as to whether your treason has saved her or not."

" You cannot be so inexorable. You have always been noble and generous," said she, embracing his knees.

" Does the Spanish spy speak of nobleness and generosity ?" cried the Leopard, with disdain. " Viper's head, you do not then know that I had to crawl over the dead bodies of my comrades to reach the magazine, and that their mouths seemed to mutter vengeance. I thought their glassy eyes turned towards me, as if awaiting that justice which treachery deserves. Do not implore me further."

" You will not kill me thus, without pity ; you would be a coward—do you hear ?—a coward. Is there any courage in becoming the executioner of a defenceless woman ?"

" I am not a child, Margaret. The Leopard has proved his courage. He is, to-day, the only one who can execute judgement on a spy. It is a sad and severe duty ; but a sacred one."

" You will, then, neither feel pity nor remorse in striking me ?"

" Was you influenced by either, Margaret, when you led to such a slaughter-house those whom you have called your children ?"

" Well !" cried she in despair, " I have deceived you, and I am glad of it. I do not repent of my treason. I had to choose between you and Carmen. I did choose. What did I care for the lives of your ferocious companions ? If they have saved me from danger, which I, perhaps, sought, have they not seen me leaning over their beds when raving in a burning or contagious fever, from which their matelots have fled ? They loved me, you say ; yes, as a physician, who could alone cure them—as a fortune-teller, whom they believed could read the future. We were quits. But leave Carmen to die, poor angel, pure as heaven, who became an orphan at her birth—who has grown up in my arms—her cradle. It was impossible : to slay her whom I had reared—impossible, I tell you. I loved her so much that at times I forgot that I had a son whom they had torn from me when an infant, and whom I should see no more. Ah ! you cannot understand these things, valiant adventurer ; you have never known the strength of those ties of the heart—such a voice has never spoken in your bowels."

" Wretched woman, you restore all my courage. Amongst those whom you have betrayed, I do not only lose brothers in arms—companions—"

" Have you heard what I said, master ? I do not repent of my treason—do your duty."

" Amongst them," continued the buccanier, without hearing her, " I count a child, whom I love, as you do Donna Carmen." All Margaret's resolution left her—a cloud gathered o'er her eyes.

" Conclude—conclude," cried she.

" Amongst them is my nephew, Joaquin Requiem, the pearl-fisher; Joaquin Montbars, the brave adventurer."

" Your nephew? You lie—you lie, Leopard. It was not so—I should have seen him—I should have known him. It is false." Her eyes shone with an extraordinary light. " I counted them all—I should not have permitted him to go with you."

" He returned to the Port de la Paix in time to join Pitrians' party in the fourth boat."

" In time—in time to be sacrificed to die!" sobbed the miserable woman.

" Like the others," added the Leopard. " Do you think I have any right now to condemn you, Margaret?"

The seigneuresse remained several minutes petrified. She then nodded her head with an air of incredulity, and burst into a wild laugh similar to that of a mad person.

" Yes, you are just, master," said she to the Leopard, " avenge yourself. It is your right. What! he also—he, too, the brave young man, who saved Carmen? He said to me the other day, laughing—' If I ever go to Europe, Margaret, you shall accompany me;' for he called me, like you, Margaret. He did not know my true name—he did not know that the seigneuresse had been once fair and happy, rich and honoured. Oh! it is a long period since that."

She pressed her forehead as if to recall her confused ideas.

" Do not spend in dreams of vanity the few minutes I have allowed you to pray to your God," said the Leopard.

" No, no," replied she, regarding the Leopard with indescribable dignity. " Margaret will not die at this time. I ought to avow my name, and reveal the secret of my life. I am about to charge you with a holy mission, and if you accept of it you may be blessed, brave adventurer. The part of the seigneuresse is done. The woman, Leopard, whom you have condemned, is no longer a wretched vagabond, without name or history. Her name is Adelaide de Rochefort."

" Adelaide de Rochefort!" interrupted the Leopard, stupified.

" Marchioness de Cossé," murmured she, in a smothered voice.

"False, false!" cried the Leopard, staggering. "Silence, silence, witch! What name have you dared to pronounce?"

"Is this name, then, branded and dishonoured in distant countries? It matters not. I ought to carry it with all its opprobrium. I repeat, I am the Marchioness de Cossé."

"Silence, silence!" cried the buccanier with violence; whilst an expression of horror deranged the visage of this impassible man.

"Why be silent? Before God, who now hears us, I speak the truth."

"The truth? On your knees; on your knees, miserable woman, and confess that you have lied." And with a powerful hand he seized her, and compelled her to kneel.

She repeated—"I am Adelaide de Cossé."

"You are the woman, then, who betrayed her young, brave and confiding husband; that husband who loved her, to become the mistress of a cowardly and conceited prince."

"Yes, I avow it; because I am about to die."

"You are an adulteress, not from love but ambition. In your blood Bernard de Cossé thought he had avenged his honour. Vile and accursed soul, what could have attached you to life without being crushed by your past infamy?"

"If I have lived, it was in the hope of expiating my fault, by force of sufferings and tears, to obtain from Bernard, not pardon, for that I was unworthy of, but some words of pity, even a look, to show that he was enraged no longer against me—and—and, must I say it? I hoped to see my child once more, whom he had carried away with him. I said, God was too merciful to separate us for ever. And how can you expect a mother to die, when one day she may expect to embrace her son?"

"Her son!" cried the Leopard, in a terrible voice. "Do you know what you have done, wretched woman?"

The seigneuresse heard him with inexplicable oppression at the heart, muttering these words:

"My God! my God! spare me—"

"No—God himself, in his just indignation, has condemned you. He has made you blind and lost you. I, also, the rough hunter who speaks to you, have been formerly a gentleman. But I have broken my sword, burned my blemished escutcheon. No one knew, until this day, what noble blood flowed in the veins of the Leopard. The Brothers of the Coast exact no other titles to nobility, save courage and fidelity. But, secret for secret; you, who are about to die, shall know who I am."

" Conclude, conclude," cried the seigneuresse, looking at him with agony.

" I am Petris de Cossé."

" The brother of Bernard," cried she, dropping her head on her breast, " Bernard, whom I have in vain sought to rejoin, and of whom all trace is lost for me in this world. They told me truly, that he had embarked for Hispaniola. But," said she, with almost a happy smile, " you, who are his brother, and who loved him, you can tell me his place of refuge. You will tell me ? You will show me my son ? He must be tall and beautiful now. You do not answer me ? Oh! I understand, Bernard still hates me. But, if it must be, they shall not see me. I will conceal myself near their dwelling, and when my son goes out in the morning I shall see him. I will not disclose myself, I will suppress my emotion, my tears and the beating of my heart. But, I shall see him, Petris, I shall be happy—oh! I must not die now. No, no," continued she, in a wild, hoarse, furious accent, " I shall not die."

" Fool! have you, then, lost your recollection ?"

" Pardon me, but what have I, then, forgotten ?" said she, in a timid, uneasy manner, like an infant detected in a fault.

" You forget that you have delivered up to the Spaniards Joaquin Montbars, and that Joaquin is my nephew."

At these words the seigneuresse felt as if a red-hot iron was shot into her brain. She stretched out her arms wildly, as if grasping something in the air :

" I shall go mad! Silence—oh! silence !"

" Joaquin is the son of Bernard de Cossé."

" Do not revenge yourself thus, Leopard. It cannot be true—say so," cried the wretched mother, dragging herself to his feet. She continued, " Say, it is not true, noble Petris. Heaven could not permit such a horrible thing—I have not sacrificed my child. Have pity on me. You know that I have expiated my crime by a life of humiliation, penitence and re‧morse. I have expiated the luxury and pleasure of a single year by a life of misery enough to frighten a Sister of Charity. Oh! why could I not have divined it was my son ?—He would have pardoned me—he was noble and good. No, I have not sacrificed him—Joaquin lives still—you deceive me. Answer me, Leopard, answer me—ah! it is cowardly to torment a female thus."

" Unfortunate !" said the Leopard, moved by her dreadful grief; " Joaquin, perhaps, lives still." The seigneuresse kissed his hand. " But, thanks to you, he is a prisoner to the Spaniards; and they will not spare him. They have still to revenge the blowing up of the pirogue."

" Thanks, generous Petris, thanks," said the poor mother, in a voice broken by her sobs. " Now, I need live no more, my destiny is accomplished—avenge your Brothers, whom I have betrayed, or I shall not tarry long before I avenge my son."

The Leopard heard her with a sentiment of pity. He murmured to himself, and seemed to reflect:

" Who knows—I may yet save him ; but Montbars and the spy must never meet—the son would despise his mother—and the mother must not be cursed by her child."

The seigneuresse only heard and comprehended these words, " Perhaps, I can save him !"

" What !" cried she, " you still hope ?"

" I hope for nothing ; but, all that the courage of one man can do shall be done, by me, to deliver Bernard's son. There is not a minute to lose, for I must return to the Port de la Paix, and from thence I shall reach San Fernando, where the Spaniards have, no doubt, transported their prisoners."

" Good, good, valiant Leopard, make haste. What! you remain motionless when there is not a minute to lose ?—when my son—courage, think of the blood of all your comrades which cries for vengeance. Do not lose such precious time out of pity for me—oh ! I do not now fear to die."

The old buccanier no longer felt strength enough to accomplish his act of justice, or to pardon the seigneuresse. He moved not. But, the seigneuresse became more inflexible against herself than the most severe judge. She gently took the Leopard's knife, and said, in a firm voice :

" Master, grant me a kiss of pity, if not of pardon, which you will bestow on my son, so well beloved, that he may not curse my memory."

The seigneuresse and the buccanier embraced silently. She then stretched her trembling hand towards the Port de la Paix.

" Hasten, hasten, Petris de Cossé," added she, with a smile. " I shall give you the signal at departure." And the courageous woman struck herself to the heart with the buccanier's knife, fell at his feet, and with her last breath uttered the name of Joaquin.

" Poor mother ! God will, doubtless, pardon her. As for me, I shall faithfully fulfil your last wish, and your soul can then be glad if Joaquin is saved."

After having concealed the body under a heap of sand, leaves, and rubbish, he walked quickly away; his mind being entirely absorbed in the rash and desperate enterprise which he had conceived.

CHAPTER VII.

THE PEST.

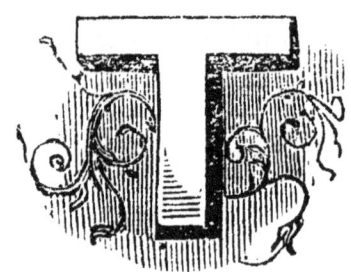 HE Leopard had taken a bold and resolute decision. He had not time to summon the Brothers, and put himself at their head, so as to save his nephew by force of arms, for the vengeance of the Spaniards was always as expeditious as it was cruel. He returned to the Port de la Paix, announced to seven or eight of the Brothers the fate of their companions, and gave them some secret instructions to Du Rossey and L'Olonnais. He then set out alone, without any other arms than his bayonet fixed in its sheath of crocodile skin, and directed his steps to the town of San Fernando.

He determined to penetrate to the heart of the town, whether he even went there as a prisoner to restore Joaquin at the risk of his life, or at least to die with him. He was greatly surprised when he encountered no lancers in the neighbourhood, and perceived no sentinels on the walls. The silence that seemed to reign around San Fernando was as ominous as a desert. However, when he reached the gate La Giralda, he saw a soldier in rags half asleep under a wooden shed, who started up at his approach, and presented his musket, crying in a terrified voice—

"The sorcerer!—the poisoner!"

The buccanier proceeded straight to him; the soldier fired; but his trembling hand made him miss his mark. The Leopard snatched the musket from him.

"Did fear so mask your eyesight, that you could not recognise the accoutrements of a buccanier?"

The soldier looked at him with a wandering and ferocious eye, continuing to cry—

" The sorcerer !—the poisoner !"

In a moment, the street La Giralda, whose houses were buried in a death-like silence, was thrown into commotion. The windows opened, armed men appeared on the balconies ; muskets glittered in every direction, and the cry of—" The poisoner !" ran along its whole length, repeated from window to window, like a death-knell.

Women and young girls, their hair floating wildly over their shoulders, and their dress deranged, as if just aroused from their siesta, pointed out the Leopard to the fury of the men with excited gestures. They repeated the terrible cry in that implacable accent of ferocity, which terror and despair can alone arouse.

The buccanier, understanding the imminence of his danger, the cause of which escaped him, decided to fight to the last, and sell his life as dear as he could ; he therefore dragged on the miserable sentinel, and used him as a living buckler for his body.

Nevertheless, the exasperation of the people seemed reaching its height, and although none attempted to pass their thresholds, the most furious were about to fire on both the men, when a gong sounded in the street, running transverse to the one where the Leopard was, who, looking back at the cause, became witness of a most melancholy spectacle.

A carriage advanced slowly, one of those conveyances, groaning and creaking every time the wheels rolled round, as the immortal Cervantes describes that of the wandering players. But, horrible reality ! this one creaked under the load of livid and hideous corpses, which hustled each other under their torn and shaking winding sheets. In front of this conveyance were seated three men, entirely clothed in yellow, laughing, and drinking from a leathern bottle, marked with blood. From time to time they struck the gong, or thrashed with a stick the two exhausted mules. On their appearance, the most of the people retired within their houses, showing signs of alarm and disgust. Several women remained immoveable, gazing intently upon the fatal cart, as if to discover there the presence of beloved victims. Amongst them were mothers and lovers, who devoured their tears, and pressed their hands on their hearts, as if to keep them from bursting.

When the chariot advanced along the street La Giralda, they forgot their terror in their anxiety to cause the conductors to stop. They, however, took no notice of the wild gestures, remaining deaf to their desperate appeals, until the unhappy women pulled their rings from their fingers, and ornaments from their necks and hair, and cast them in the street. Then the cart stopped, and the yellow alguazils, having picked up their harvest, uncovered the bodies.

It was dreadful to behold the violet-coloured swollen faces of the dead. But none of the women were seized with horror. Those who recognised well-known and beloved features amidst the heap, looked fixedly at them with a dry eye, as if they wished to impress the recollection more firmly on their minds. Others threw out their arms, and seemed to say—" We shall soon rejoin you." Finally, all those who saw only unknown faces, fell upon their knees, and prayed.

The Leopard understood their grief, for he shuddered at the idea which suddenly entered his mind.

" Perhaps Joaquin is there, asleep, amongst the others."

He determined to know, and threw down the sentinel. The chariot was already progressing; the yellow alguazils had covered the bodies, and several inhabitants had again appeared on the balconies, musket in hand, determined this time their vengeance should be gratified. But, to their infinite surprise, at the very moment that several of the most determined were about to fire on the supposed poisoner, our brave adventurer leaped forward, and instantly he was upon the terrible chariot.

" Done like a reckless buccanier," cried one of the yellow alguazils.

" Worthy to join our brotherhood," said the second.

" Sorcerer, pirate, or poisoner," said the third, " you are welcome ; our trade is the best at present," and he laughed, and showed rings and rosaries which had been thrown to him. The Leopard did not answer ; he examined the bodies.

" We are kings of the town," said the first, again ; " for we alone raise our taxes, and we alone are feared."

" Here," said the second, throwing a sheet over the buccanier's shoulders, " here is your royal mantle."

" And this your sceptre," said the third, handing him the leathern bottle.

Joaquin was not amongst the dead. The buccanier grew calm ; he turned to his companions, and said coldly—

" You love piastres, masters ? Well, I am the Leopard ; conduct me to the Governor Don Christoval de Figuera. I have nothing in common with such as you. Obey !"

The insolence and effrontery of these men sunk before the

coolness of the celebrated buccanier. One of them proceeded to the governor's palace, to announce the important capture. But Don Christoval was so much occupied with the calamity which had desolated the town during several days, that he merely ordered the Leopard to be confined with the rest, who had unfortunately survived the explosion of the pirogue.

CHARLES . PETERS . Sc.

San Fernando was, at this time, in dreadful confusion on account of a pest which had invaded it suddenly, and without apparent cause; and in which scarcely any one could believe. The people preferred to attribute the terrible evil to human and criminal causes; in which case hope could afford some relief to their agony. The subtile poison necessarily implied a

11   M

poisoner, and the credulous multitude ferociously shouted—
" Death to the wretch !—death to the poisoner !" The medical
men avowed their ignorance of the cause or cure of the pest ;
they were discouraged on beholding men, apparently in good
health, all at once complain of a dreadful heat in the head,
then the eyes become red and inflamed, the respiration irregular,
and the skin yellow, or livid ; and death ensued generally
after a night of agony and burning fever. The black-vomit
which had ravaged the Indian tribes, had not yet visited the
isles. One doctor, alone, conceived he saw a similarity in this
epidemic, and attributed it to the miasma produced by the last
earthquake ; but his opinion was not listened to, and it wanted
very little to make the multitude treat him as the real poisoner.
Victims are always wanted where delirious suspicion reigns
amongst the mass ; it is the only remedy in which their fears
have any faith. The pest had so effectually discouraged all,
that the capture of eight pirates, amongst whom was Joaquin
and Pitrians, produced no sensation, or sign of triumph in
the town. The governor caused them to be numbered, and
ordered two to be executed each day, so as to prolong the joy
of the Spaniards, always greedy of such spectacles. When
the Leopard entered the narrow and naked cell, where the
prisoners were crowded together, he only perceived calm and
even joyous countenances ; all the adventurers were familiar
with the face of death ; besides, there are few spirits that
do not rise before a solemn and public danger : they might
tremble and grow pale if sent alone to the gibbet, but when
companions in the same cause march together, each has courage
for all and through all.

On seeing the Leopard, the Brothers uttered a dolorous cry.
Joaquin ran to him and pressed his hands with tenderness :

" Uncle, we hoped that you were more fortunate than us—
had escaped ; and, now, you are here a prisoner—condemned,
like us, to death."

" Oh ! I succeeded in escaping alone, Brothers, because I had
a duty to perform. My vengeance accomplished, and not being
able to deliver you by force of arms, I said to myself that
I might be as useful to you in prison as on the field of battle,
and here I am."

" Alas !" said Joaquin, " your generosity will only serve to
sacrifice you."

" I promised your father, that in the hour of danger, I
would never abandon you, lad. Besides, I am charged with

another mission, a sacred one, for you." He hesitated, scarcely knowing how to confide what he wanted to Joaquin.

" Who, then, interests themselves in me, a poor adventurer?" asked Joaquin, with a melancholy smile.

" And who should it be, if it was not an unhappy woman, who has, doubtless, been very culpable, but who has been as cruelly punished for her faults as her mortal enemy could desire? A woman who has only survived years of humiliation and suffering because of your memory, and of the hope she had of seeing you once more."

" I do not understand you," said Joaquin, with agitation; " a mother could only love thus, and mine is dead, as you know, long ago, and died a horrible death."

" Your mother lived, Joaquin; your father fled so hastily after his furious transport of vengeance, that although he thought her dead, she still lived."

" My mother lived?—and now I am only told of it!" said Joaquin, in a hollow voice. " I had a mother, like others whom I have envied, and yet I never saw her!"

" No feebleness, lad; we are not alone here."

" Oh! my God!—my mother lived; my mother indeed lived, her who smiled over my infancy, and now she is dead."

" Dead; and, in dying, she begged that her son would not curse her, as she had loved him well."

" Curse her!—me?" cried Joaquin: " but, why did she not seek me out? Can a mother be guilty with a son? Oh! how happy I should have been to have said only that single word—mother!"

" God did not will it, Joaquin. She, too, would have been happy only to have seen you alive; but in dying she had, at least, the consolation of having seen her son although without knowing it at the time."

" How is that, uncle?"

" Never curse the seigneuresse!"

Joaquin was stupified. He pressed his burning forehead and wept. He comprehended all. He dare not ask any more.

CHAPTER VIII.

THE VISIT.

EANTIME, the Spaniards visited the prisoners, and were surprised to see them playing at dice without sorrowing for their position, or caring for the fact that each bore in his bonnet the number, according to the order of their death. Joaquin was number six. The Leopard came last, and stood ninth on the roll. The next day the young man felt himself much troubled on observing amongst the prisoners a visitor. It was a veiled lady, attended by a monk, whose visage was almost entirely concealed under his capuchon. His heart gave a bound, as he remarked to the Leopard, in a smothered voice—" Do you not recognise Donna Carmen and Friar Eusebio, uncle ?"

" Ah ! I see you are not yet entirely cured : poor fellow ;" and the buccanier good-naturedly nodded his head.

" Are you now satisfied ?" said the monk to the young woman, who was weeping under the veil. " No human power can save your accomplice. As for you, senorita, you promised me that if I allowed you to see this wretch once more, you, on entering a convent which would become your tomb, would convey all your property to the order to which I belong. I have kept my word. Will you abide by yours ?"

" Yes," replied she, in sa tifled voice. " But since nothing in this world can now save Joaquin, allow me to speak to him and bid him a final adieu, so that he may not suppose that I have sacrificed him, or forgotten him in a cowardly manner."

" No !" said the friar, coldly; " for I have sworn by my brother's name that the pearl-fisher should never see your face, except at the last moment of his life, so that he might be the more afraid to die."

" Let me speak to the Leopard," insisted Donna Carmen.

" To the Leopard, who considers you the cause of his nephew's ruin, I consent."

An imperceptible flash of joy passed from the young girl's eyes whilst a gaoler opened the iron gate which separated the prisoners' cell from the curious.

The buccanier hesitated to obey Donna Carmen, but he could not resist the pressing request of Joaquin. The moment she saw the Leopard approach she withdrew from the friar and went straight to the adventurer, saying, in a low tone, " You are all about to die, and you know it."

" Yes; and we shall die bravely, as our Brothers did upon whom your executioners commenced."

" Bravely !" repeated Carmen, bitterly. " No—no; but as cowards, whose limbs shake as they go to the scaffold."

The buccanier looked at her severely.

" You are a Spanish woman, senorita; but I believed you had a nobler heart. There is little generosity in thus casting insult in the faces of those who are condemned."

" I tell you, master, the Spaniards are too knowing to permit you to march with a lofty look and a high head to death. That would be a mean revenge. I tell you they wish to see you trembling and cowardly at the last moment."

The buccanier shuddered, and replied—

" Explain yourself, senorita ; explain yourself."

" Now do you suppose that they will permit you to ascend the scaffold like heroes on a pedestal ? No, no, no. They know how, by ennervating drinks, to put a pale mask on the brow of the bravest, feebleness and agony in the hearts of the most reckless, and how to elicit the cry of fear from their lips."

" Infamous !" interrupted the buccanier.

" Silence ! Silence ! Yes, your nephew himself, even you, the Leopard, will allow yourself to be dragged to the scaffold in place of marching there boldly." Then, seizing the rough hand of the buccanier, she slipped into it a small silver flask, which he mechanically grasped. " This is laudanum, master. Thanks to this flask, you can die without shame or feebleness before the fatal hour."

" Thanks, Donna Carmen. I now pardon you all the evils of which you have been the innocent cause."

" But wait before you apply the fatal poison; let all hope first be extinct. A rumour is afloat that an expedition of pirates is directed upon San Fernando, with the view of delivering you; and if they arrive in time—"

" Who is the chief ?" asked the buccanier, whilst a joyous expression animated his countenance.

" L'Olonnais."

" In that case, those who are to suffer to-morrow will be

saved, and those whom chance has left to-day may assist at the execution of their judges."

" Yes; but amongst those condemned to-day, Joaquin may be amongst the number."

" Perhaps," replied the buccanier, with a strange smile.

" Have you, then, any hope ?" asked Carmen, whose heart beat violently.

" Come, senorita," interrupted the imperious voice of the monk ; and he advanced towards her.

Poor Carmen allowed herself to be dragged away, pale and sinking, whilst the friar cried out—

" After to-morrow, the prison will be empty."

CHAPTER IX.

THE SELF-SACRIFICE.

JOAQUIN, in the meantime, was in despair that he could not speak to the young Spaniard. All his thoughts were concentrated on her. At times, he felt his heart oppressed in thinking that death was about to separate them for ever. His uncle's exhortations were disagreeable; at times, he answered even in an irritated tone.

"The son of Bernard de Cossé," said the Leopard, "ought to meet death calmly."

"If I had only spoken to her once more, death would have been sweeter. Her image pursues me incessantly. I wish to be always with her in thought, and to dream of nothing else. This generous young woman is the sole loadstone that attracts me to life. Air is not more necessary to my lungs, than her image to my memory."

"More serious thoughts ought to occupy the mind of one who is condemned."

"More serious thoughts?" repeated he with a bitter smile. "Uncle, this prison only contains the most miserable portion of me. All that is full of life, uncle, wanders around that pale figure, so lively and interesting in suffering. To think that shall see her no more, and that my heart will beat no more with love to her!—my brain burns. I even think that the idea inspires me with a fear of death."

"Unfortunate, dare you thus speak before me?"

"Do not fear, uncle. Donna Carmen will not make me a coward; she for whom I would traverse a town in flames. But I believe at times that I shall not die. The sinister words of the monk sound in my ears like a fortunate prediction."

"Compose yourself, lad. Sleep, and calm this agitation which upsets you."

"Yes, I am agitated; for I await in hope—of what I know not—life, liberty, Carmen—all, perhaps. Oh! I shall go mad!" And he laughed in a strange fashion.

"It is excessively hot here," said the Leopard; remarking with uneasiness the perspiration which covered Joaquin's brow.

"Oh!" replied the young man, going to the wicket to catch a breath of fresh air. "There is something infernal in a prison, when doubts and hopes assail the mind. My God my God! can it be possible that I shall never see Donna Carmen! My blood boils in my veins, uncle. I am thirsty.' And the countenance of the buccanier brightened.

"I have still a little brandy, Joaquin. You can empty my gourd. It will keep up the heart."

He seized the gourd when speaking, and poured into it several drops of laudanum from the silver flask. Joaquin was too much absorbed to see anything. The Leopard's hand trembled as he handed the gourd to Joaquin. Joaquin put it to his lips and the buccanier shuddered. Perhaps, he had not correctly calculated the dose to which he resorted so desperately Joaquin had, however, already drank life or death—God only knew which. He speedily was asleep, and lay down in a corner, pale but calm. The Leopard kissed his forehead with parental joy. Several tears shone on his weather-beaten face as he watched with anxiety the breathing of the sleeper. He did not know whether he had killed or saved him, but a secret voice whispered—

"You have done well."

An hour had scarcely sped before the brutal command of the alguazils was heard at the wicket of the prison—

"Come along, pirates ; up, and be marching."

The Leopard looked at Joaquin with alarm.

"Numbers six and eight."

Joaquin moved. A cold perspiration damped the Leopard's brow. Number eight left the cell.

"Number six !" cried the alguazil, impatiently. "Must we come and seek you, my brave man ?"

Joaquin murmured the name of Donna Carmen. His countenance bore a smile. He dreamed, and slept on.

"Still her. He loves no one else," said the Leopard. "But the Spaniards want their number. They shall have it.'

He took Joaquin's bonnet, left his own in its place, which had the figure nine inscribed, squeezed the hands of Pitrians and Jean David, who remained admiring his self-sacrifice and noble generosity. He then joined the alguazils, saying—

"My brother Bernard will have nothing of which to accuse me when I rejoin him on high. I have given up life for the sake of his son, as I would have done for himself."

Before he proceeded to the place of execution, he emptied,

along with his companion, the flask he received from Donna Carmen, for he did not wish to afford them the satisfaction of seeing the Leopard die with a pale face and a shivering frame. Hence the vengeance of the Spaniards could only be exercised on two corpses, and instead of attaching them to the gibbet, they were obliged to throw them along with their own dead on the sinister chariots which we have described. The pest increased and its fury redoubled, although several supposed poisoners were torn in pieces. Terror might be read in every look. Every mouth was full of denunciations. The medical men proposed to establish a lazaretto, or pest-house, but the Bishop of San Fernando ordered a nine days prayer and a procession, which latter mode of safety was preferred by the inhabitants. Not a joyous cry was heard in the streets during many days; no perambulating traders; no young mounted cavaliers; no mendicants begging for charity at the corners; no workmen proceeding to their labour, chaunting a national song; and no young girls laughing at the threshhold of their homes.

San Fernando was converted into an immense hospital. The dead silence was only broken at intervals by the funeral knell from the churches, the groans of the afflicted, the curses of the yellow alguazils, and the creaking of their chariots. On the balconies and at the windows bloody garments and winding-sheets were hung out to dry. All that the doctors could succeed in doing was to have the doors of those houses nailed up whose inhabitants were either dead or afflicted with the pest. A cross, marked with chalk, indicated to the alguazils where the bodies were to be found. The sudden death of the Leopard and his companion turned the suspicions of the crowd upon the adventurers. According to some, all the adventurers were infected with an epidemic, which God had sent to them in punishment of their crimes.

According to the opinion of the majority, the Brothers of the Coast had secretly introduced themselves into the town, and had rubbed over the walls of houses, churches, and monuments some venomous matter, so that the whole town exhaled it, and the people breathed it in with the air. Terror always borders on the extravagant. The governor, Don Christoval, seizing on this delirious supposition, wished to give greater importance to the execution of the three last buccaniers. To make it a spectacle which would content and soften the savage disposition of the multitude.

CHAPTER X.

THE RESCUE.

EXT evening, when the hour approached for execution, the town assumed the aspect of a *fête*. All the balconies were illuminated. The terraces were covered with orange and citron plants. The walls were covered with green branches, splendid tapestry and stuffs figured with gold. The most precious furniture was piled on the balconies; and, to witness the eager looks of the crowd leaning at the windows in their rich costumes of silk, satin, and velvet, diamonds glittering on the heads and dresses of the females, who would not have believed the crowd to be joyous and happy? Who would have thought that fear lurked at the bottom of their thoughts? —only those, perhaps, who remarked the houses shut up here and there, offering a dark and gloomy contrast to the surrounding illumination. At the windows of these houses the sick watched with a saddened air the turbulent crowd rushing past, and then, fixing their fading eyes on the golden crosses of the churches, which sparkled in the blue sky, they prayed deeply.

In the street marched, two and two, the religious fraternity with their banners and varied costumes. The nuns were there, too, their eyes shining through their silk masks, and the clergy singing mournful hymns, their sonorous voices mingling with the church bells. All combined to form a spectacle terrible and grand. In the middle of the procession advanced a chariot, groaning as it rolled, on which was placed the condemned. Joaquin was between Pitrians and Jean David. When Joaquin awoke and searched in vain for his uncle, and when he understood the sublime sacrifice of the heroic buccanier, he was lost in surprise, and affected with profound grief.

" He thought I was afraid to die, and has taken my place. Ah! I ought to have foreseen it; but I shall soon have my turn," added he, with an expression of melancholy satisfaction. He smiled with disdain at the Spaniards, whose suspicions rendered them more pale and frightened than the certainty of death produced amongst the buccaniers.

Joaquin sought again and again to discover a look of commiseration beneath the masks of the females who surrounded him. He sought to surprise, amidst the crowd of penitents, some fugitive emotion, some involuntary gesture, one of those signs invisible to others, but which goes straight to the heart of the being beloved. But, alas! all was menacing and disdainful. Amongst the voices, solemn and plaintive, which rose in chorus to the heavens, he could not distinguish the tone of his beloved. In a short time his attention was forcibly directed in another channel by the storm of yells and hooting which proceeded from the crowd in the streets. At this point there was an ascent in the street, and the chariot moved more slowly along. The common women, the beggars, and ragged urchins perceiving Joaquin glancing his eyes from balcony to balcony, conceived that he was dazzled with the sight of the immense wealth the Spaniards had dragged forth to adorn the bloody ceremony, and opened upon him a fire of biting and vulgar sarcasm.

"Oh! oh! pirates," cried a young girl, "if you have an itching palm there is plenty of booty for you. Do not stand on ceremony."

"Damnable heretics!" shouted a scolding shrew. "You see that, in spite of your robberies, there is enough left behind to buy rope enough to hang the whole of your thieving band."

"Ah! friends," cried a water-carrier, "you will find on the place San Isidora some old acquaintances."

"With her Royal Highness the Lady of the Gallows-tree," shouted another, amidst laughter and applause.

"Look how wan and pale these brigands are."

"They are afraid. Why don't you weep, my hearties? But God forgive me if the old one is not drunk. His head rolls as if it did not belong to his shoulders."

In truth the condemned were horribly shaken by the jolting of the carriage, indeed, so violently and incessantly as to make them lose their breath. The unfortunate trio could with difficulty maintain their original firmness. Old Pitrians experienced such a dreadful headache that he could not avoid exclaiming, in a subdued voice—"Infernal torture."

All at once Joaquin perceived a female, motionless, on a balcony which was without ornaments or torches. He felt a chilliness at his heart. It was Donna Carmen! By a powerful effort he stood up and saluted her in a gesture full of grace and sadness. He only uttered these few words in a firm and and solemn accent: "May happiness await you!" But the young girl pointed to the barricaded door, and answered with a melancholy smile—

" There will soon be a cross on this house."

The crowd, at first, was silent, expecting to find in this unforeseen interview, some fresh food for their cruelty, or hear some insulting or fierce raillery from the young Spaniard. But, understanding nothing of the meaning of the few words exchanged, they interrupted the touching scene by their yells. Friar Eusebio, who walked at the side of the chariot, remarked to Joaquin, pointing at the same time to the house—" Donna Carmen will never leave it alive. Did you understand her aright ?"

The young man turned away his head without answering, and the monk made a sign to the conductors to increase the speed of the chariot, which threatened every moment to be upset by the shocks and jolting it received.

" Oh ! how I suffer," murmured Pitrians, whose brain was on fire.

" My God ! have courage," replied Joaquin. " Do not tremble now and afford sport to the wretches."

" Die as you have lived," said Jean David, " and fear nothing."

When they arrived on the place San Isidora Neuva, the theatre of the execution, and when Pitrians wished to descend, he staggered, and was seized with an ungovernable tremour.

" Look at the old brigand," cried one; " see how he is frightened."

" However, he has killed plenty of Spaniards without pity or mercy. He did not tremble then."

" Now an infant could beat him."

" You will see they will have to carry him."

" Drink—drink; I want to drink," stammered the condemned.

" Untie his hands," cried a woman, " he could not hurt a fly."

" Drink—drink," repeated the adventurer, in a sinking voice. The crowd pressed around the chariot.

" Pitrians," said Joaquin, " have courage; are you mad ? In two or three minutes all will be over. Stand up—up, man !"

" I cannot—I cannot; there is a mist before my eyes, and my limbs are powerless. Drink—drink."

" Coward ! coward !" exclaimed the crowd, every eye being directed upon him.

" Stand up—stand up," cried Joaquin, forcibly.

At the word coward—at this insult, the old Pitrians opened his haggard eyes. He tried, at first, to maintain himself on his trembling limbs, then attempted to step towards those who had insulted him. It was his last effort. He threw out his arms, and fell heavily, saying—" Sustain me, Montbars."

The crowd laughed.

" The pirate will slay no more Spaniards."

Friar Eusebio leaned over the body of Pitrians, and shook hands with him, a triumphant smile irradiating his countenance ; but he started back in a moment, his eyes fixed, terror depicted in his face, and cried aloud—

" It is not fear ; it is the yellow fever !"

This was the first time since the commencement of the pest, that the terrible word had been uttered ; all the Spaniards of Hispaniola knew from tradition this frightful scourge was the twin-sister to the black vomit, which had cruelly ravaged the Brazils, Chili, and of late years, also, Barbadoes and Martinique. Every one withdrew with terror. The wax candles fell from the trembling hands of the penitents. The fatal word circulated in a low murmur from one end of the procession to the other, which unrolled itself like a gigantic serpent. The chanting ceased ; none dared to face the yellow fever, that invisible murderer, which never threatens, but which, as they thought, mingled with the breath, and was conveyed by a touch of the hand, or the contact of the clothes. The disordered crowd seemed to be paralysed. It was afraid of itself. One single word isolated every heart. The sight-seers recoiled from each other as if they were enemies. The tolling of the bells seemed more melancholy. The mass melted silently away.

" Friar Eusebio," said the governor, severely, " you were wrong publicly to pronounce such a secret ; now, we must make haste, and get rid of these brigands." Then he added, in a loud voice, " Let them resume the chant of the dying. Friar Eusebio has been deceived."

" No—no," replied the monk, still terrified. " See, my lord, how yellow the adventurer's face becomes."

" The crowd magnifies the danger," said the prior of a convent.

" The yellow fever is conveyed with the rapidity of lightning," said the governor's doctor.

The prior instantly retired, without waiting the governor's

answer, and, accompanied by all the monks, they shut themselves up within the walls of their convents. The fraternity
disappeared the moment the crowd fled. Several ragged-
looking characters alone wandered about the place of execution. Don Christoval was only surrounded by a few terrified
lancers. At his order, they approached, with a very bad grace,
the chariot, from which Joaquin and Jean David had not descended. The latter smiled, and said—

"Come on, my brave fellows, and be quick, otherwise I
shall escape you, like Pitrians." The lancers stopped, he continued—"God be praised! the blood fills my eyes, and rings in
my ears. It is the yellow fever announcing itself. Come, my
brave fellows ; let my death even be fatal to the Spaniards—
come, the fever will not wait your pleasure."

At these alarming words, the lancers looked at each other,
hesitated, and trembled before the prisoner, who swayed backwards and forwards, seeming to sink into himself. The more
feeble he became, the more they were alarmed. The more the
violence of the attack bent him down, the farther they retreated.
Finally, when the black blood burst from his eyes and ears,
they fled, leaving Joaquin, bound upon the chariot between his
two hideous companions. There he stood trembling with impatience, but still entertaining a final hope.

Don Christoval and the friar then saw several men, who
were scattered about, approach towards them. The governor
cried out—

"These beggars will, perhaps, be more courageous than my
soldiers, and will assist me to perform my duty."

But the monk having scrutinised the countenance of one of
them, exclaimed instantly—

"Fly, my lord! these are the Brothers of the Coast, who
have introduced themselves into the town under cover of this
tumult, and disguised in these rags."

The governor was thunderstruck; but before either he or
the monk could stir, they were surrounded, seized, bound, and
secured by the adventurers.

Joaquin believed himself free. His manacles would be cut
off. He shouted in a loud voice—

"Help—help, Brothers ! Here, brave L'Olonnais."

For it was him whom the friar had recognised, and who
commanded the expedition. For the first time, terror seized
upon the buccaniers. They looked at the dead and dying
stretched out together, and not one of them dared move a step
towards the fatal chariot.

" What do you wait for, Brothers ?" asked Joaquin, with surprise.

" The courage and arms of men cannot contend with such an enemy as the yellow fever," replied L'Olonnais, hesitating.

" Are you afraid ?" cried the young man, in a tone of doubt.

" Hear me, Montbars ; we are not come here to deliver you, but to save our companions. Did you not become a maroon when you were the servant of Michel le Basque ?"

" Yes," replied Joaquin.

" You have violated our statutes; none of us is compelled to risk our lives for you. You are condemned."

" You also against me !" murmured Joaquin, and he bowed his head on his breast with resignation.

The adventurers gathered together, threw a look of hesitation on the chariot, and then formed in order to depart.

All at once, Joaquin was seized with a new idea, and addressed L'Olonnais—

" Hear my last request, and let it be a recompense for all the services I have rendered you."

" Speak !"

" In the street San Isidora you will find a house shut up. The door has been sealed up like a coffin on a living woman, out of pure vengeance : you understand. Is it not horrible thus to be revenged on a young, beautiful, and innocent girl ? Well, promise me that you will open the door, and promise me that you will restore the poor child to air, life, and liberty."

" Your wish shall be accomplished. Adieu, Brother," said L'Olonnais, quite easily.

And the adventurers moved away slowly, almost ashamed of their feebleness, but influenced by an indefinable terror. They looked without desire on the splendid textures hung upon the walls, at the vases and other precious objects glittering on the balconies, in short, at all that luxury piled up in the silent streets, which bore a strong resemblance to the city of the dead described in the " Arabian Nights Entertainments." Having reached the barricaded house, the Brothers stopped. A few blows of an axe soon burst the door open.

Donna Carmen had remained motionless and drowned in despair on the balcony. When she saw the ragged men smashing open the door, she imagined they came to slay her, and that the friar had denounced her ; she trembled and descended the stairs to meet the adventurers.

When the monk saw her appear, he said—

" Joaquin believed he would save her, but I can still sacrifice her. Senorita," added he, with a sinister smile, " hear me."

" He is dead, is he not, since you smile in that manner ?"

" No, Donna Carmen, he is alive; but he is still a prisoner, condemned and chained alone to the cart in the place San Isidora."

The adventurers interrupted him—

" Silence, foolish monk, or we will cudgel you."

" March !" commanded L'Olonnais. " Every moment's delay may be fatal to us in this pestiferous town."

Friar Eusebio could not avoid adding—

" You alone, senorita, dare release him."

The troop marched on, but the monk had time enough to see Donna Carmen proceed as rapidly as her failing strength would permit in the direction indicated, and he jeeringly murmured—

" My brother, Don Ramon, is avenged—avenged upon both, for she will perish with him."

In the meantime, Donna Carmen proceeded onwards to the place of execution, pale as a phantom. She was stupified at the appearance of the singular scene before her, illuminated, and yet silent as the grave; the gallows without the condemned, and the tolling of the church bells.

When she perceived Joaquin standing upon the chariot, conspicuous amidst all the twinkling lights, and the only living creature in that place where such a great crowd was assembled a short time previously to see him die, she imagined that the incidents of a dream were passing before her eyes—

" Perhaps the monk has deceived me. Perhaps Joaquin has perished along with his companions under the hand of the executioner. Can it be a deception of vision that places him now before me ? My God ! I do not dream ; I have all my senses about me." She paused about ten paces from the chariot. " Joaquin ! Joaquin !" murmured she.

" Who is that ?" said the young man, starting and raising his head. " Who remembers me ?"

" Cannot you guess ? do you not recognise me ?" cried she, in a transport of joy, extending her arms towards him.

" Donna Carmen free ! torn living from her sepulchre, and now standing before me ? My brave companions, then, have been true to their promise ; may a thousand blessings attend them !"

The young creole advanced.

" And as soon as I was free I came to seek you, Joaquin," said Carmen.

" You—you have not, then, forgotten me?" said he, in a soft voice. " But, do not approach me; do not come near this cart," added he, in terror.

" Why not? I am alive, and can I leave you to die? Could you believe it possible?"

" You do not know the danger; fly—fly, quickly. I have alone frightened the whole people; you do not know that these my two Brothers have been struck down with yellow fever! These are fitting witnesses whom you choose for our nuptials. Oh! fly, Donna Carmen. In a brief space my countenance will be like theirs, horrible to look on; my breath will be fatal. I feel already as it were a cold perspiration on my brow."

Donna Carmen came nearer and nearer to the chariot, shuddering at the sight of the two bodies, but she subdued, by strength of mind, the instinctive fear which assailed her.

" Joaquin," said she, calmly, " what do you love in me? If I was not so fair, if suffering extinguished the brilliancy of the eye and destroyed my looks, would you abandon me? Could you only love the young and smiling girl?"

" How can you, Carmen, ask me such a question? You are to me life itself. It is not Donna Carmen de Larates that I love; it is you yourself: why I love you so, I cannot tell. If you were a queen I should dare to love you; and if you were the poorest of the poor, it would be the same. You may hate me, but you cannot prevent my love."

Donna Carmen, without reply, advanced between the two bodies, which were leaning towards the earth, and supported her fair and emaciated hand on the chariot.

" I do not wish to see you die, Carmen. I do not wish you to be placed beneath my winding sheet; my love is not so cowardly or selfish. I love you, Carmen, as a sacred idol; life is still lovely for you; oh! live on. Do not come near! There is a mist gathering over my eyes—it is a terrible symptom."

" You are suffering," said Carmen; and, ascending with difficulty, she put her trembling hands on the cords which bound the condemned. She felt a burning tear. She continued in a tone of deep emotion, " Joaquin, a woman's courage may sink before naked swords, she cannot then overcome the instinct of fear; but there are times when our courage rises when the most resolute men are afraid. Joaquin, I have to expiate the offences of pride towards you. We shall now live or die together."

" Alas! Carmen, you would die, then, through me. It is dreadful to destroy those we love. I should have died happy in knowing that I was beloved." The young Creole smiled. " Shortly, that lovely smile, Carmen, will be displaced by the writhings of agony—ah! my hands grow icy cold."

Donna Carmen then hastily untied, detached, and tore asunder the cords, which pressed tightly on the adventurer's wrists. Then, kneeling down, she detached those which encircled his ankles, and rising up, proud of the heroic action, she said :

" Joaquin, you are now free !—embrace your wife ; for, before God, I now solemnly swear, that I shall have no husband save you alone."

The young man looked at her doubtfully, not daring to credit the truth of such sweet words ; but when he noticed the colour which blushed on the cheeks of the pale Spaniard, he passionately embraced her, exclaiming—

" Ah ! I am too happy to die now !"

" Well," said she, " if you have any strength left, or if happiness can restore your courage, let us forsake, without a moment's delay, this accursed spot. Gongora, the boatman, has become, since the pillage of Rancheria, one of the most renowned fishermen of San Fernando. He is still faithful to me, and in a few hours he will transport us in his boat to the hatto, where you, Joaquin, first began to love me."

The young man without reply descended from the chariot. Donna Carmen took his hand and allowed him to conduct her towards the port. In an hour afterwards they were at sea, the adventurer assisting Gongora actively in the management of the boat. The next morning they quietly disembarked at the hatto of Rancheria, where, as the young girl predicted, all their misfortunes ended where they had begun.

CHAPTER XI.

CONCLUSION.

BOUT six months after these events, on a beautiful evening which, in the Antilles, is generally gilded like a fairy scene, Donna Carmen attended by some slaves awaited Joaquin's return from the chase, for which he had set out in the morning. She rested in the same clearing where she had first seen the Leopard—she studied with a dreamy look two tombs that occupied the ground where the drying hut formerly stood. These sepulchres contained the remains of the Marquis Bernard de Cossé and his wife the seigneuresse. At intervals, Donna Carmen hearing vague noises in the forest, despatched some of her slaves on the look out. Finally, the joyous sound of horns was heard in the distance, and a smile shone on her countenance. The sound approached—she then seemed motionless, as if indifferent; at length Joaquin appeared in a splendid hunting dress, and followed by the hunters and the hounds.

" Thou here, Carmen, at this hour ?" cried he, with emotion. " How imprudent !"

" I was uneasy at your long absence," said she, looking at him affectionately; " and I came here to await your return, for I know that you pause here for a short time every day you are out."

" Are you jealous of the dead, dear child ?" replied Joaquin, with a melancholy smile; " I am, indeed, late; but I persuaded myself that I heard the hillo of the buccaniers in the woods, and an involuntary curiosity led me on."

" Ah ! you have not, then, entirely forgotten your fine life as an adventurer ?" interrupted Carmen, playfully. " You would like to see your old acquaintances of the Port de la Paix."

Joaquin was about to reply, when they suddenly heard several ringing cries, and perceived an unfortunate slave, emaciated and ghastly, bursting upon the clearance and rushing towards them.

" Help ! help !—have pity on me, good people. I am a Spaniard ; save me from the pirates."

Joaquin and Carmen at first looked upon him with compassion ; but, suddenly starting back with a feeling of abhorrence, they mutually exclaimed :

" Friar Eusebio Carral !"

The wretch, in his turn, lifted up his eyes ; and a deep expression of surprise and rage darkened his countenance, on recognising the young people, and perceiving the evident happiness which they enjoyed.

At the same moment a buccanier, around whom bounded several setters and hounds, boldly advanced without being intimidated by the presence of Spaniards, and applying his lash to the monk, he cried :

" Cowardly sluggard !"

" Why do you beat this unfortunate man ?" asked Joaquin.

" The fellow remembers, too often, his old trade," answered he, without looking at the questioner. " He declares he ought not to work on a Sunday ; I, however, allow him to kill buffalo six days in the week and sell them on the seventh."

" I see that L'Olonnais is still the same," said Joaquin, holding out his hand to the buccanier. The latter looked with surprise at his old companion.

" Joaquin ! is it possible ? Is it indeed you ? and in this brilliant costume !" Then looking at Donna Carmen, who blushed, " I see—a woman had more courage than all the Brothers of the Coast. You are now a lord, Joaquin ; I am still the free buccanier—rich to-day, poor to-morrow. What is the use of piastres in the pocket of a dead man ?—and our lives are never safe. Adieu, Joaquin. He pressed his hand, and rudely pushing the monk before him, he said :

" As for thee, thou may'st take an eternal leave of Rancheria ; thou shalt die a slave, for thou wilt never have merit enough to become a free buccanier."

The adventurer, with his slave and his hounds, were soon lost from view in the woods.

Joaquin sighed as he watched L'Olonnais disappear.

" Do you regret forsaking that vagabond life, Joaquin ?" asked Carmen.

" Are you not the universe itself to me ?" replied the young man, tenderly. " Our union has been purchased by the death of all who loved us. But, Margaret is at least avenged, since the monk, whose hatred pursued us with such untiring fury, has received from Providence such a cruel chastisement in his present destiny; and, above all, in witnessing our happiness. The married lovers slowly pursued their way towards the hatto, under the light of the stars, which were scattered, like glittering dots of gold, in the deep azure of the sky.

It is almost needless to add, that Donna Carmen and her now fortunate husband, Joaquin, long continued to enjoy every blessing which wealth and affection could confer—their happiness more than ordinarily unalloyed by the petty annoyances of life, by the remembrance of the great trials they had undergone.

THE END.

London: Geo. Peirce, Printer, 310, Strand.

LIBRARY OF FRENCH ROMANCE.

Select Works of the celebrated Alexandre Dumas.

Now Publishing, in small 8vo., with Steel Frontispiece and Vignette, 2s. 6d. sewed; 3s. cloth gilt, the Historical Romance of

MARIE ANTOINETTE;

OR, THE CHEVALIER OF THE RED HOUSE.

A TALE OF THE FRENCH REVOLUTION OF 1793.

Also, 2s. 6d. sewed; 3s. cloth gilt, with Steel Frontispiece and Vignette, the Historical Romance of

MARGARET OF NAVARRE;

OR, THE MASSACRE OF THE HUGUENOTS.

Also, 2s. 6d. sewed; 3s. cloth gilt, with Steel Frontispiece and Vignette, the Historical Romance of

THE PRISONER OF IF;

OR, THE COUNT OF MONTE-CHRISTO.

Also, price 1s. sewed, the celebrated Romance of

PASCAL BRUNO,

THE SICILIAN BANDIT.

WORKS OF VICTOR HUGO.

In small 8vo., uniform with the above, price 2s. sewed; 2s. 6d. cloth gilt, the celebrated Romance of

LA ESMERALDA;

OR, THE HUNCHBACK OF NOTRE DAME.

Steel Frontispiece "The Cathedral of Notre Dame de Paris," Steel Vignette "La Esmeralda dancing in the Place du Grève;" and upwards of forty superior Engravings on Wood.

Also, price 1s. sewed,

THE NOBLE RIVAL;

OR, THE PRINCE OF CONGO.

A TALE OF SAINT DOMINGO.

Steel Frontispiece and Vignette, and numerous Engravings on Wood.

Also, price 1s. sewed, the Romance of

HANS OF ICELAND;

OR, THE DEMON DWARF.

Steel Frontispiece and Vignette, and numerous Engravings on Wood.

Complete, 1s.

THE BLACK MENDICANT.

BY P. FEVAL.

Just Ready, small 8vo., price 1s.,

THE FAIR CIRCASSIAN.

FROM THE FRENCH OF ALEXANDRE DE LAVERGNE.

Also, price 1s.,

THE POISONERS.

" 'Tis cool, deliberate, conducted malice,
A deep, a secret, settled scheme of death."

In small 8vo., 1s.,

THE MYSTERIES OF THE INQUISITION.

In small 8vo., sewed, 2s.,

VICTOR HUGO'S celebrated work,

LA ESMERALDA;

OR, THE HUNCHBACK OF NOTRE DAME.

Steel Frontispiece "The Cathedral of Notre Dame de Paris."
Steel Vignette, " La Esmeralda dancing in the Place du Grève." And
upwards of forty superior Engravings on Wood.

" Decidedly the best translation of this beautiful story that has yet
appeared. There are several chapters added which did not appear in the
first translation."—*United Service Gazette.*

In small 8vo., sewed, 1s.,

THE NOBLE RIVAL

OR, THE PRINCE OF CONGO.

BY VICTOR HUGO.

Steel Frontispiece and Vignette, and numerous Woodcuts.

In small 8vo., sewed, 1s.,

HANS OF ICELAND;

OR, THE DEMON DWARF.

BY VICTOR HUGO.

Steel Frontispiece and Vignette, and numerous Engravings on Wood.

*** The NOBLE RIVAL and HANS OF ICELAND in one
volume, cloth gilt, price 2s. 6d.